The Fatal Sip

Anita carefully sets a tray of empty stemware on the counter, a strand of hair escaping her ponytail. She tucks it behind her ear and nods toward Gaskel's empty barstool.

"How's it going with the fancy critic?" she asks.

"Okay," I answer vaguely, adding Gaskel's glass to the collection destined for the dishwasher.

"I bet it's going better than you think." Her cheeks are glowing with the sheen of naïveté. "I already sold a case of the cab to the group of guys, and the couple in the corner bought a bottle of the Ski Lodge Cherry." Anita dashes off to package the recently sold wine.

Hope balloons in my chest and I feel a surge of determination to convince Gaskel to give my wine another chance. By any means necessary. I'll grovel if I must.

I pour a sample of the Mile High Merlot and then idle near the bathroom door, glancing at the grapevine clock hanging over the hallway table. Gaskel has to be done soon.

A customer with dark brown curly hair and a prominent nose fidgets in line behind me and I become even more aware of the time. In fact, the longer I wait, the more worried I get, especially when I remember the way Gaskel's chest heaved wh̶ ̶ ̶ ̶ ̶ ̶p.

I knock on t̶h̶ ̶ ̶ ̶ ̶ ̶ ̶

No a̶ ̶

"Mr. ̶ ̶ ̶ ̶ ̶ ̶ ̶ ̶ ̶ ape of my neck risin̶ ̶

I try the doorknob and find it unlocked. My unease grows as I slowly push the door open.

I gasp, bringing my hand to my chest. There's a shattering of glass and, faintly, I realize I've dropped the merlot. Burgundy wine dribbles over the Tuscan-tiled floor.

And there's Gaskel.

His ego would take a major hit if he knew he'd been discovered in such a messy state. He's sprawled ungracefully on the floor, his legs bent at awkward angles. It looks like he'd almost made it to the toilet before he threw up, vomit all over his face and starched shirt. One hand cradles the expensive watch strapped to his other wrist. A piece of paper sticks out of his front pocket like a flag of surrender, and his eyes stare glassily at the ceiling.

There's a stillness emanating from his body. Somehow, I know he's dead.

Killer

Chardonnay

Kate Lansing

BERKLEY PRIME CRIME
New York

BERKLEY PRIME CRIME
Published by Berkley
An imprint of Penguin Random House LLC
penguinrandomhouse.com

ISBN: 9780593100189

First Edition: May 2020

Printed in the United States of America
1 3 5 7 9 10 8 6 4 2

Cover illustration by Samantha Dion Baker
Cover design by Farjana Yasmin
Book design by Alison Cnockaert

To Sophie
May all your wildest dreams come true

Acknowledgments

There are so many people who helped bring this book to life.

My agent, Pamela Harty. Thank you for believing in me and championing this story.

The entire team at Berkley, especially my brilliant editor, Miranda Hill. Thank you for your expert guidance, editorial insights, and encouragement. Among many other things, it was definitely the right call to save that truffle.

My local chapters of Sisters in Crime and Mystery Writers of America. Thank you for providing me with such an inspiring writing community.

My friend and beta reader extraordinaire, Abby Reed. Thank you for all the brainstorming sessions and invaluable feedback on early drafts.

My mom and dad. Thank you for instilling me with a deep appreciation for reading, igniting my imagination, and always encouraging me to pursue my passion.

My husband, John. This book absolutely wouldn't have been possible without your constant support. Thank you for always being there for me, filling my life with laughter and love, and all the adventures tasting wine around the world.

And Sophie, my darling daughter. Thank you for all those gloriously long naps as a newborn. Your sweet smile motivates me more than you know.

Chapter One

I arrange open bottles of wine behind the hard maple countertop from lightest to heaviest. A crisp white blend on the left, a jammy cabernet sauvignon on the right, and me, a cluster of nerves, right smack in the middle.

Today is the grand opening of my winery—I still can't believe I'm saying that—*my winery*, Vino Valentine. The world will finally get to taste the fruits of my labor, which is equal parts exciting and panic-inducing.

Because this is really happening.

My crazy pipe dream is becoming a reality. Although, as I'm all too aware, my reality could very well turn into a nightmare.

"Parker, where would you like these?" my assistant, Anita, asks, brandishing two baskets full of palate-cleansing crackers.

Towering over me, her willowy frame is accentuated

by wedge sandals, long blond hair pulled into a high ponytail, and a flowery tunic dress.

"One on each end of the tasting bar," I answer.

Anita places them as directed and then returns to my side. She caught me in the back earlier hyperventilating into a paper bag that was meant for packaging goods. Ever since, she's kept an extra-close eye on me. Which I appreciate. Really. Except sometimes a girl needs to have a meltdown in peace.

She pushes thick-framed glasses up her nose. "So, are you ready?"

"No. Yes. I don't know." I bury my face in my hands and then peek through my fingers. "What if no one shows?"

True story, my parents couldn't even fit my opening into their busy schedules, as they so kindly informed me this morning via text. And it's a Saturday. Which begs the question, if my own mom can't make time for me, what hope do I have for the general public?

"This is Colorado, the land of handcrafted concoctions; they'll show," Anita says with a confidence I wish I felt.

Colorado may not be the first place that comes to mind when people think of wine tasting, but it's a burgeoning destination thanks to the high altitude and cooler climate, which give the fruit a more concentrated flavor.

She continues, "People are going to flock here like internet junkies to viral kitten videos. I mean, look at this place."

I must admit, the cozy area is picturesque. Shiny blue letters on the storefront window gleam with the name Vino Valentine. The interior is arranged with oak-barrel tables, simple espresso folding chairs, and wine-bottle lanterns overhead. More baskets full of crackers and pillar candles—unscented so as not to interfere with the delicate aromas of the wine—dot the tables, and photographs of vineyards from around the world adorn the walls.

"Maybe you're right," I concede.

"Oh, I'm definitely right." Anita's eyes sparkle with such good humor they rival the polished glasses lining the open shelves above the tasting bar.

"Okay," I say, clapping my hands together. "All that's left to do is light the candles. You do that and I'll get the door."

Anita flits away with a lighter, the candles giving the space a warm ambience.

As I make my way toward the storefront, I tug at the delicate beaded necklace around my neck. As always, it makes me think of my late aunt Laura. I wish she were here to see her investment come to fruition. What I wouldn't give for her steadfast support, to hear her tell me everything will work out as it's supposed to. My chest aches for how badly I miss her. But instead of dwelling on my sadness, I focus on making her proud.

The sign on the door is made of varnished oak and features a design of clinking glasses. It's heavy with importance as I flip it from CLOSED to OPEN.

And nothing happens.

There's no great tilt to the universe, no angelic chorus overhead, no stampede to get trampled in.

There's only me, unlatching the door and taking in my surroundings.

When I was deciding where to set up shop, I immediately landed on Boulder. It's where my heart is. I love the majestic mountain backdrop, sprawling blue skies, and ever-present scent of pine trees. The distinct city vibe but with trailheads practically in my backyard.

My parents balked when I chose this location for my winery, but I saw potential in the industrial part of North Boulder. I leased space in a modern shopping center with white cement siding, charcoal awnings, and floor-to-ceiling windows that let in plenty of light. The trendy café next door keeps me in caffeine, and across the street is a nursery with rows of shrubs laid out like a welcome mat to the rolling foothills.

With a sigh, I pad back to the tasting bar to wait for someone to show up. *Please,* I think, *someone show up.*

Then the bell over the door jingles.

I spin around as my first customer traipses through the door.

Of course, it's my best friend, Sage.

A petite redhead with a penchant for fashion and nerd canon, Sage is dressed in sky-blue capris, a drapey silk shirt, and her prized Khaleesi dragon-claw necklace.

My face splits into a huge grin. "Thank you for coming."

"Wouldn't have missed it." She shoves her giant sunglasses on top of her head and looks around in awe. "You did it. You effin' did it."

My eyes swim with tears at the pride in her voice.

"I had no doubt, obviously," she says. "But it's even more amazing than you let on."

Sage's live-in boyfriend trails behind her like an anchor. Jason is unremarkable in every way—mousy-brown hair, pale freckled skin, and eyes that are a little too close together. I've never understood what Sage sees in him. Nonetheless, I'm glad he's here. I tell him as much.

The bell jingles again and a group of college-age

guys come through the door, followed by a chic couple who look vaguely familiar, and then my older brother, Liam, with a friend I've never met.

Liam envelops me in a giant bear hug, lifting me an inch off the ground.

"Set me down," I say through clenched teeth, swatting at him. I smooth my pencil skirt after my feet are back on solid ground.

"Relax, Parker," he says. "The party has arrived." He takes a mock bow, clearly expecting me to fall over myself with gratitude.

I roll my eyes.

Anyone would peg us for siblings with our matching raven hair and blue-gray eyes. But our looks are where the similarities stop. What Liam lacks in ambition, he makes up for by having this weird sixth sense for where to find the next good time. Which I suppose bodes well for my opening.

I scan my suddenly bustling winery, nerves prickling.

The group of college-age guys commandeers a long table made of three oak barrels smooshed together, the couple settles in at a private two-top in the corner, Sage and Jason tuck in near the front window, and my brother and his friend pick a table center stage.

Just like that, I'm open for business.

Anita and I hop to. We pour tasters, talk through the winemaking process, and give pairing tips for different varietals. Wine bottles deplete and new ones are opened. Baskets of crackers are replenished, and glasses swapped out.

I feel myself easing into a groove, the butterflies that have filled my stomach for the last week finally subsiding. That is, until two things happen.

First, the couple, who are apparently chic only in appearance, begin to bicker. Loudly.

They raise their voices as accusations fly.

"Not my fault—" the woman cries, getting to her feet. Anger radiates off her, from her clenched fists to her narrowed eyes.

The man cuts her off, speaking in a continuous stream of angry French.

"Taste this," she shouts as she raises her glass and, proof that real life is every bit as dramatic as a soap opera, throws the contents at the man.

Time seems to slow as every eye turns to them.

Drops of the Ski Lodge Cherry wine dribble down the man's chiseled face, onto his cream-colored sweater, and all the way to my pristine hardwood floors.

That's when the second thing happens: another customer walks through the door.

He has the stocky build of someone who enjoys a good meal, and is every inch the intimidating figure his reputation suggests. In slacks and a pressed collared shirt, he clutches a leather-bound tablet, his keen eye taking in every detail of my winery, lingering on each of my customers in turn.

I recognize him immediately based on his pictures from social media, news articles, and, more important, his popular food and wine blog.

Gaskel Brown, the most reputable critic in the Front Range, is in my winery. At the exact moment chaos descends.

Chapter Two

All sorts of problems can arise in winemaking—oxidation, tartrate crystals, overpowering aromas of vinegar or must. The tricky part is pinpointing the cause, like playing a fermentation detective, and course-correcting before the entire batch is ruined. The same is true in life.

I glance desperately at Anita. She understands my silent plea for help and dashes toward the imploding couple.

Greeting the esteemed new arrival in a frazzled gush of niceties, I escort Gaskel to the tasting bar and wave him onto a barstool. "Best seat in the house."

I don't think I've ever heard someone actually *harrumph*, but I swear Gaskel does. "I suppose this will do." He pulls out the stool and wipes a fleck of nonexistent dust from the seat.

"Take a look at our tasting menu and I'll be back in

a jiff." I'm not sure which is more shocking, that *the* Gaskel Brown is here or that I used the word *jiff* unironically.

I tag in for Anita, who has procured a towel for the spilled wine and directed the man to the restroom to freshen up. She mops up the last of the pink liquid and disappears to check on the other tables.

"I can't believe I did that," the lady says.

She sinks into her chair, her eyes rimmed in red. Her tanned skin flushes so deeply it almost matches the funky yet tasteful maroon highlights streaking her hair. She's decked out in a fashionable sheath dress, gorgeous suede kitten heels, and a statement necklace.

I still get the sense I know her from somewhere, but no matter how much I strain my mind, I can't place where.

"Please don't worry about it." I continue, in a tone I hope comes across as both stern and soothing, "Only, let's try not to let it happen again."

She nods sullenly and I feel a pang of pity for her. Unfortunately, I know what it's like to experience a relationship going south. "Let me know if you need anything."

She finally meets my gaze. "I will. Thank you."

It's my turn to nod.

Then I shift my attention to Gaskel. He's settled in at the bar, waiting not so patiently with an empty glass before him.

I scoot around the maple countertop and to the other side of the bar, flashing him my most winning smile. "Let's get this tasting started."

My success or failure hinges on a glass of chardonnay. I've poured everything into opening my own winery—my savings account, the better part of my twenties, my social life. If this doesn't pan out, I'm not sure who I am anymore. Just a wannabe entrepreneur with an overfondness for wine on the fast track to spinsterhood. I can't blow this.

Gaskel lifts his glass of golden liquid to the light, admiring the legs dripping down the sides of the crystal bowl. He breathes in the aroma, a tiny crease forming between two rather bushy eyebrows.

"I detect peaches," he grumbles. "These grapes must be from the Western Slope."

"You have a good nose," I say in a champagne-bubbly voice.

"Of course I do."

"Right. Well, the grapes are from Palisade," I say, fiddling with my necklace.

I don't own my own vineyard and instead order grapes from growers outside of Grand Junction. Which means if Gaskel doesn't like my wine, it's because I didn't do the fruit justice, didn't manage to extract the full flavor profile. In short, it's all on me.

I continue, "In addition to peaches, there are hints of melon, honeysuckle, and an oaky finish."

"We'll see about that." Gaskel takes a sip with the trademark gurgle of an expert.

I hold my breath as he swishes the wine around in his mouth. The moment stretches on to an eternity. My stomach flips as I study his stoic face, scarcely daring to move.

In the background, my winery is a flurry of motion. Absently, I notice the man of the Wine-Tossing Incident has returned to his table, now in an undershirt, his cream-colored sweater resting on the windowsill, blotched with pink. Thankfully, he and his counterpart seem to be behaving.

I refocus on the distinguished figure before me, honored Gaskel deigned to show up for my opening. Honestly, I don't even know how he heard about it, although apparently, he has his ways.

From the hottest places in town to the hidden gems, there's a mystique to how Gaskel selects which establishments to feature on his website. Some say it's a new way of preparing food or wine that attracts him, others surmise it's the promise of a free dessert, but I've always figured he must follow his stomach. Regardless, his presence could be huge for my business. Or an utter disaster. Gaskel is notoriously hard to please.

He swallows with a shudder and dumps the remaining wine into a decorative vase. A vase not meant for disposing of wine, hence the daisies.

I wince but then force myself to smile, recalling the thousands of devoted subscribers who regularly read his blog and follow his recommendations. The daisies are a necessary casualty.

Gaskel taps a note into the tablet before him, his jaw clenched into a frown. That can't be a good sign.

"Can I get you a taste of something else?" I ask with more than a hint of desperation. "The Mount Sanitas White or the Pearl Street Pinot?"

The names of my wines pay homage to the locale. The most popular parks, streets, and even the mascot of the local college in Boulder. It seemed like a good idea at the time. Now they just sound silly rolling off my tongue.

"I'll just cleanse my palate first." Gaskel bites into a

cracker, crumbs sticking to his silvering hipster goatee, a stark contrast to his otherwise meticulous appearance. He glances around my winery, his disapproval palpable.

I try to squelch the panic rising in my chest. Maybe his tastings always take forever. Maybe the fact that he's taking so long is actually a good sign. Maybe I can sneak a peek at his tablet.

No, that's a horrible idea.

Gaskel looks from side to side, craning his neck so intensely that I worry for his fitted collared shirt. At first I think he's checking out the ambience, but then I notice the way his eyes nervously flit about, landing on nothing in particular.

"Is everything okay? You seem distracted."

"Fine," he says gruffly. "Just waiting for someone."

"What do they look like?" I ask eagerly. "I can help keep an eye out for you."

"No," he says a little too quickly. He coughs and stands up abruptly, a light sheen of sweat breaking out on his forehead. "Where's your bathroom?"

"In the back and to the left." I purse my lips in concern as he stumbles. I didn't realize he'd had that much to drink but his rosé-red face says otherwise. He steadies himself and continues.

The bright screen of Gaskel's tablet catches my eye. In his hurry, he forgot to close it. I refrain from snooping only by straightening the tasting menus for the umpteenth time and realigning the open wine bottles behind the hard maple countertop.

Chatter and laughter waft from tables. Sage's voice rings out above all the others. She catches my eye and raises her glass to me with a wink. She's out in full force, maintaining a conspicuously loud running commentary on how amazing I and my wine are, in case anyone needs extra convincing (her words, not mine).

Her compliments are sweet, and beyond the call of duty. But they mean nothing if my wine isn't up to snuff.

Surely one peek at Gaskel's tablet wouldn't hurt . . .

I glance at the restroom; he's still in there with the door shut. Carefully, I lean over the bar, curiosity winning over logic. Even upside down, I can see his notes are acerbic. The words *sour*, *bitter*, and *amateur* leap off the screen.

I clench my hands into tight fists, outraged. Then I remember the harsh truth about this business: taste is subjective. What's well balanced and buttery to one person could taste like vinegar to someone else.

My face flushes in shame. Why did I think I could do this?

"Say cheese," my brother's voice says at my side. I nearly jump out of my suede ankle boots as Liam snaps a picture of me.

Stars dance in my vision from the flash. "No offense, but this really isn't a moment I want captured on film."

"I've gotta document my little sis's big day," he says, snapping another picture with his vintage Nikon camera. A bag of extra lenses and accessories is slung over his lanky frame. "Besides, I need the practice."

I shouldn't be surprised that Liam somehow manages to make this about him. He notoriously flits from hobby to hobby, his most recent interest being photography.

"Seriously, cut it out," I hiss at him in annoyance. "Gaskel will be back any minute." Unless he decided to slip out the back.

Liam slouches onto a stool. His friend follows suit.

I learned the hard way that my brother's friends were off-limits. That doesn't stop me from eyeing this one's expertly mussed sandy-blond hair and the thin scars etched up his toned forearms.

"Parker Valentine," I say, reaching out my hand. His grip is strong in mine and his fingers are rough, like he uses them for hard labor every day. He holds on a second too long.

He has broad shoulders, at least a day's worth of scruff on his chin, and a confident demeanor. "Reid Wallace." His lips flinch into a frown as he reads the tasting menu. This guy definitely needs to loosen up.

"What kind of wine do you enjoy?"

Reid cocks his head to the side as if in challenge. "Surprise me."

"And I have yet to meet a drink I don't like," Liam says, needlessly. He attempts an artsy close-up shot of the signature Vino Valentine labels I spent months perfecting, crisscrossing grapevines punctuated by the sun.

I study Reid's indie-band T-shirt and slate-green eyes. "The Campy Cab," I finally say. I pour them each a taster, trying to instill confidence in my voice. "Smoky and fruit-forward with just a hint of tobacco. Pairs especially well with s'mores."

Anita carefully sets a tray of empty stemware on the counter, a strand of hair escaping her ponytail. She tucks it behind her ear and nods toward Gaskel's empty barstool.

"How's it going with the fancy critic?" she asks.

"Okay," I answer vaguely, adding Gaskel's glass to the collection destined for the dishwasher.

"I bet it's going better than you think." Her cheeks are glowing with the sheen of naïveté. "I already sold a case of the cab to the group of guys, and the couple in the corner bought a bottle of the Ski Lodge Cherry." Anita dashes off to package the recently sold wine.

Hope balloons in my chest and I feel a surge of determination to convince Gaskel to give my wine another chance. By any means necessary. I'll grovel if I must.

I pour a sample of the Mile High Merlot and then idle near the bathroom door, glancing at the grapevine clock hanging over the hallway table. Gaskel has to be done soon.

A customer with dark brown curly hair and a prominent nose fidgets in line behind me and I become even more aware of the time. In fact, the longer I wait, the more worried I get, especially when I remember the way Gaskel's chest heaved when he stood up.

I knock on the door. "Mr. Brown?"

No answer.

"Mr. Brown?" I try again, the hair at the nape of my neck rising. "I'm coming in, sir."

I try the doorknob and find it unlocked. My unease grows as I slowly push the door open.

I gasp, bringing my hand to my chest. There's a shattering of glass and, faintly, I realize I've dropped the merlot. Burgundy wine dribbles over the Tuscan-tiled floor.

And there's Gaskel.

His ego would take a major hit if he knew he'd been discovered in such a messy state. He's sprawled ungracefully on the floor, his legs bent at awkward angles. It looks like he'd almost made it to the toilet before he threw up, vomit all over his face and starched shirt. One hand cradles the expensive watch strapped to his other wrist. A piece of paper sticks out of his front pocket like a flag of surrender, and his eyes stare glassily at the ceiling.

There's a stillness emanating from his body. Somehow, I know he's dead.

Chapter Three

I practically sprint from the bathroom, nudging past the guy still waiting outside.

My vision blurs from the blood pounding in my head. I hunch over a large floor vase in the hallway, clutching the ceramic edges while my stomach churns.

I can't believe what I just saw. Can't even begin to process what happened.

I force myself to take deep yoga breaths—in through my nose, out through my mouth—until, finally, reason returns.

The police. I need to call the police.

Fumbling for my phone, I manage to dial 911, my fingers tingly from adrenaline.

My head spins from the surrealism of the situation. I almost feel like I'm watching myself from above: a panicky, freaked-out winemaker scrambling to do the right thing.

The operator is calm and soothing when she answers, "Boulder, 911. Where is your emergency?"

Tripping over my words, I eventually manage to rattle off the address.

"What is the nature of your emergency?"

"I don't know what happened, but there's a man here, a critic, he's—" I swallow and whisper, "Dead." The word is foreign in my mouth.

"Is anyone else in danger?"

I peer toward the bathroom with a shudder. "I don't think so." Still, goose bumps prickle my arms.

"Officers are on their way."

She keeps me on the phone while, blindly, I return to the tasting room.

You would never know something catastrophic occurred for how normal everything seems. Patrons are still settled around oak-barrel tables, merrily imbibing and enjoying a lazy summer weekend afternoon.

Until the authorities arrive.

Then a fearful hush falls over my winery. Necks crane to see what's going on, the force of curiosity too strong to deny.

Safe to say, this is not the grand opening I envisioned.

I perch behind the tasting counter, clutching my head with both hands, while a police officer and an EMT barricade themselves in the bathroom. I stubbornly cling to hope even as a shiver runs up my spine, the image of Gaskel's body branded in my mind.

No one is allowed to leave the premises. My hard-earned customers clump together, their impatience growing steadily. Ever the helpful assistant, Anita flits through the room like a butterfly, her long ponytail swinging behind her, checking to see if she can get anyone anything. I make a mental note to give her a raise as soon as I can afford it. If I ever can.

I feel the eyes of Liam and Sage fixed on me in concern, but I ignore them. I just need a minute to process all of this.

The bell over the door jingles and a man in a navy suit makes his way toward us. His eyes are clear instead of bloodshot and he's considerably more built now, but I still recognize him from eons ago.

"Eli Fuller?"

"Parker?" he asks with equal astonishment.

I haven't seen Eli since high school graduation. He was four rows in front of me, *F* coming well before *V* alphabetically, but I remember the Birkenstock sandals he wore all the time, even with his cap and gown.

I stand to greet him. "What are you doing here?"

"I'm a detective now." He flashes his badge with pride. His hair is clean cut and slicked back, a far cry from the shaggy style he used to sport. "I need to ask you a few questions."

All I can do is nod, taken aback that the renowned stoner of the Boulder Cineplex somehow became a detective.

"You discovered Mr. Brown, correct?" Eli starts, pulling a tiny pad of paper from his jacket pocket.

"Yes, he'd been in the restroom a long time," I manage to stammer. "I went to check on him."

"Did he seem nervous or act unusual?"

"I'm not sure. This was the first time we'd met." I

hesitate, thinking back to our brief interaction. "He was looking around and said he was waiting for someone, but no one ever showed."

"Can you describe the events leading up to when you found him?"

"He got here around four thirty, sat down, and took a sip of wine followed by a bite of a cracker to cleanse his palate. The next thing I knew he was sweating, red in the face, and staggering toward the restroom. I figured he had more to drink than I thought, but then . . ." I trail off.

"Which wine did he try?"

"The Chautauqua Chardonnay." I point to the bottle, sitting unassumingly behind the counter. "Usually a tasting would start with a lighter white, but I didn't know how many chances I'd get to impress him."

Eli continues, "Did you see anyone tamper with his drink?"

"It went straight from my hands to his glass." My mouth goes tannin-dry as I connect the dots. "Why are you asking so many questions about his wine?"

"I can't answer that." His eyes flick to mine and a jolt of fear courses through my body.

I lean against the barstool for support, reveling in the touch of cool metal against my palms. "Did he—" I swallow and lower my voice to a whisper. "Was it poison?"

"We won't know for sure until we get the coroner's report." But it's clear that's exactly what he thinks.

I push my bangs off my forehead and blink back tears. That's when a terrible thought enters my mind. One I almost can't acknowledge in case it proves to be true. Fighting back the bile rising in my throat, I force myself to confront the awful possibility.

Could I be responsible for Gaskel's death?

Did I mess up the fermentation process or was the bottle infected with some new deadly strain of cork taint? But I was so meticulous, testing the temperature and acidity every step of the way. Moreover, other people tasted from that same bottle and are still standing. I gnaw on my bottom lip, perplexed.

I'm so preoccupied, I barely register Eli's next question. "Do you know of anyone who would want to harm Mr. Brown?"

There's a snort behind me. I'd forgotten that Reid was at the bar, too. "Only every restaurant owner in the Denver area," he interjects. "Did you ever read the guy's blog?"

"What's this about a blog?" Eli asks.

Reid finishes the last bit of his wine, seemingly unconcerned that someone has recently died from drinking my craftsmanship. "Gaskel Brown trashes almost every restaurant he goes to," he says. "Do you know how many people would love to get back at him?" The scars on Reid's arms combined with his nonchalant attitude mark him as a bad boy.

"Are you one of those people?" Eli asks evenly, his stance turning predatory.

"Definitely not," Reid responds. There's something incomprehensible in his expression, almost like irony, but it's gone a moment later. "He gave me a rave review."

I frown, wondering exactly who my brother's friend is.

Eli relaxes his shoulders and returns his focus to me. "Where is the glass Mr. Brown was drinking from?"

"Probably about halfway through the rinse cycle." The color drains from my face. "I had just gotten him a fresh one. I didn't want any remnants of the chardonnay in the glass since he didn't seem to like it."

"How do you know he didn't like the chardonnay?"

I cross my arms over my chest, not wanting to admit to my snooping. "I, uh, could just tell."

"That'll be all for now," Eli says, jotting down one last note. "I'll let you know if I have any other questions."

"Can you do me a favor, for old time's sake?" I ask, although honestly I was never close with Eli. We navigated in different circles, only briefly commingling at the occasional house party or show at Red Rocks.

He raises one eyebrow at me. "That depends on the favor."

"This is my first day of business and I don't want to scare anyone away. Is there any way you can keep the whole poison thing to yourself?"

His gaze softens. "I'll do what I can." Then he continues, "But this is an open homicide investigation."

The words hang in the air between us, thick and heavy like the sediment at the bottom of a good bottle of cab. "Wait, did you say homicide? As in murder?"

"Good to see you, Parker," Eli says, the corner of his mouth twitching. "Although I wish it had been under different circumstances."

Oh God, my business will never survive this. And that's the least of my concerns. I start to hyperventilate.

"This can't be happening," I say to no one in particular.

Liam plunks a glass of wine in front of me. "Drink this. It'll help." At my skeptical look he adds, "Don't worry, it's not the chardonnay."

A half sob, half chuckle escapes my throat.

"Too soon, man," Reid says. He picks up the tasting menu and scans it silently.

Flashing blue lights of emergency vehicles give the scene a nightmarish quality as the coroner leads a stretcher supporting a body bag through the door, the happy jingling of the bell overhead belying the bleakness of the situation. My fingers go tingly from taking too-short breaths. To think just a little bit ago, Gaskel was tasting my chardonnay and tapping the beginnings of a review into his tablet, doing his job like he always did, and now he's gone.

I take a large gulp of wine. Somewhere in the recesses of my mind, I recognize the floral notes of Ralphie's Riesling. After another sip, I'm able to breathe, and the tension in my shoulders eases a fraction.

Eli and his band of crime-scene technicians slowly file out of my winery, leaving behind a muddy trail of footprints. At some point, it started raining. Through the storefront windows, raindrops glisten on my newly planted petunias and clouds drift down the mountains, so thick I can barely see the angled peaks of the Flatirons.

Sage wanders to my side with her boyfriend, Jason, following close behind. "Okay, whose ass do I need to kick?"

A smile plays at the corner of my lips, no doubt my friend's goal. "I wish I knew."

"It was going so well," she exclaims, her strawberry-blond hair practically bouncing with positivity. "We overheard the table next to us talking about how impressed they were."

I shake my head. "If—when—people find out *the*

Gaskel Brown actually died in my winery, I'm done for." I don't voice the other tidbit haunting me: Gaskel didn't like my wine. I know that's the last thing I should be worrying about, but it still stings.

She squeezes my shoulder reassuringly. "You can crash with us tonight if you don't want to be alone."

"What about the game?" her boyfriend grumbles, looking like he took a bite of something unpleasant and was forced to swallow it. He kicks the toe of his sneaker into the floor, his shoulders slouched in self-pity.

Because of Sage's small stature, she often gets labeled as being cute or sweet. But don't let her appearance fool you. She's fierce. Especially when her wide blue eyes flash with anger, like they are right now.

Sage elbows him in the ribs. "Jason, that doesn't matter right now." She turns her attention back to me. "And if you need a lawyer, I've got your back."

My girl is a law clerk for the most respected judge in Boulder County, an esteemed position that will eventually land her her choice of lucrative job offers thanks to all the connections she's making. But for now, she works crazy hours with an even crazier workload, which she endures by pretending to be someone else on the weekends via cosplay. If you look close enough, she usually has at least one piece of nerd canon hidden among her professional attire; today it's her elfin thumb ring and dragon-claw necklace.

"No," I say quickly, not keen on spending the evening having to hide my frustration with Jason. "I'll be fine tonight, but I may take you up on your legal advice."

"You can stay at my place," Liam offers, throwing a glare at Jason. He tucks his camera safely into its case, jaw clenched.

Liam has always seen himself as my protector, even if I hardly need one as an adult. Although with a murderer on the loose, perhaps I do.

"You live in Mom and Dad's basement. Your place is technically theirs," I say, crinkling my nose at him. "Seriously, guys, I'll be okay."

To prove to them just how fine I am, I get to my feet and smooth the front of my eyelet pencil skirt. It's time to put my business hat on. Hiding all emotion behind a look of polite hospitality, I hustle to the front door as customers trickle out, their moods ranging from annoyed to morose to blithely tipsy depending on how much they imbibed.

I hand out cards for a free tasting. It's a catch-22—I need them to spread positive word of mouth, but I'd rather not invite a potential killer to visit again.

My face is starting to hurt from fake-smiling when Liam and Reid pause before me, the latter studying a particularly vibrant vineyard photograph hanging on the wall beside the entrance.

My brother goes to punch me lightly on the shoulder but, distracted by something at the bar, ends up smacking my chin.

"Hey, watch it," I say. I check to see what he's looking at, but only find Sage and Jason hovering around a barstool, and Anita collecting remaining glasses from tables.

"Sorry." He clears his throat. "Sundowner, anyone? I've gotta let off some steam." My brother's specialty is letting off steam at his favorite dive bar on Pearl Street. Steam from doing what, nobody knows.

Liam continues to his car, but Reid hangs back. "It was nice to meet you, Parker," he says, and I can tell he actually means it. "For the record, I thought your wine was well balanced with just the right amount of jammy-ness, and I don't give compliments lightly, especially when it comes to food and wine."

"Thanks," I say, a warm feeling spreading through my chest. "Did Gaskel really give you a rave review?" I blurt out.

"I'm the executive chef at The Pantry. I got two en-thusiastic thumbs-up." He gives me a roguish wink. "But I try not to let it go to my head."

The Pantry is a popular farm-to-table restaurant, ru-mored to have been started by a famous Silicon Valley tech genius. "You should be proud," I say in awe, and with a smidgen of disbelief. "That's quite the accom-plishment for someone so . . ." I trail off, giving him a once-over.

"So, what?"

"Young," I finish, although even I'm not convinced that's what I was going to say.

He shrugs, slipping his hands into his jean pockets. "You weren't aware of Gaskel's reputation, were you?"

"Only that he can make or break a business." I tug at my beaded necklace. "I'm afraid he's going to break mine."

"I wouldn't be so sure about that. You've got a good product in an up-and-coming area."

Reid takes a step toward me and continues, "But the service was the best part."

My cheeks warm. I press a card into his hand, our fingertips brushing. "Come back for a free tasting. It's the least I can do."

"Count on it." He slips my card in his wallet and is halfway out the door when something catches his eye.

"Hey, do you mind if I take one of these?" he asks, snagging a tasting menu from a nearby table.

I'm not sure what this guy's fascination is with my tasting menu, but I give him the go-ahead. "I'm yours—I mean, it's yours." I wave him off, mentally kicking myself for the verbal flub, and for the flirting. I really can't ruin another one of my brother's friendships.

Sage and her boyfriend walk to the front of the store. I hear Jason whisper, "I want to be home by the first pitch."

Sage rolls her eyes, readjusting the strap of her purse. "We have to go. Promise you'll call if you need me." She gives me a quick hug.

"I will. Thank you for coming," I say, and then nod at Jason. "Both of you. I appreciate it." They bicker on their way to the car and I wonder, probably for the hundredth time, how to tell someone they deserve better.

I lock the dead bolt and slowly survey my winery, empty but for Anita and me. The air-conditioning rumbles, its echoes sounding like whispers in the cool, dry air. I shiver.

"What a mess," Anita says. She wipes her hands on a towel and then redoes her ponytail, holding her hair tie in her mouth, chunky bangles clanking on her wrists.

"There's nothing for it but to get started." I let out a long sigh. Small-business owners perform multiple roles, and right now, whether I like it or not, that means I'm the janitor.

I wander into the back to grab a broom, the cavernous space an ode to viticulture. I run my hand along the stainless-steel equipment—the grape-sorting table, crusher de-stemmer, the giant wine vats that nearly touch the ceiling, and the state-of-the-art bottling system. There's a makeshift cellar sealed by a stainless-steel door with a double-glass-paned window that keeps the humidity at 60 percent and the temperature at a crisp fifty-five degrees Fahrenheit, ideal for aging wine.

Bins for future harvests line the eastern wall. I need to put in my grape orders soon. As long as I'm still in business, that is.

I push a broom over the stained concrete floors, the mundane chore keeping me grounded, working my way to the storefront. Without my asking, Anita begins efficiently tidying each of the table centerpieces and then moves on to the bar.

I lucked out when Anita applied for the assistant job, especially given the other opportunities she has as a senior at CU Boulder. Citing a dual interest in operations management and wine, she said this would give her the most hands-on experience. In truth, I see something of myself in her, and not just because she's attending my alma mater.

After college, I worked at a marketing company before trading in my cubicle for a tasting bar. It was worth it to pad my savings account, but I would like to imbue Anita with the confidence to pursue her dream straightaway, whatever that might be.

"How were sales?" Anita asks, arranging bottles and stemware on open shelving.

"I won't know until I go through invoices later." A reminder of the long—and no doubt depressing—night ahead of me. "I'm more worried about tomorrow than today."

She pauses and looks right at me, a surprising amount of emotion in her eyes. "That's the nature of business, isn't it?"

"I suppose so," I say in acquiescence, sending a desperate prayer to Bacchus that the future of Vino Valentine doesn't involve any more death. I pause and lean on the broom handle, shaking my head somberly. "That poor man."

"Yeah," Anita says with an equally dazed look.

We fall into the uneasy silence of two people trying to make sense of the unfathomable.

Chapter Four

There are flowers waiting outside my apartment when I get home that night. An extravagant bouquet of lilies, peonies, and lavender. The card reads: *Congratulations on your big day! Love, Mom and Dad.*

I crumple the note into a fist.

The flowers are a nice gesture, thoughtful even, but they don't make up for the fact that my parents weren't there today. I get that they have demanding careers, but I would have appreciated their choosing me over their jobs.

Growing up, I accepted my parents were important, my dad being head of the computer science department at CU and my mom a chemical engineer at NIST Laboratories. I was proud of them, what they were doing, even as Liam and I routinely came home to an empty house. To make up for it, we would go camping at the Rocky Mountain National Park during spring breaks and spend every holiday together—time that let us know family came first. Only now, I'm not so sure.

I don't know if they're genuinely slammed at work or if they're so blinded by my brother's screw-ups that they think my winemaking business is nothing but a passing fancy.

Either way, I want to prove to them my passion for making wine is legit.

Murder aside, that's still the case.

My phone buzzes. As if on cue, it's my mother. How is it she knew to call at this exact moment, but her mom-senses couldn't pick up on the fact that I needed her earlier?

I set the vase of flowers on the entryway table and answer my phone with a swipe. "I got your flowers." I sniff a sprig of lavender, the aroma not nearly as calming as it usually is. "Thank you."

"Of course, sweetie. I'm sorry we couldn't be there." To her credit, she sounds genuinely apologetic.

"What happened?"

"Oh, I got called into work and your dad decided to wait so we could go together." She carries on, ignorant of my silent seething, "Was it everything you dreamed it would be?"

Tears spring into my eyes and, all of the sudden, I can't do this. "Is Liam there?"

She lets out a sigh. "Always."

"Why don't you ask him? I have to go." I'd rather beg Liam's forgiveness than relive the events of the day.

"Talk later. Love you."

"Love you, too," I say, and then hang up.

I reposition the flowers—they really are lovely—before greeting my cat, Zin. She's named after Zinfandel, a grape with unknown origins, kinda like her. She's a sweet rescue kitty who hates the sound of aluminum foil and loves batting corks across the kitchen floor. The shelter had no idea where she came from but speculated she lived on the street because of the tiny bit of one ear that's inexplicably missing. I try my best to give her a life of luxury.

Zin nuzzles deeper into the afghan blanket I set up for her on the couch, moving one paw over her eyes in protest of being woken. Apparently that's the only greeting I'm going to get.

I scratch behind her ears, her silky gray fur and rolling purr a comfort.

My apartment isn't much, really more of a hallway with its skinny living room and oblong-shaped bedroom, but I've managed to make it cozy. Vintage art prints hang on the white walls, funky lamps from various art festivals give the space a worldly vibe, and a Persian rug and russet velvet sofa ooze relaxation. But the best part is the view.

I unlatch the French doors to my private balcony, the night air rife with the smell of damp earth and wet concrete after the rain. Resting my forearms on the railing, I appreciate an unobstructed view of the Flatirons, the slanted rock formations that overlook Boulder. Under the pale moonlight, they look like giant slabs of stone being tugged in opposite directions, much like my life.

My phone buzzes; it's my mom calling again, probably checking in after Liam delivered the bombshell about the murder at my winery. I send her a text letting her know I'm fine and that I'll call her tomorrow. She tries once more before giving up. I push aside the pang of guilt I feel for ignoring her.

I refocus on the mountain backdrop and give myself one more minute of reflection, and maybe an iota of self-pity, before I pad into my cramped kitchen and open the bottle of champagne I'd chilled for the occasion.

The *pop* of a cork has to be one of the happiest sounds on the planet. I pour myself a glass of bubbly and curl up next to Zin.

"Here's to Vino Valentine," I say, tilting my glass toward her squashed face. Zin head-butts my hand in response.

And I'm toasting to my business with a cat. Great.

To distract myself from my lagging romantic life, I get to work. I open my laptop and log in to my payment-tracking software. As expected, sales today were lower than projected, but that alone doesn't spell doom. Control freak that I am, when I initially developed my business plan, I factored in every contingency. Well, almost every contingency. Who could have predicted a dead body?

Point is, I went conservative.

Clicking on the analytics tab, I see the bottom line: if I sell half the wine I currently have bottled at market value in the next two months, I should be able to stay afloat until fall harvest.

A good review in *Gaskel's Gastro* would have done wonders. Heck, I'd even have settled for a mediocre review. But now . . . I shake my head.

I need to come up with something to take the heat off that bottom line. Something big enough to garner attention but still affordable.

Sipping on champagne, I log in to Instagram, Twitter, and Facebook. I scan my streams for news of Gaskel's murder, letting out a sigh of relief when I see nothing, and then post from my Vino Valentine account. Social media may be a no-brainer for advertising, but unfortunately it isn't very effective. Maybe I should look into buying ad space with a synergistic publication like *Westword* or *5280*. The problem is those don't come cheap.

"Think, Parker, think," I say to myself, but of course come up empty. Zin gazes at me with her orblike eyes, as if somewhat worried about my mental capacity.

Reid seemed in tune with the food industry; perhaps he could help me brainstorm. Admittedly, I might also be looking for an excuse to call him.

Speaking of a certain off-limits hottie, I search for Gaskel's review of The Pantry. His blog has a separate section for places that have achieved five-gastro status, a cutesy way of saying stars. There aren't many. Gaskel was known more for his scathing keystrokes than his praise, his followers appreciating his merciless candor, even if it spelled doom for restaurateurs.

The review pops up, featuring Reid smoldering in chef's attire. It's almost too good to be true. Gaskel gushes over his impeccably seared scallops, creamy corn chowder, and curry-roasted vegetables.

Envy churns in my gut. What I would give for that sort of endorsement, and Reid shrugged it off like it was no big deal.

I force myself to let it go and am steadily scrolling through electronic credit card receipts when I see it—a name I recognize. Moira Murphy. Of Murphy's Bend Vineyards.

It hits me then exactly how I knew the chic couple

from my opening. I hadn't recognized them, having only visited Murphy's Bend once, back when Vino Valentine was a wisp of a daydream.

Their winery is well established and located mere miles from mine. I'd be flattering myself if I called us competitors, but it is curious Moira and her husband—I never did catch his name—made an appearance today. And even more curious is the fact they made a scene right as Gaskel arrived.

Moira purchased a single bottle of the Ski Lodge Cherry. I wonder what she thought of it, if she even had a taste before tossing it in her husband's face.

With more than enough swirling through my mind, I finish my glass of champagne and call it a night.

I wake up feeling jet-lagged. My brain is so sluggish I have to convince myself the disaster that was yesterday actually happened. Reality finally settles in, though, making me want to nestle beneath the covers and ignore my alarm clock. Alas, I have a business to run, my vintner reputation to salvage, and a hungry cat to attend to.

Zin head-butts my arm and kneads the comforter until I finally sit up. I don't know if it's a remnant from her days on the street or a personality quirk, but she always acts like if it weren't for her constant reminders, I would inevitably forget to feed her. As if.

"Don't worry, sweet girl," I coo, scratching behind her ears soothingly. "It's time for breakfast."

Zin trails after me as I pad through my apartment, opening curtains and switching on lights. I pour a cup of kibble in her bowl and she meows a thank-you.

Ravenous kitty seen to, I go about fixing myself a bowl of granola topped with fresh berries and yogurt. I nibble breakfast on my balcony, watching the pink rays of the rising sun hit the Flatirons. By the last bite, I'm confident I can handle the day. Or at the very least, survive it.

Dressing with careful precision, I pair an airy floral dress with knee-high leather boots and dangly windcatcher earrings. I tease the locks of my A-line bob and add a touch of lip gloss to round out the look.

Lastly, I clasp my beaded necklace around my neck, a fine white-gold chain with tiny crystal grapes. It was a gift from my aunt Laura. She was the first person I told about my dream of opening a winery. I expected her to laugh, but instead she wrote me a check. Enough for a down payment on the gorgeous stainless-steel equipment currently occupying the back of my shop. If it weren't for her, it would have taken me ages to open Vino Valentine.

It's been nearly two years since she died. It was sudden, unexpected. One moment she was easing forward at an intersection, the light having just turned green, and the next she was gone. Hit by a drunk driver.

She'd been on her way home from a friend's book signing. Aunt Laura was supportive like that; always there when someone needed her. Sporting events, big presentations, birthday celebrations, if she was invited, there was no doubt Laura would attend. Likely with a foam finger.

And, as Liam and I can attest, she was the cool aunt everyone wished they had.

She took trips to remote corners of the globe,

marched in protests to make sure her voice was heard, and, in general, strove to make the world a better place than the way she found it.

I wear the necklace she gave me as a reminder to live the way she did: without regret.

I miss her like crazy every day, but feel her absence even more keenly now. What advice would she give me if she were here?

I can practically hear her chiding me to buck up and keep looking forward.

I intend to do just that.

With my head held high, I march through my front door, ready to face the world.

It's an unspoken rule in Boulder: always thank the bus driver. After a quick jaunt on the Skip RTD line, I bid the driver adieu and then flounce into the Laughing Rooster, the coffee shop neighboring my winery.

The café is packed with sleep-deprived college students, stereotypical Boulder hippies, and working professionals like myself. Perhaps I come here too often because the barista automatically starts preparing my large skinny latte.

While I wait, I peruse a table holding brochures for local businesses, noting that the stack of Vino Valentine postcards is infinitesimally shorter than the last time I checked. It may not be the huge win I need, but every little bit helps.

Caffeine in hand, and thankfully soon to be in my bloodstream, I go about one of my favorite tasks, unlocking my winery. There's something about the scent of the space—a heady mixture of freshly painted walls and aged oak barrels—that I find comforting. But today the silence only makes me twitchy.

After an hour spent jumping at every creak, I'm overjoyed when Anita arrives. And even more excited when my first batch of customers trickles in, grateful that nobody seems to have heard about Gaskel yet.

They're a group of cyclists who, from the looks of it, just finished a late-morning ride. They're surprisingly confident in spandex shorts and polyester jerseys, their table littered with water bottles and energy bars. They look thirsty, and for more than just water. The notoriously steep Lee Hill is nearby and if that was their route, they certainly deserve to kick back. I bring them an extra basket of palate-cleansing crackers, the only food we have on hand, when I go to take their order.

Anita is helping me pour their requested flights of wine when Eli—Detective Fuller—makes a smooth entrance. He's sporting another dapper suit, a crisp white shirt against navy-blue slacks and a matching jacket. It's still strange to see him clean cut and without the trademark eau de skunk. I swallow my nerves, unsure what his presence here means.

Eli spins in place, his penetrating gaze seeming to take in more than the tasteful decor. I greet him with a smile and a wave, hoping the cyclists assume he's merely another customer.

"Parker, I need to ask you a few more questions," he says.

"Of course," I answer, passing Anita the last tray to deliver to the cyclists.

The delicate glasses rattle on her open palm and she falters. It takes a lot of practice—and muscle—to carry a laden tray one-handed. Anita's a natural, though, her dish-breaking record nearly perfect.

"Have a seat at the bar," I say to Eli.

"I'd prefer to stand." He tucks a hand in his pocket, flashing me a glimpse of his gun.

"Your call." I wipe down the counter with a cloth, mostly to keep myself from fidgeting. "Did you find out any other information? Was it for sure the wine?"

"Forensics is still testing, but initial results showed high levels of aconitine in Mr. Brown's bloodstream." He rests one arm against the back of a barstool, every inch the cool and calculating detective. "We can't tie it to his glass since that went through the dishwasher, but it's a fair assumption given the wine bottle was clean."

A quick glance at the table of cyclists shows they're absorbed in recounting a particularly difficult climb from their ride. Still, law enforcement officials tend to make people nervous; best get this over with quickly.

I'm careful to keep my voice low. "What does that mean?"

"It suggests Mr. Brown was poisoned, and it was a fast-acting one." He pauses, shifting on his feet. "There's nothing anyone could have done."

My shoulders droop as I release the breath I'd been holding. "At least it was quick."

"That's more than can be said for a lot of my cases." He continues, deep lines forming around his jaw, "Did you notice anything unusual about Gaskel? Even the most insignificant detail could be important."

"You mean besides the whole murder thing?" I ask, cocking my head to the side.

Eli doesn't appreciate my sarcasm.

Tucking a loose strand of hair behind my ear, I think back to the way Gaskel's body looked, lying unmoving on the cold tiled floor. His head twisted to the side, his hand holding his fancy watch, and then I recall the piece of paper. "He had a brochure or something sticking out of his pocket like he'd recently tugged at it. I wonder what it was for."

Eli sucks in a breath. "His pockets were empty. Someone must have searched him before officers arrived on the scene."

My eyes widen. Someone didn't want the police to find whatever Gaskel was carrying, which means it likely pointed to their identity. Too bad I lost my cool, and almost my lunch, and vacated the bathroom to call 911.

"Was there anything on the ground around him?" I ask. "Anything at all in his wallet?"

"Nothing resembling a brochure. There's only your word for it." Eli narrows his eyes and pulls out his notebook, referencing something in its pages before turning his attention back to me. "Were you upset by his negative remarks on your wine?"

"You're assuming that I snooped on his tablet."

"How else would you know he didn't like your chardonnay?" Eli levels me with a stare. "It wouldn't have been that hard. He left it open to the draft of his blog post."

I shift from one foot to the other. "Fine, yes, but I don't see what that has to do with anything." Then I realize what he's implying and blanch. "You're kidding, right?"

"You were the one who poured his wine. You had access, a clear motive. It's not that far of a leap, is it?"

"But I didn't even know he would be at my opening, didn't see his comments until he was already in the bathroom. There wouldn't have been time for me to add the . . ." I trail off, something dawning on me. "Wait, does the aconit-stuff taste like anything?"

"Aconitine? I have no idea. Why?"

I whisper under my breath, "Maybe it changed the flavor. That could explain why he didn't like it." I'm ashamed to admit how relieved I am by this prospect.

"Back to the matter at hand," he says sharply, attracting the attention of the cyclists and Anita. "A man was poisoned. By your wine—"

"Technically it wasn't my wine," I clarify. "It was something *added* to my wine."

"Regardless, my job is to figure out how this happened." Eli's baritone voice echoes through my winery.

The health-conscious athletes make a hasty retreat, throwing cash on the oak-barrel table, their flights of wine only half-finished. My stomach plummets faster than my ego.

The door clicks shut behind them. I smack a hand against my forehead and groan. "Dammit, Eli, do you have to scare my customers away?"

Anita pushes the tasters toward me across the bar top and then retreats to clean their table.

"Sorry," Eli says, having enough sense to appear sheepish. He sinks into a stool. "This must be hard for you."

"You have no idea." I dump the remaining tasters of wine down the drain one at a time, each one a jab to my pride. Sweat equity, and plenty of real equity, went into every swallow. A lump lodges itself in my throat.

"This seems like a cool place," Eli says, finally resembling the boy from my past.

"Thanks," I murmur. "Would you like a taste of something? On the house." I'm surprised by how much I hope he agrees.

"Another time. When I'm not on the clock." His lips twitch into a lopsided smile.

"So how'd you get to be a detective? Last I remember, you ran with a pretty different crowd."

"Long story. Suffice it to say, people change." I never noticed it before, probably because they were always bloodshot, but he has soulful eyes the color of dark caramel. "Are you still into climbing?"

"I haven't gone in a while. Starting Vino Valentine has kept me pretty busy." I rub the back of my neck, a knotted mess of tension. "I really should, though. It's always helped me relax."

"That would be smart. Investigations can last awhile, especially after we pass the twenty-four-hour mark. That being said . . ." He trails off with a meaningful glance at the clock. "Can I borrow your assistant?"

"Just promise to return her in one piece," I answer. "And can you ask your questions in the back?"

Eli nods and approaches Anita, who's still wiping down that same table, ponytail swinging. If she's not careful, she'll buff her way straight to the ground.

Anita jumps in her wedge sandals when Eli addresses her and teeters away from him. She visibly gulps and stammers an answer before following Eli into the back of my shop.

The skittish way she's behaving makes me wonder: Does Anita know something about Gaskel's murder?

My next customer is wholly unexpected.

The bell jingles as a slim woman with deeply tanned skin and a warm smile enters my shop. Her long hair is braided down her back, blond with textured maroon highlights. I recognize her as half of the chic, yet dramatic, couple from my opening.

"Moira Murphy," she says, holding out a hand, a tennis bracelet dangling on her wrist. "Of Murphy's Bend Vineyards."

"Right," I say as if this is news to me. Her grip is like the vise I use to crush grapes. "Parker Valentine. Nice to meet you."

She plops her slouchy leather purse on the bar top. "How long have you been making wine?" She has the silky voice of an automated message system.

"For about six years, although it really started as a hobby."

I think back to my very first glass of the hallowed beverage, a Chianti in Florence while I was studying abroad at the ripe young age of nineteen. It was love at first sip. The complexity of the flavors and how a winemaker can manipulate them enthralled me.

My ever-observant aunt got me a winemaking kit for my twenty-first birthday and even offered up her garage as a space for me to prep it in. By the time my first batch of wine—a merlot I was probably a little too proud of—was complete, I was hooked.

With the idea for Vino Valentine a spark in my mind, I spent two glorious weeks in Napa touring vineyards, fawning over delicate thin-skinned grapes. The winemakers patiently answered my questions, sharing their earned wisdom about maceration times, oak versus steel aging, and blending varietals to enhance flavor. When I returned home, I was like a mad scientist, beakers strewn about my apartment, testing the methods I'd learned with new fervor.

I continue, "I didn't seriously consider it as a business venture until a couple of years ago."

Moira nods as if she understands perfectly, but then purses her lips. "I want to apologize for my husband's and my behavior yesterday. Trust me when I say it was very out of character."

"It's fine. Really." I fiddle with the tasting menus, stacking them neatly on the countertop. "It was hardly the worst thing that happened."

"About that—"

My heart plummets to somewhere around my naval. She only left with a bottle of the Ski Lodge Cherry, after all. "I can give you your money back if you want," I offer hurriedly. "It was terrible—"

"That's not why I'm here," she interrupts, giving me a stern look reminiscent of my second-grade teacher. "Never offer to give a customer their money back. Honestly, that's no way to conduct a successful business."

"Guess I'm a little trigger-happy with damage control." I click my tongue. "So why are you here?"

"I just had to stop by and tell you in person how much I loved your wine."

My jaw drops and I stammer, "R-really?"

"Really," she says, dimples forming. "The chardonnay was divine, nice and buttery, exactly my preference. I left with a bottle of the cherry so my husband and I could actually taste it instead of using it as a missile." Her cheeks dot with color, but she continues, unabashedly, "We still can't figure out how you achieved such a depth of flavor."

"That means a lot coming from you." I smile nervously, and then sigh. "It may end up being a vintage edition."

Concern etches her face. "Why do you say that?"

"You were there, you know what happened with Gaskel." Voicing his name leaves a bitter taste in my mouth and a hollow ache in my chest.

"Oh, pffft." She tugs at her long braid, draping it over one shoulder. "In my opinion, the restaurant world is better off without *Gaskel's Gastro.*"

No doubt there are those who heaved a sigh of relief at no longer having to worry about Gaskel's critical pen, but to say so out loud is rather tactless. I mean, he was still a real person with family and dreams for the future.

There's an awkward silence as I steal a glance at the doorway behind me, grateful that Eli is still in the back questioning Anita. This is a tidbit he might find interesting. I fiddle with my beaded necklace.

"You've gotta admit Gaskel brought attention to restaurants others might miss," I say.

"Oh, I didn't mean to sound callous," she says hurriedly, her eyes darting around. "It's a sad affair, and you're right, Gaskel's reviews certainly helped with press coverage, but they weren't the be-all end-all."

I nod, only slightly satisfied, and make a mental note to check if Gaskel ever reviewed Murphy's Bend, curious to discover if Moira has an ulterior motive for stopping by. I hope not, because I kinda like her.

"I've been to your tasting room, too. The Bend It Red is delicious." I lean forward, lowering my voice to a conspiratorial whisper, "Any chance you'll tell me what varietals are in it?"

"Cab franc, merlot, syrah, and one more secret ingredient I can't share," she says with a wink. "Have you thought about hosting a VIP tasting?"

That idea, along with roughly a dozen others, has

indeed crossed my mind. "Unfortunately, I don't have a clientele built up yet."

"Carrick and I threw a party a couple years ago for a few top-tier clients and it was very successful." She taps her chin with one finger, considering. "Why don't I send you the contact information of some avid wine lovers I know who would appreciate something like this?"

I'm beyond flattered she would even offer. "That would be amazing, but are you allowed to share their contact info?"

"I'll only include people I consider friends, and I'll even give them a heads-up."

"Wow, thank you," I gush. Really, who am I to pass up any opportunity that comes my way? My brain is already churning through plans and possibilities. This could be the big break Vino Valentine needs, only . . . "Why are you doing this?"

"We need to work together to put Colorado wines on the map. Plus, like I said, I enjoyed your wine. You have passion, spunk." She clutches her purse and holds my gaze. "Don't pay any attention to the headlines. The media exaggerates everything."

"Headlines?" I ask with a gulp.

I fumble with my phone, my fingers shaking as I open the *Denver Post* app. In bold black letters, the very top story reads: *Food Critic's Fatal Sip*. The article weaves a narrative where yours truly, in a fit of desperation, poisoned Denver's premier critic for not liking my wine.

Hesitantly, I open social media. Vino Valentine has been mentioned and tagged in hundreds of posts, and #KillerChardonnay is currently trending. I scroll through my Twitter notifications, my temperature rising at the rage behind the tweets.

> @MilesHPoole: Why hasn't an arrest been made,
> @BoulderPD? @VinoValentine is obviously
> GUILTY #LockherUp #KillerChardonnay

> @CORealScene: Shocked @VinoValentine is
> allowed to stay open for business
> #JusticeforGaskel #KillerChardonnay

> @JKLemon2: .@VinoValentine's wine was so bad
> it literally killed @GaskelsGastro
> #KillerChardonnay #WineFail

I drop my phone as if it were responsible for this virtual horror.

"Oh my God," I say, holding one hand over my mouth.

Damn the media. Damn whoever killed Gaskel and caused this mess.

"Chin up, dear," Moira says. "This will blow over in no time." With those parting words, which are far from uplifting, she leaves.

I don't know if I'll ever be able to put Gaskel's death behind me. Even if my business miraculously survives this, finding his body, with his pale face and glassy eyes, is like a scar on my psyche. As much a part of me as the lightning-shaped scar on my shin. I got it at the end of a long day of climbing in Eldorado Canyon. The sandstone cliffs and bubbling creek were too enticing for me to quit when I should have. Someday it may make for one helluva story, but there will always be a tinge of lingering fear at being faced with my own mortality.

I'm still staring after Moira when Eli resurfaces from the back. "That's one loyal assistant you have."

I nod numbly. "Thanks."

"I didn't say that was a good thing." A frown slides into place. "Ms. Moore wasn't very forthcoming, but it seemed like there was something on her mind. Any idea what it could be?"

I shrug my shoulders. "The usual stress of an uncertain future? She only has a year left of college, which is a scary spot to be in."

"Perhaps," he says but doesn't take his eyes off of mine, clearly not buying that answer. "I don't know if you're aware, but it's obstruction of justice to keep something from the authorities."

"Whatever happened to innocent until proven guilty?"

"This isn't a courtroom." He hesitates and then asks, "Did you ask her to cover for you in any way?"

"Of course not. I want this case solved as much as you do. Probably more, actually."

"If you say so." He knocks twice on the counter. "I'll be in touch."

I don't bother with a response.

The truth is that I can throw VIP parties or revamp advertising, but there's really only one way to salvage my reputation: prove that I—and my wine—had nothing to do with Gaskel's murder.

Chapter Five

The first rule of economics is that there's no such thing as a free lunch. When I offer to treat my brother to a sandwich at his favorite deli, it's because I need something in return. Something he probably won't want to give me.

Pearl Street is hopping, as it usually is. Paved with brick and lined with quirky shops selling a wide range of goods from sports gear to upscale kitchenware to kites, the pedestrian street is the heart of Boulder and has something for everyone.

May is my favorite time of year to walk the outdoor mall, the suffocating dry heat of summer yet to settle in. Marigolds, petunias, and geraniums add splashes of color to green foliage, and a large rock sculpture doubles as a burbling fountain. I navigate around street performers—a contortionist folding himself into a tiny box and a trio of musicians playing alternative pop songs on classical instruments—and the crowds each has attracted.

My lunch destination is a place called Snarf's located down a quieter side alley, a hidden gem renowned for its homemade spicy pickles and peppers. I order our usual sandwiches—portobello and swiss for me, and turkey on rye for Liam—and, once they're ready, snag the last table outside.

I check my phone. No texts from Anita. I left her in charge of my winery with instructions to alert me pronto if she needs help. Not that I expect many customers after getting demolished in the news and on social media. I cringe inwardly.

Liam sinks into the chair opposite me, über casual in jeans and a white undershirt. The dirt caked on his work boots makes me wonder, even as he carefully sets his camera bag at his feet, if photography is on the way out and there's a new hobby on the horizon. This is about the life span of one of his so-called passions.

Liam's past hobbies include but are not limited to: day trading in the stock market (the real reason he ended up back in Mom and Dad's basement), wanting to *make it* as a musician (his angsty period, complete with grunge jeans and obscure lyrics), and hosting a podcast that pitted popular fictional characters against one another (which was actually pretty entertaining).

"How's the photography?" I ask, trying to be as pleasant as possible. I do need something from him, after all.

"A work in progress," he answers, a gleam of excitement in his eyes. "I'll have shots from your opening soon. There should be a couple for your website."

My ears perk up. Maybe Liam managed to capture

something—or someone—incriminating. "Remind me again why you don't do digital?"

"Because film makes me feel more creative, and it produces crisper images with a starker light contrast."

"Yeah, yeah, yeah," I grumble. My brother, the analog purist, is potentially slowing down the investigation. I suppose I should be grateful he managed to get pictures at all. "Let me know when they're ready."

"You're not the only one interested. That detective wants to see them, too." Liam was two grades ahead in high school so he doesn't have the same memories of Eli that I do.

"Any chance you can give me a peek before you turn them in?"

"Sure," he says with a shrug and unwraps his sandwich. "So what do you want?" he asks before taking a large bite.

I shrug, munching on a spicy pickle. "Maybe I just wanted to have lunch with my brother."

"I call BS." He wipes his mouth with a napkin and starts messing with his phone.

"Excuse me, we're having lunch here." I gesture between us.

Liam levels with me. "Do you want Reid's number or not?"

I open and close my mouth several times, sputtering, "That's just preposterous." Liam watches me, unblinking. He knows me too well. "Fine. Yes, I want his number."

"I knew it." He throws his napkin on the table in triumph. "Only if you promise this won't be another Guy situation."

I flinch at my ex's name. Guy was my last and longest relationship. I honestly thought we would be together forever, but when he moved out of state to pursue his career as a political consultant, long distance proved to be tough. Too tough. After a few strained months, he presented me with an ultimatum: either I move to D.C. and abandon my winery plans or we break up. It wasn't a difficult decision to make; guess that means it wasn't true love.

Guy took it harder than I did. He assumed I'd pack my bags and go play supportive girlfriend to his leading man. When I didn't, he not only cut me out of his life, he cut my brother out, too.

As a result, Liam lost one of his oldest friends and I lost someone who I thought would always be in my corner. And sure, it was Guy's fault he behaved the way he did. But I didn't have to pretend moving on would be easy. Or end things by sending him that meme of Ruth Bader Ginsburg dropping her microphone.

I haven't been on a date since. Between opening Vino Valentino and now with Gaskel's murder, there hasn't been time. At least that's what I keep telling myself.

"I promise," I say. "This is purely a business matter."

"Yeah, right," he says, entirely unconvinced. He taps his phone and then turns the screen toward me.

"How did you meet Reid, anyway?" I ask, copying the number over. "He seems more driven than most of your friends."

"I resent that." He waves a chip in my direction before tossing it carelessly into his mouth. "I have very driven friends."

"Just no drive yourself." I always thought an older brother was supposed to be someone to look up to, a role model. The only things I've learned from Liam are what mistakes to avoid.

He just shrugs and looks away. "We met when I subbed for his bassist. He's the drummer for a band called Spatula." We chew our sandwiches in silence for a minute before Liam speaks again. "I feel like it's my brotherly duty to warn you, Reid isn't the commitment type."

"Good thing I'm not interested in him romantically," I say, secretly wanting to hear more. I lean forward in my seat.

"Don't get me wrong, he's a great guy and all, but he's—how do I put this lightly—a total player."

"Noted," I say, one eyebrow raised. I shouldn't be surprised. That basically secures his bad-boy image. "Seriously, I'm only reaching out to pick his brain on marketing for Vino Valentine." And to find out if he knows anything about Gaskel's murder.

"Can't Sage help with that?" he asks, crushing his sandwich wrapper into a ball.

Sage would be more than happy to help me brainstorm, but it wouldn't be very fruitful. She's the best friend and coconspirator a gal could ask for, and brilliant in her own right, but she doesn't have insight into the restaurant biz.

"She's busy with work and Jason," I say by way of an explanation.

Liam frowns, creases forming on his forehead. He really doesn't want me to contact Reid. I chew the last bite of my sandwich, savoring the mingling spicy and savory flavors. "What made you bring Reid to my opening?"

"He heard about it and, once he found out we were related, asked to tag along." He says this like it's no big deal, but it sends my mind reeling.

Here I'd assumed my brother dragged him along, but Reid knew about my opening ahead of time, had sought out an invite. Now, not to sell my wine short, but what if he had an ulterior motive for attending? Like exacting revenge on a certain critic. Only, Gaskel gave him a glowing review. If Reid was involved, there must have been another reason, perhaps having to do with the reputation he alluded to.

Liam continues, interrupting my thoughts, "If I thought you'd be into him, I would've said no. I'm not Tinder."

"Big left-swipe on that," I say cheekily.

He exaggerates a flinch. "I don't want to know anything about my little sister's swiping."

We continue our sibling banter, but there's something simmering below the surface, a forced nonchalance emanating from Liam that sets me on edge.

I only have two customers that afternoon, if you could even count my parents as customers.

They sit at an oak barrel table near the front window. My mom pushes cat-eye glasses up her nose and drums her fingers on the tabletop, her frizzy hair bounding out in all directions. My dad quietly studies the tasting menu, his smartwatch glinting in the sunlight. He likes to stay up-to-date with the most recent technology, which is at odds with the layer of chalk usually coating him.

I steel myself and greet each of them with a hug. My mom gives me an extra squeeze before letting go.

"Welcome to Vino Valentine," I say. My heart clenches as I gesture to my barren winery. If only the other tables were full of happily imbibing customers.

"It's lovely, sweetie," my mom gushes, patting my hand. She readjusts the sparkly grape brooch I gave her for her last birthday. "Your aunt Laura would be proud."

Her glassy eyes mirror my own.

"This is some place, kid," my dad says. It's not easy to impress him—many a student has tried and failed—but he raises his eyebrows so high they're encroaching on his receding hairline. "I hope you're not staying open just for us."

Something lodges itself in my throat. Probably my pride. "No. It's been pretty dead around here after the excitement of yesterday."

I force a smile on my face, not wanting to worry them. They get enough of that from my brother.

"That's so sad about that critic," my mom says, as if *sad* can even begin to describe the injustice. "We couldn't believe it when Liam told us what happened. Have the police found who did it?"

"Not yet," I say glumly. "The detective was here again this morning."

"They'll catch him and people will forget, move on to the next thing," my dad offers encouragingly.

"Hopefully sooner rather than later," I mumble, and then switch gears. "Did either of you read Gaskel's blog?"

They both shake their heads. I shouldn't be surprised; restaurant trends aren't really their forte.

"I met him once at the dean's house," my dad says. He regularly gets invited to schmoozing events pandering to potential university donors. "If I remember correctly, he spent the majority of the party complaining about the temperature of the stuffed mushrooms."

"That sounds about right," I say, recalling the sting of his harsh words about my chardonnay. "Well, what can I get you both?"

"White wine for me," my mom says. "And sparkling water."

I scratch my forehead to cover my wince. "At least taste the wine before you make a spritzer. Please."

Spritzers are delicious in their own right—fizzy and refreshing—but they change the flavor of wine. Ice cubes effectively water down the drink and carbonation masks intricacies of the grapes. After all the time and effort I've put into making my wines, it's honestly a little insulting.

She purses her lips and wriggles in her seat. "Women haven't worked for generations to have our freedoms snatched away from us . . ." I roll my eyes. This isn't the first time I've heard her feminist spiel, usually reserved for more meaningful matters than cocktail preferences. Luckily, she cuts it short. "No one is here to see anyway."

"Red wine," my dad interjects with the even tone of a referee. "Whatever you recommend."

Grinding my teeth, I seek sanctuary behind the tasting counter and pour their drinks. The Mount Sanitas White for my mom and Campy Cab for my dad. On the house, of course.

I deliver their orders and linger while they sip. They barely swallow before showering me with compliments and, for a minute, I feel like I might be able to do this, like a chink in my battered confidence has been restored.

Maybe my winery actually has a shot.

Then, as I walk away, I hear the telltale sound of ice cubes plunking into a glass and the fizz of carbonation. My mom is making a wine spritzer.

I'm not good with uncertainty. In winemaking, I get to decide which varietals to blend and how long to let the juices macerate, ferment, and age in oak or steel. Every step is science blended with art, yielding results largely under my control.

This is all to say, I spend way too long debating whether to contact Reid.

After a dismal afternoon and with no sales on the horizon, the spritzer incident fresh in my mind, I get desperate. I need to know if he had something to do with the murder, or at the very least, can elaborate on Gaskel's reputation. If he happens to have marketing ideas, too, all the better.

I carefully construct a text: *Hey Reid. This is Parker Valentine, Liam's sister. Would you be up for grabbing a cup of coffee? There's something I want to discuss with you.*

My pulse quickens as I press send; it's been ages since I felt nervous about texting a guy. I distract myself by checking social media, which is so utterly depressing I want to chuck my phone into the trash bin.

Luckily, Reid doesn't make me wait long: *Sounds great. Name the time and place.*

I type: *Tomorrow 9 am, the Laughing Rooster?*

He responds in the affirmative, complete with a winking emoji.

That settled, I sit at an oak-barrel table and scroll through electronic receipts to see if any other customer names leap out at me like Moira's did. No such luck. I'll have to research each one individually, a task best done in the privacy of my own home. I'd hate to be caught creepily stalking customers, even if it is for a good cause.

"Do you mind if I take off a little early?" Anita asks, startling me. Her apron is already stored beneath the counter and she fingers the straps of her embroidered purse guiltily. "It's so quiet, I figured . . ."

"As long as it's not for a job interview," I respond, only half-kidding. "I'd hate to lose you as an assistant."

"Of course not," she says, dimples forming in her round cheeks. "It's an early yoga class."

Anita does strike me as the yoga type, lithe and graceful, and with the calm disposition of someone who meditates regularly. "Then absolutely."

She beams at me in thanks. "The winery will be fine. This is just a storm that needs to be weathered." With her white cotton dress, thick glasses, and long wavy blond hair, she gives the appearance of someone who's never experienced hardship.

I suddenly remember her strange behavior with Eli. "Hey, what questions did Detective Fuller ask you?"

"If I saw anything suspicious." She shifts her weight from one foot to another. "But most of them were about you. How long I've known you, what kind of boss you are, that sort of thing. Honestly, he seemed kinda into you."

I can't help the laugh that escapes my throat, even as my face flushes. "He's only interested in me because he thinks I poisoned Gaskel."

"That makes absolutely no sense. Why would you self-sabotage?"

Loyalty like hers is hard to come by. I give her an appreciative smile. "Because he didn't like my chardonnay."

She holds a hand to her chest, her eyes widening. "The Chautauqua Chardonnay? No way."

"They think the poison was in his glass, but since it went through the dishwasher they can't be sure it wasn't my wine."

"Oh, em, gee." Her lips tremble and color drains from her face, but her tone takes me aback, almost like she's saying what's expected instead of what's really on her mind.

"Why were you so nervous around the detective?"

I expect her to shrug it off, deny her strange behavior, but she surprises me.

"I guess it's like when you're driving, you can't help but slow down when you see a cop, even if you're only going the speed limit." She pauses, twirling a strand of hair around one finger. "You try so hard to act normal, afraid they'll think you did something wrong, that you end up coming across as, well, *not* normal."

"Totally," I answer. "Too bad, though. I thought you might've seen something."

"I wish," she says, sniffling. A single tear trickles down her cheek. She wipes it away and tries for a smile, but it doesn't reach her eyes. "I feel helpless."

The only way to examine the true colors in a glass of wine is to hold it up to the light. The same could be said for people. I consider Anita afresh, her polished exterior, polite demeanor, and youthful innocence. She's smart—she would have to be to manage her course load—but obviously sheltered.

"Had you met Gaskel before?" I ask, leaning back in the espresso folding chair, the metal cool and grounding.

"No, but I've followed his blog since I was a kid. My parents introduced me to *Gaskel's Gastro*." She casts a wayward glance toward the bathroom. "They praised it for promoting Colorado businesses."

"True," I say with a sigh. What a harsh reminder that a local legend was destroyed in my winery. "Where are you from?"

She swallows nervously. "I feel like I'm being interrogated. Did I do something wrong?"

"No," I say quickly, forcing a smile on my face. "I was just curious. You get out of here and enjoy your class."

Anita hesitates. She grasps the strap of her purse with white knuckles and rocks on her feet—backward and forward—and then shakes her head. "See you," she finally says with a fake cheeriness and leaves.

One thing is for sure: there's something she isn't telling me.

After I close up, I stop by the climbing gym hoping to burn off a bit of lingering stress. The gym has a solid combination of bouldering and climbing walls, and the art deco murals feature peaks from around the Front Range.

Dressed in cargo pants, tank top, and a headband, I strap a chalk bag around my waist and squeeze into my tiny shoes. I've always loved the way my feet look in climbing shoes, like they're meant to careen mountains.

I decide to start with bouldering. No ropes, no harness, no spotter. Just the puzzle of how to get from point A to point B by leveraging your body in certain ways and using the path of bright-colored grips. It's a practice in balance, patience, and knowing when to take a leap of faith.

Traipsing across the thick cushioned floor, I dust my hands with chalk and select a challenging purple route. I start in the corner at eye level and maneuver myself from one grip to the next, pausing between each move to calculate the next. My back and arm muscles are taut and my legs contract and straighten, every muscle working in unison.

My fingers grow sweaty, so I dip them back into my

bag for more chalk, letting my body dangle by one arm with my feet supporting me from below.

I lunge with my arms and the image of Gaskel's body flashes through my mind. As I pull myself to the next grip, I think about how someone could have done it. There'd been a glass waiting in front of Gaskel when I'd approached him to start his tasting. I didn't think twice about it then, but Anita and I had both been busy. Who could have gotten it for him?

When I kick my leg out wide to reach the next foot-hold, I think about what would make someone desperate enough to resort to murder. Was it a bad review or something else that drove them to kill? Was the murder carefully planned or a spur-of-the-moment decision? Did the killer mean to take my business down, too?

I reach the end of the route and let myself fall back onto the cushioned floor with a soft thump. My brain is still buzzing with questions, but it's quieter than before.

My next step is clear. I need a better understanding of the suspects, and for that I need Sage. While she may not be a restaurant guru, she has a natural affinity for reading people from her experience in trial as a court clerk.

I dust off my hands and call my friend.

Sage and I are like an unexpected food and wine pairing. Green chili and chardonnay, grilled cheese and brut, or peanut butter and pinot noir. Our friendship shouldn't work but, for some inexplicable reason, it just does.

We've been friends ever since we were assigned as roommates freshmen year of college. Whereas I'm more outdoorsy and willing to take risks, she's the stereotypical indoor kid, into reading, video games, and cosplay.

But our styles mesh.

We both like things tidy but not too tidy, know what it means to work hard, and have a perspective that allows us to not sweat the small stuff.

Sage must have come straight to my apartment from court because she's still in her power suit—gray slacks, pumps, and a fierce blouse that brings out the red in her hair.

She's carrying a reusable grocery bag. "I stopped by the farmers market for provisions," she says, procuring Haystack Mountain goat cheese, rustic oat crackers, and a carton of fresh-picked raspberries from the bag.

"Well played, counselor." I carefully assemble our snack onto a plate, mouth salivating, and pour us each a glass of pinot.

Zin eyes our nibbles curiously, her pink nose sniffing in approval as I set the plate down on the coffee table. I pluck her up and move her to a pillow I deem a safe distance from the vittles, sinking into the couch next to her. She gives me an affronted look, but is quick to forgive when I pet her silky fur. Zin's steady purring sets the backdrop for our conversation.

"So what's up?" Sage asks, a pained edge to her voice. She winces as she reaches for a cracker and slathers it with a healthy layer of chèvre.

Maybe it's the events of yesterday, but I'm immediately on guard. "What's wrong?"

"I was moving furniture before work this morning," she answers, taking a large swig of wine.

"Hey, that's my favorite pinot. Take your time and

enjoy its flavors." I've been trying, and failing, to get Sage into wine tasting since college.

"Tastes like wine," she says cheekily before leaning back with a contented sigh. I decide not to push it.

I pop a raspberry in my mouth and chase it with a sip of wine, the freshness from the berry pairing perfectly with the smoky undertones. "What furniture were you moving?"

"Jason's recliner."

"Wait, why were you moving Jason's *man chair*?"

"It wasn't angled correctly to see the TV and his back was bugging him," she answers with a shrug. "Which is why he needed the damn recliner in the first place."

"That's convenient."

"We can't all be an island like you." She gives me a pointed look over her wineglass. "You know, some people ask for help when they need it. Even The Manual"—Sage's nickname for the esteemed Judge Manuel Acosta for his encyclopedic knowledge of the legal system—"needs assistance sometimes. As he proved when he threw an intellectual property case on my desk at the last minute today."

I roll my shoulders, which are already tightening from climbing. "Actually, that's why I called you. I need your help."

"You're not personally liable, if that's what you're worried about." Her phone buzzes; she checks the screen briefly before silencing it and putting it in her bag. That's the thing about Sage: whenever I need her, she's there for me with her one-hundred-percent laser focus.

"I hadn't even thought of that," I say with a groan. I take another sip of wine, letting the fruity flavors roll over my tongue, and then continue, "I need you to tell me what you noticed from yesterday."

"Why don't you ask Liam?" she asks. "He was there with his camera. Photo documentation would be more credible."

"I'm fully planning on combing through his pictures." I take my headband off and rub my temples. "But Liam doesn't know people like you do. Did you notice anyone who was off, or who gave off a strange vibe?"

Sage gets cozy on the couch on the other side of Zin, removing her lavish black strappy shoes. I make a mental note to borrow them for my next night out, whenever that might be.

"There was the couple who got into that very public, and messy, fight," Sage starts, scratching behind Zin's ears. "They continued to bicker the rest of the time, although quietly, and did not seem happy about being stuck there while the officers did their once-over."

"That would be Moira and her husband, Carrick. They own Murphy's Bend Vineyards. She stopped by earlier to apologize for all the drama, and to offer some friendly business advice."

"Maybe she felt guilty for offing the critic and dooming your business. Not that it's doomed," she adds hurriedly. "But her advice could've been a sort of karmic olive branch."

"True." I cock my head to the side. "Guess I'll be paying them a visit and trying their wine. A tasting is the perfect cover to probe for information."

"Let me know when you're going and I'll tag along."

"Deal," I say, giving her an appreciative smile. All it took was a murder investigation to pique her interest in wine tasting. "Okay, what else?"

"Jason knew one of the guys from the table of recent grads, said he was acting strange, almost like he was embarrassed about something. He did seem a bit"—she takes a sip of wine while searching for the right word—"twitchy, I guess. But that could be who he is. Either way, the twitchy ones always cave."

I stifle a groan. I'll have to ask Jason for the customer's name, a task for tomorrow. "Anything else?"

"That Reid guy is interesting. He really doesn't care what anyone thinks of him." She munches on a cracker, musing. "But I didn't get the sense he was hiding anything. Plus, your brother can vouch for him."

"We both know Liam's never been the best judge of character. Remember Penny?" I ask, referring to one of my brother's worst moves, bringing a girl to Thanksgiving dinner. Let's just say Penny made off with more than her namesake. "Luckily I'm having coffee with Reid in the morning, so I can find out for sure."

"Ooh, intrigue." She nudges me with her foot. "Let me know how it goes."

"Of course." I clink my glass with hers. "Cheers."

Later that night, I sit alone at the small bistro-style table on my balcony with my laptop open in front of me. Crickets chirp lazily in the darkness and a cool breeze grazes my cheek. I zip up my hoodie and twirl the drawstrings between two fingers.

I start by typing *aconitine* into a search window and click on the top hit, a summary of the horrible side effects of the poison: numbness of the feet and limbs, extreme nausea, difficulty breathing, confusion, and worse.

My stomach twists and sweat beads on my forehead,

almost like I'm experiencing phantom pity pains. I shake it off and study a picture of the delicate purple flower aconitine stems from, also known as wolfsbane, or monkshood because of the way its petals curl together like a hood. Every part of the plant is extremely poisonous and it just so happens to grow especially well in mountainous regions of the northern hemisphere—that would be Boulder.

I let out a long exhale and open a fresh tab before I make myself sick.

The homepage of Gaskel's blog pays tribute to the man behind the reviews. There are hundreds of messages—fans sending condolences and wishes that he rest in peace.

But there are other messages, too. Unexpected ones calling him a fraud and worse.

Like *FlavorVille55,* who says: *They say those that can't, teach. I say those who can't, review. The only thing you* could *do was tear others down.*

Or the mildly threatening *devils_food99,* who claims: *You ruined my family. I was orphaned because of you. You deserve what you got.*

And even an accusatory comment from *Flygurl15,* who says: *I know about the kickbacks u got. Glad ur gone.*

Now, I know the internet is full of trolls, but I wonder if there's any truth to their charges.

I read Gaskel's bio twice. It seems only fair that if you see someone in death, you should know something about their life.

He was a Colorado native from Breckenridge, where his sister still resides. Gaskel was always passionate about food, but was never interested in becoming a chef. After earning a degree in journalism from Syracuse, he moved back to Colorado and started blogging about food and wine. He worked for various news publications until they slowly puttered out of print, at which point his blog had gained enough followers for him to pursue it full time. No significant other is mentioned; in fact, he always dined alone at establishments he reviewed. The bio closes with a picture of him in a casual fleece sweater posing with his terrier named Pico.

Gaskel clearly worked hard for his success, his solitary lifestyle indicating he likely chose his profession over a personal life, something I can relate to.

I glance at Zin, my companion extraordinaire, who is waiting patiently on the other side of the kitchen window, swishing her tail and staring wistfully outside. I pluck a leaf of catnip from the plant I keep on the balcony and slip it inside, much to Zin's delight. Through glass panes in the balcony doors, I watch as she munches on the leaf. Soon she's rolling around on the ground, batting at the curtain cord. I smile at her playfulness and then get back to work.

The archives of Gaskel's blog include reviews for hundreds of restaurants, diners, wineries, and even a few microbreweries. Seriously, the guy was so prolific he could have hosted his own show on the Food Network.

Fleetingly, I wonder what made him attend my dinky opening. Was he legitimately interested in reviewing it, or was there some other purpose to his visit? I may never know.

I find his review of Murphy's Bend and sink lower into my chair. As I read, my fingers tingle and a chill creeps up my spine.

His words are scathing. He wrote that their wine—

with the exception of the Bend It Red—tasted artificial and one-note, and he was especially harsh on their cab, which he referred to as a *viable substitute for battery acid*. Ouch.

Scrolling through the numerous comments, I get a sense of the toll his review must have taken on their business.

Moira Murphy certainly had a motive, but what she lacked was opportunity. She couldn't have slipped something into Gaskel's wine; she never left the table. But her husband did.

Carrick went to the restroom to freshen up after his wife threw her wine at him. He could have easily made a detour to the bar without Anita or me noticing. We'd both been so scattered, cleaning, keeping up with tables, and, of course, pandering to the esteemed critic.

What were they fighting about that escalated so quickly? I mean, that level of drama is usually reserved for prime time, not real life. Unless the whole interchange had been staged, it was a clever way to take the focus away from the bar. But then what was with the hushed bickering Sage overheard?

I gnaw on my bottom lip, changing gears. Even if I don't trust Moira or her husband, I'd be a fool not to heed her tip. As promised, sent to Vino Valentine's business account, is a list of VIP clients from Murphy @MurphyBend.com. She included a warm salutation and brief note wishing me luck.

I've always believed hard work trumps luck, but I'd need both to resurrect my business.

I start formatting an invitation, picking this Thursday as a date, figuring I can do a classy spin on Thirsty Thursday, a common utterance in our college town.

With no time to waste, I select a black-and-white photograph to push it over the top—make it more VIP—and draft the verbiage. I want it to sound upscale but not snooty.

My phone buzzes, causing me to jump and bonk my knee against the table. It's a text from Sage: *don't check social media.*

I send a quick reply: *ignorance isn't an option for me right now.*

She responds with the monkey emoji covering its eyes.

It can't possibly be that bad, right? The upside to social media is that it has a short attention span. There's always a shiny new story.

Bracing myself, I log in to Twitter, Facebook, and Instagram.

Not only is #KillerChardonnay still trending, but now Vino Valentine and my personal account are both being mentioned, and slammed. Over and over and over. By users who don't realize there's a real person reading their notes, a person who had no part in what happened to *the* Gaskel Brown.

I slam my laptop shut when I can't take any more, feeling even more determined to track down Gaskel's killer. Not only will they have his fans and the justice system to contend with, but they'll also have to answer to yours truly.

Chapter Six

I get to the Laughing Rooster early the next morning in a pitiful attempt to calm my nerves. Having been up since dawn, I've already consumed more than my fair share of caffeine. Still, I greedily slurp my latte as I search for a suitable table.

I choose one tucked away in a private corner with a view of the entrance, stashing my purse and climbing bag underneath. Vibrant paintings by local artists hang on the walls, price tags dangling from each one, and the scents of espresso and freshly baked pastries waft through the air.

My foot bobs along with the bluesy music playing over the loudspeakers. I can't stop fidgeting. I smooth my hands over my striped pencil skirt and make sure my blouse is tucked in just the right amount.

Then, all at once, I freeze.

Reid saunters into the café, the sunlight highlighting the amber and gold tones in his mussed sandy hair, reminding me of a glass of port. In slim-fitted jeans and a T-shirt, he appears relaxed as can be. He scans the café—his eyes lazily roaming over study groups and mommy playdates—until they land on me. I start and give a sheepish wave.

He puts in his order with the very smitten barista before making his way toward me.

"Thanks for meeting me," I say by way of a greeting.

His lips twitch as he takes the seat across from me and rests his elbows on the table. Again I notice the scars lining his forearms, only now I recognize them for what they are: oven burns.

"Gotta admit," he says, "I'm intrigued, and that doesn't happen often."

The barista delivers Reid's coffee, a warm sticky bun dotted with pecans, and two forks. She winks at Reid before retreating, her neck flushed.

"I've never even gotten a smile out of her, let alone table service," I muse.

He flashes me a devilish grin, I imagine the same one that made the barista swoon.

"That won't work on me," I say, taking a sip of my latte.

"It was worth a shot." He turns his attention to the sticky bun. "No serious talk before breakfast. Help yourself." He takes a large mouthful, chewing thoughtfully.

My eyes are drawn to his lips and, too late, I realize he's watching me. I shift under his gaze and, picking up the other fork, take a tiny bite. The morsel melts on my tongue, sweet, tangy, and nutty. "Oh my God, it's unfair how amazing this is."

I can practically see the wheels in his brain whirring. "They must make their dough in-house. It's flaky, buttery, and the cinnamon permeates every layer. I'll have to ask for the recipe."

We devour the rest of the sticky bun, matching each other bite for bite until only one remains. Reid insists I take it and after a halfhearted refusal, I succumb to the sweetness.

It's not until I'm daintily wiping my mouth with a napkin that I realize I just shared a pastry with a potential murderer, one whose go-to is poison. The only thing that keeps me steady is the fact he would have had to poison himself to get to me, and he's too smart—and too cocky—to do that. Nonetheless, I really need to keep my guard up.

"So, you said you wanted to discuss something," Reid says, resting one arm over the back of his chair. If he noticed my momentary freak-out, he doesn't let on.

"Yes," I say, scooting to the edge of my seat. "I need your advice."

"How about we make a deal?"

"What sort of deal?" I ask, apprehensive. Reid doesn't seem like someone I want to hop into bed with. Business-wise, of course.

He digs in his pocket and removes the Vino Valentine menu he took from the opening. There are deep creases like it's been folded and unfolded many times, and there are notes scribbled next to each wine even though I'm pretty sure he only tried the Campy Cab.

Before I can decipher his handwriting, he pulls the menu away. "I'll help you if you do me a solid."

I purse my lips, running a finger around the rim of my mug. "You don't even know what I need your help for."

He cocks his head to the side, considering me. "You're Liam's sister, I trust you."

Reid has a lot of faith in my brother, arguably too much. "I'm not agreeing to anything, but go ahead. You've got my attention."

"I liked your wine. It was bold, full of flavor." He says this with such authority I can't help but feel flattered.

"Where did you hear about my opening, anyway?" Maybe it was the same place as Gaskel, which would solve at least one mystery.

He leans forward and whispers, "There's this thing, you may have heard of it, it's called the internet."

"Oh, *that*." I click my tongue and match his sarcasm. "Newfangled technology, hashtags and such. Yes, I've heard of it."

Reid clears his throat and continues, "Anyway, as I was saying, I liked your wine. I have no doubt the rest are just as delicious."

I raise one eyebrow. "I guess I should be relieved someone feels that way."

"What do you mean? You had a roomful of people enjoying your craftsmanship."

Reid wouldn't know about Gaskel's notes. The only silver lining to this whole mess is that Gaskel's blog was never published. Reid has no idea Gaskel used words like *sour*, *bitter*, and *amateur* to describe my wine.

I let out a sigh and say, "Let's just say Gaskel wasn't particularly fond of my chardonnay."

"And that bothers you because . . ." He twirls his finger, eyes narrowed in puzzlement.

My pent-up frustration soars like a cork ready to

pop. "He is—was—notorious for his palate. Of course it bothers me."

Reid shakes his head and takes another sip of coffee, looking amused.

"You wouldn't understand," I snap. "Gaskel gushed over your cooking."

Anger flashes in his green eyes and he leans forward lightning quick. "You're putting too much weight in his opinion. There's a reason I got such a good review and it has nothing to do with my cooking."

Now we're getting to the good stuff, the crux of what I really want to know. "What did it have to do with, then?"

"Money," he says, clenching his jaw. "But I don't want to talk about Gaskel."

"Well, I do." I cross my arms over my chest. "Did he accept bribes? Is that the reputation you were alluding to?"

Reid stares at me for so long I'm convinced he's not going to answer. Luckily, I grew up with an older brother who's also a stubborn pain in the ass. I hold my ground.

Finally Reid sighs and says, defeated, "Gaskel gave good reviews to restaurants that paid well, and to those that didn't, or couldn't, he'd ruin with a few taps at his keyboard." He clears his throat. "So I'd forget what he said about your chardonnay."

I lean back, completely stupefied. "That makes no sense. He didn't approach me for money."

"Maybe he never got the chance to."

"How do you know this?" Although what I really want to ask is how long he's known. Gaskel may have solidified Reid's reputation as a chef, but Reid seems like the type to resent its having been bought.

"That's between me and my employer, which is what I want to talk to you about." Reid pierces me with his eyes before continuing, "I want you to sell me your wine at a wholesale price."

Laughter bubbles out of me, the kind where I'm momentarily afraid it might turn into a sob. "Why would I do that? I'm struggling to make ends meet as is."

"Because I want to open my own restaurant," he says, giving me a look of sheer determination. "And I want to feature your wine."

"You can't be serious."

"I never joke about food. Your wine has the local flair I've been looking for." He pushes the menu across the table so I can read what's scribbled next to each wine. They're dishes. Succulent farm-to-table dishes that would pair beautifully with each varietal. Leek and chive frittata topped with Provençal goat cheese, trout roasted with dill and cherry tomatoes, and Burgundy beef with mashed celery root and fresh-cut asparagus. "These are based on your descriptions of each wine. They'll need tweaking after I taste them, but it's a start."

I lean back in my chair, blinking several times. This could be huge for my business. Only, this kind of thing takes time, time I most certainly don't have. "How soon?"

"I already have the space and the bulk of the plans drawn up. Opening would be in September."

That's four months away and I was already worried about surviving the summer. "I would love to. Really, I would. But I'm not sure I'll be in business then." The harsh reality makes my shoulders slump forward. I think back to the trending hashtag on social media and shudder. "People aren't exactly lining up to taste wine where someone was murdered. I'm not sure how to recover from this."

He's quiet for a minute, sipping his coffee before answering, "This is free publicity. Maybe there's a way you can spin the narrative in your favor."

"The only way I can think of to do that is to figure out who killed Gaskel." I let my words sink in, monitoring his reaction carefully. "Where exactly were you when he was poisoned?"

"Very subtle," he says with a snort. He rubs his bicep, a fork tattoo peeking out from under his shirt sleeve. "I was helping your brother get some shots, holding lenses, lining stuff up, that sort of thing."

That's easy enough to verify with Liam. "Did you see anything?"

"Just the regrettable actions of the intoxicated."

"What do you mean?"

"The chick who dumped her wine on her date, a guy getting shot down by your assistant, the usual fare of restaurant life."

"Huh," I say, my foot bobbing again, this time in thought. "Any idea who got Gaskel his wineglass?"

Reid shakes his head and lowers his voice to a hurried whisper. "Look, poking around in Gaskel's death is a terrible idea. First off, it could be extremely dangerous. Secondly, what if you get caught interfering with the police investigation? That could backfire."

I speak with a confidence I wish I felt. "It's a risk I have to take."

"I can't in good conscience let you do this alone." He runs a hand through his mussed hair and lets out a sigh. "I'll chat with the owner of The Pantry. He's in town and might have more insight into how Gaskel conducted his—er—side business."

"Thank you," I say, relieved to have someone on my side.

"Don't thank me yet." He reaches his hand across the table. "If we can keep your business from failing, will you work with me?"

I hesitate, eyeing his outstretched hand, my brain reeling through pros and cons. There are no cons except that I don't entirely trust Reid. Or maybe it's that I don't trust myself around him. Either way, dare I turn down this opportunity?

In the end, Reid's offer is too good to resist. I force myself to ignore the electricity that travels up my arm at his touch when we shake hands. Now that we're working together professionally, it's even more imperative we don't get involved romantically. And that I prove he's not a killer, of course.

We spend the rest of the meeting discussing ways to keep Vino Valentine afloat. I even tell him about the VIP party, which he offers to prepare dishes for, a sort of trial run for his restaurant. We part ways with a promise to schedule a time for him to taste the rest of my wines ASAP.

After I get settled in at the winery, I shoot Liam a text asking for an ETA on the pictures from my opening. Bonus, I'll be able to pick his brain about the deal I just struck with Reid.

It doesn't take him long to respond: *Stop by tomorrow AM, not too early. Bring coffee.*

I send him a thumbs-up and then turn my attention to the VIP party.

Given the party is only a few days away, I need to finalize the verbiage for the invites, now able to boast food pairings along with wine. Which is why I'm currently perched at my tasting counter—why go in the back when I don't have customers, anyway?—tapping away on my laptop.

Before I second-guess myself, I click *send*, casting the invites into cyberspace. There's no backing out now. I immediately refresh the screen, already obsessing over RSVPs.

Jeez, Parker, give people a second.

To distract myself from compulsively checking my email, I make note of what supplies I'll need to procure, putting in an order for extra banquet tables, utensils, and linens with a rental company.

Anita pretends to stay busy, although I catch her playing with her phone whenever she thinks I'm not watching. There's no need for the act; I know there isn't enough work to justify her being here, but I don't have the heart to send her home. Plus, I like having the company.

The bell above the door jingles and I hurriedly close my computer and stash it under the counter. Anita nonchalantly slips her phone in her pocket. We paste matching smiles on our faces to greet the new customer. But it's not a customer. In fact, it's one of my least favorite people.

My smile falters as Jason walks through the door. I nod at Anita to let her know I'll handle this. She waltzes into the back with a shrug, ponytail swinging behind her, already palming her phone.

I'm not used to seeing Jason without Sage as a buffer. He's wearing khakis with a collared boating shirt and puka-shell necklace, which is odd since, to my knowledge, he's never been on a boat or to Hawaii. It makes me wonder if there's anything authentic about him.

"Hi," I say, the greeting sounding more like a question.

He peers around the winery, shifting awkwardly. "It's dead in here."

Thank you, Captain Obvious. I cross my arms over my chest. "Can I get you a taste of something?"

He grunts and slouches onto a barstool. "The sweet one."

I pull a glass from the floating shelf of pristine crystal stemware and pour him a taster of Ralphie's Riesling, wracking my brain for a polite conversation topic. Then I remember what Sage said the night before about how Jason knew one of the recent graduates who had attended my opening, and that he was acting strange.

We start talking at the same time. "Sage said—" I start.

"I know—" he says.

I chuckle nervously and wave for him to go ahead.

"No, you first," he says, fidgeting with the stem of his glass, not taking a sip. I wonder if he believes the morbid rumors flying around social media. Or if he even knows how to use social media. "I insist."

"Sage mentioned you recognized someone at the opening."

He looks confused for a moment, but that might also just be how his face is naturally. "You must mean Max," he says. "We're on an ultimate team together."

Ultimate Frisbee is a popular, and serious, pastime in Boulder. There's nary an evening when two teams aren't facing off with a disc in local parks, goals identified by colorful cones or whatever environmental markers are available. I know from Sage that Jason takes ultimate Frisbee very seriously, his mood entirely dependent on whether his team wins or loses.

"The Frisbros?" I ask, the name of his team somehow lodged in my brain.

"Yeah."

"How's your season going?"

He shrugs and grumbles, "It'd be better if the rest of the team would make the same level of commitment I do."

"Right," I say. Too bad he can't put the same level of commitment into his career, relationship, and general upkeep. "Did Max do or say anything . . . unusual?"

"I dunno, I guess. He seemed nervous, like he didn't really want to talk to me."

Well, that's not terribly surprising given this is Jason, but I should still do my due diligence for the sake of the investigation.

"Any chance you could give me his contact information?"

"Going for a younger guy?" he asks with a smirk.

"Hardly." I hesitate, my need for Max's number trumping my (entirely justified) trust issues. "You said it yourself, my winery is dead. Unless I can figure out what happened to Gaskel, which is why I'm tugging on every loose thread."

"I was with Sage the whole time," Jason says, trying for a joke.

I chuckle halfheartedly as he scrolls through the list of contacts on his phone.

"Have you had any more computer issues?" he asks without looking up.

Jason works in the IT department at CU, the same job he's had since we were undergrads. A few weeks ago, he tried and failed to troubleshoot a bug with the billing software installed on my laptop. Sage forced him—and me, for that matter—into it. He poked halfheartedly at the keyboard for twenty minutes before advising me to try a different piece of software. Having already invested a decent chunk of change into the one I had, I rebooted as a Hail Mary and *presto!*, problem solved.

"Thankfully, no," I answer. "That is one area of my life that's going smoothly."

Jason grunts and turns his phone toward me.

Once I've secured Max's number, I rest my elbows on the countertop. "Okay, so what did you want to talk about?"

Jason downs his wine in one gulp. "Look, I know you don't think I'm good enough for Sage."

The truth hangs in the space between us. I don't deny it, curious to see where he's going with this.

Jason continues, "Truth is, I don't feel good enough for her most of the time, but I want to be." His eyes are glassy and for a second I'm worried he's going to cry.

I sigh heavily, not meeting his gaze. "Sage could do worse."

As the product of a scumbag dad and a doormat mom, Sage has scars that run deep when it comes to love. Which is why she's clinging to her first love, the first guy who asked her out in high school and then followed her to college and beyond. It's why she won't put up with crap from anyone, but for some reason has blinders on when it comes to Jason.

"She deserves the best," Jason says.

"I agree wholeheartedly." *And that most certainly is not you*, I think to myself.

He exhales and I can tell he's circling around telling me the reason he stopped by. "I can't wait for my career to get on track to show her I'm serious. Especially when there's something I can do right now."

I can see his point; he'd be waiting a long time. In order to get his career on track, he needs to actually have a career. Not that there's anything wrong with IT; it requires patience and being on the bleeding edge of technology. It's just that I don't get the sense Jason actually likes it. In fact, even after all the time I've known him, I don't know what he *is* passionate about. Besides the Frisbros, of course.

"And what's that?" I ask.

Jason messes with his phone again and holds it up so I can see the screen. "Which of these rings do you think Sage will like better?"

I feel like I've had the wind knocked out of me. I pour myself a small glass of the first wine I can get my hands on, the Pearl Street Pinot, and, against my upbringing, know-how, and respect for wine, I down it in one gulp.

I pull myself together and refocus on Jason. "You do realize these are engagement rings, right?"

"Come on, Parker, give me some credit."

"Just checking," I say, taking his phone from him. He's flagged two rings, neither of which is right for Sage. Her style is classic with a modern twist, or something of the elfin variety, while both of these rings scream *gothic grandma*.

I hand back his phone, buying time. How do I tell him these rings are all wrong? That, in fact, *he* is all wrong? "Mmm, tough choice."

"I'm leaning toward the one with amethysts. Chicks dig purple, right?"

"Oh, absolutely. However . . ." I squint, not sure how to break it to him. "I'd go for a square-cut diamond— make sure they're humanely sourced since that's important to Sage—thin gold band, minor gem accents, maybe green to contrast with her hair."

Jason looks like he just swallowed something sour. "I only wanted to know which of these you'd pick for her. Apparently, that's too much to ask of her best friend."

"Fine," I snap, hands on my hips. "The one on the right, only because it's the less dreadful of the two. Are we done here? Because I'm clearly very busy." What I would give to have a bustling winery right now.

"Thank you," he says curtly. "Now that's settled, I have one more favor to ask. Don't pit Sage against me."

"What?" I ask, genuinely confused.

"You're her best friend, she listens to you, respects your opinion. Let her decide this on her own."

"Sage is a strong woman." *Too strong for you*, I want to add. "She'll answer for herself. Is that all?"

"Yeah." His eyes bulge like a bug's. "Good luck with everything, and tell Max I said to drag his lazy ass to Frisbro practice." With that, he stalks out of my winery, letting the door slam shut behind him.

It's not until he's gone that I wonder about the timing of his proposal, and his quick assertion of an alibi. Perhaps I need to consider Jason more seriously as a suspect.

"What a douche," Anita says, returning to the front

of the store, shaking her blond head. "By the way, I re-arranged the labels."

I ignore the fact that Anita somehow managed to find something to organize. "What am I going to do? I promised to stay out of it."

My head thunks against the counter, raven hair splaying around me, a sense of helplessness seeping in. Am I really going to lose my best friend to that jerk?

"There's a loophole," Anita offers. "A couple subtle questions would be acceptable."

I lift my head and look at her.

"Ask about other fish in the sea, that sort of thing."

"You're right," I say, smoothing out my hair.

Inspired, I send Sage a text: *Are you still up for that tasting?*

She must not be in court because she responds a minute later: *Tomorrow? I'm slammed with a case, going to be a late night . . .*

Hopefully Jason will wait a couple of days to make his big move. I send back a thumbs-up along with: *6:00. I'll meet you at Murphy's Bend.*

"Murphy's Bend, huh?" Anita asks, peering at my phone. She dips her chin in embarrassment. "Sorry, I didn't mean to snoop."

I set my phone upside down on the counter. "It's okay. I figure I can do a little recon while warning Sage."

Anita rests her elbows on the counter, draping her ponytail over her shoulder. "Isn't it, like, more important to focus on Vino Valentine than worrying about what the competition is doing?"

"In business, you have to balance both. You know what they say: *'Keep your friends close and your enemies closer.'*" Especially when murder is involved.

"Please be careful." She levels me with a steely gaze, one that says she has more backbone than I've given her credit for. "You're a good person and an awesome boss."

I nod, my throat constricting, and quietly watch the people strolling by the Vino Valentine storefront window, none of them even glancing inside. In fact, they seem to be trying awfully hard *not* to see us.

To avoid sinking into a pit of despair, I take a deep breath and channel my energy into my studious mentee. "Let's talk about you, Anita. Have you thought more about your plans after you graduate?"

"I'm considering grad school. It's a tough market right now; I need an advanced degree to set me apart if I'm going to land a decent position."

"What about opening your own business?"

"I've seen how hard you've worked to open Vino Valentino and I guess I'm not sure it's the life I want anymore." She shrugs, plays with the end of her ponytail, her eyes flitting to mine nervously. "Is it worth the sacrifice?"

I don't have an answer for her. This is by far the hardest thing I've ever done, and most of the time I feel completely insane for going for it. But I'm not sure what my life would be like without my dream. The prospect terrifies me, almost more than confronting a murderer.

"You'll have to decide what's right for you." I pause, taking in the space I've worked so hard to create. "As for me, I'm proud that I'm living my dream. If I were to die tomorrow, at least I'll know I tried."

Chapter
Seven

The afternoon lull grates on me like an insult, cutting deeper the longer it takes me to formulate a comeback. It gets under my skin and makes me restless. At this rate, my winery won't make it through the week.

I have to take action.

I decide to pay Jason's friend Max a visit, figuring it's the quickest way to cross one suspect off my list.

I'm quite proud of the way I got his address, by cold-calling and pretending to be a recruiter for the new Google campus. He took the bait immediately, doling out his address like it was his final lifeline.

Max lives in a large house on the Hill, just a couple of blocks west of campus and a short walk from the café I used to haunt during finals when I was a student. By the crushed PBR cans and discarded red cups littering the porch, I can tell he has roommates, which is further proved by the guy who answers the door in nothing but boxers and a graduation cap. The deep bags under his eyes tell me he's still hungover from a big night of celebrating.

"I'm looking for Max," I say, peering around the guy.

"Jackwad, your girlfriend's at the door," he shouts upstairs. To me he says, "Come on in."

Max has the unfortunate last name of Jackard, exposing him to a plethora of nicknames. And apparently none of his roommates have met his girlfriend, which works in my favor.

I gingerly step over the threshold and into a quasi-foyer, careful not to touch anything for fear of needing a tetanus shot. Boxer guy stumbles down a dark hallway, leaving me alone, the scent of stale beer and weed in the air.

The stairs to my right creak as Max descends. I faintly recognize his dark curly hair—very Jon Snow—and prominent nose. And suddenly I realize he was the fidgety customer who was waiting with me outside the restroom while Gaskel's body lay lifeless inside. That he was so close to where the murder took place is unnerving. I take a small step back, comforted by the open door behind me, an escape route if one is needed.

Max is in black skinny jeans and a T-shirt sporting Shakespeare's profile, pegging him as a drama nerd. His goofy smitten grin disappears when he registers that his girlfriend is nowhere in the vicinity.

"I'm Parker Valentine; you were at my winery the other day."

Color seeps from his face, leaving behind a white mask. "I remember."

"I'm friends with Jason Valleres. He says hello, by

the way," I say, paraphrasing Jason's less than cordial message.

Max grunts, running a hand through his shaggy hair.

"I'll cut to the chase and let you get back to celebrating graduation." I wave toward the empty spirit bottles on a nearby card table.

"Not me," he says, his chest puffing out. "I'm busy prepping for the Shakespeare Festival." The Shakespeare Festival takes place at the beginning of every summer at the outdoor theater on campus. I've only been to one show, but it was thoroughly entertaining.

"Right, well, I'll let you get back to it." I hold my purse close to my side. "Jason mentioned you were acting funny, that you didn't seem to want to talk to him . . ."

"The guy isn't exactly the most popular on our team. It was a bit awkward," he says, chewing on his thumbnail. I'm tempted to offer him hand sanitizer.

"What do you mean?"

"He's always razzing us when we can't make practice. He doesn't get that we've got other stuff going on," he says. "Like, why doesn't he join a team with guys his own age?"

Jason is a few years Max's senior but chooses to hang with the younger crowd in a pitiful attempt to feel cool. Poor guy doesn't realize he may get voted off the Frisbros soon.

"With the Shakespeare Festival coming up, and a new girlfriend, I bet you're pretty busy," I say, cocking my head to the side.

"She's volunteering for the festival, too, so at least we get that time together." He gets a dreamy, faraway look in his eyes. He's obviously enamored.

I bite back a smile. Oh, to be young and in love. Involuntarily consumed with the other person; the nervous butterflies, fervent texts, and stolen moments. And none of those pesky adult realities that hinder relationships. You know, like credit scores, forty-hour workweeks, or, in my case, cross-country moves.

For a second, I wonder about his girlfriend. I hope she's as excited about their burgeoning relationship as he is.

"So what brought you to my winery?" I ask, and then add, "It helps to know which bit of advertising works."

"I heard about it from a friend." His eyes dart around like a frightened animal, landing somewhere over my left shoulder.

"Who?"

He hesitates, his gaze glued to a spot over my shoulder. For a theater buff, this guy really needs to work on his acting skills. "A guy from my house. Grant."

The thing is, Max's house is on Grant Place. When people lie, they tend to grasp for inspiration. My guess is he doesn't know anyone named Grant and thus doesn't want to share where he found out about my opening, which is suspicious, to say the least.

"Grant? Are you sure?"

"Yeah." He shuffles his feet.

"Is there anything you noticed while you were at my winery, anything at all?" I bite my bottom lip and try to rustle up some tears; all I have to do is imagine using the bathroom in this house. "You see, I've given everything to open my own winery. If this doesn't succeed, I'm done for." I tuck a strand of hair behind my ear and sniffle, playing the guilt card.

"No, I didn't notice anything." He chews his thumbnail again. I stay silent, letting him sweat. "If I did see something, I couldn't say anything, anyway. But I didn't. Really."

"Why couldn't you say something?"

He opens and closes his mouth. "Because there's nothing to say."

God, he's either incredibly naive or a complete idiot. Regardless, he and Jason deserve each other. All I wanted to do was cross this dude's name off of my list of suspects and instead he's giving me every reason to think he was involved in the murder.

"What about when you were waiting outside the restroom?" I ask. "Was there anyone else around?"

"That wasn't me," he denies, a touch too quickly.

I replay the memory in my head and grow even more certain that it was, in fact, him. But why would he lie?

Since tapping into his guilt didn't work, I try for intimidation. "The detective working this case is an old friend," I say, exaggerating. "I wonder what sort of illegal substances he'd uncover in this house. Marijuana might be legal in Colorado, but I'm willing to bet there's more than that here."

If possible, even more color drains from his face. "Screw you."

I cross my arms over my chest and roll my eyes. "Very original."

"'The silence often of pure innocence persuades when speaking fails.'"

"Who said that, Shakespeare?"

"It's from the *Winter's Tale*."

I'm not familiar with that play, but the quote far from convinces me of his innocence.

"Fine. Well, if you remember anything, call me at this number." I give him one of my Vino Valentine cards, scribbling my cell number on it.

The door shuts in my face. It's clear Max is hiding something, and I intend to find out what it is.

Like a good red wine, sometimes you need to let a problem breathe—decant—to better understand its flavors.

I seek clarity on the bouldering wall, letting my mind wander. I move from grip to grip. Jason's timely proposal, Max's secret source, Moira and Carrick's fight. Everything must fit together, it's just a matter of sorting the grapes from the stems.

I fall back on the mat and gaze up at the pinholes in the ceiling until a familiar face appears in my line of vision: Eli Fuller.

I start, sitting up so fast I bonk my head with his.

"Sorry," I say, rubbing my forehead.

"Guess I deserved that." Eli winces as he touches his own forehead. "I shouldn't have startled you."

"I've been extra jumpy lately." I get to my feet, leaving two chalk handprints on the knees of my tie-dyed leggings, and give Eli a once-over. He's decked out in cargo shorts and a Nirvana T-shirt, and his dark hair is mussed instead of slicked back, one stray lock falling over his temple. His chalk bag, climbing shoes, and harness dangle from one hand.

"You took my advice." Warmth seeps into his voice. "Has climbing helped with the stress?"

"It has, although you wanna know what would really help? Solving this damn case so my winery has a fighting chance."

"Trust me, we're working on it." He clicks a cara-biner open and closed. "I was watching. You're pretty good."

"Thanks." I stand a little taller. If there's one place I feel especially confident, it's the climbing wall. "When did you start climbing?"

"At the Police Training Academy. I excelled at the climbing wall on the obstacle course. It stuck as a hobby." He plops down on the cushioned floor and laces up his shoes. "Interested in a game of add-on?"

"Sure, if you think you can keep up," I say with a wink. Add-on is a game where you and another person take turns tacking new moves onto a sequence until one of you can't complete the route.

He chuckles. "How about this: if I win, you join me for dinner later."

My bravado falters. "A date?"

"Not a date. Dinner," he clarifies.

"Okay," I say. "But if I win, you have to share a tidbit about the investigation."

"I can't do that," he replies instantly, only instead of looking frustrated, he seems amused.

"Then you'd better not lose. I'll even let you go first to warm up." I nod at the wall, rubbing more chalk between my hands.

I can tell Eli climbs regularly. His body is fluid, all muscles and clean lines as he picks the first move, one that favors his height and broad shoulders. I give him a slow clap when he finishes and he bows nonchalantly in response. It doesn't escape my notice that a couple of girls standing nearby blatantly ogle him.

I hop on the wall and stretch my body diagonally to complete the first move, my fingertips barely reaching the hold. Then I consider a different angle, choosing a foothold that constricts my body into a tight ball, shifting my weight so one side leans against the wall. This move isn't so much about muscle as it is about finesse, which gives me an advantage. I flash Eli a grin as I dismount.

We go back and forth like that, each of us leveraging our strengths, until eventually Eli says, "Let's call it a draw."

Inside, I'm relieved, my muscles screaming for a break, but I put on a brave face. "That means you've gotta give me something on the case."

"Hey, we tied."

"No, we didn't, you conceded." I flutter my eyelashes, faux-sweetly.

He exhales and checks that no one can overhear our conversation. Luckily, the oglers have moved on. "This was a premeditated crime. It took careful planning and precision." He pauses, stretching his forearms by pulling back on his fingers with the opposite hand. "The first thing I learned when I became a detective was to never underestimate your adversary. There's clearly someone very intelligent working behind the scenes."

A pit forms in the bottom of my stomach. "The poison that was used . . . it sounds terrible." I shake my head.

"It's vicious," he practically growls. "Whoever did this wanted Mr. Brown to suffer."

The echoes of laughter around the gym sound like they're coming from a world away. "How do you do this for a living?"

There's a numbness in his eyes, a wariness, as he answers, "It's not easy, but I like what I do, and I'm good at it. I'll catch whoever did this."

I nod, only slightly reassured by his words. I roll my shoulders to loosen my neck. "Have you talked with Max Jackard? Seems like he's hiding something."

Eli freezes mid-stretch and drops his arms to his side. "How would you know that?"

"No reason," I say quickly, sensing the change in his demeanor. "You up for the climbing wall?"

"Sure," he says, eyeing me suspiciously. "I'd better not find out you're interfering in the investigation."

"Understood, Detective. Forget I said anything." Note to self: don't share my extracurricular sleuthing with Eli.

"This isn't high school, Parker. This isn't a class for you to ace." The reference to my perfectionism surprises me, especially since I never thought he was paying attention.

"I'll go first," I say to change the subject.

I step into each leg loop of my funky orange harness and pull them up until they're nestled around my upper thighs. Then I fasten the belt around my waist and attach my chalk bag to a gear loop with a carabiner. When I was a beginner, I found all the buckles and straps to be intimidating. Now, though, they're routine.

I attach the rope dangling from the climbing wall to both tie-in loops on my harness with a figure-eight knot and pass both ends of the belaying rope to Eli.

His deft fingertips brush my waist as he checks my knot. He nods his approval but stays where he is, his head bowed. I study the hard lines of his face, his sculpted cheeks and strong chin. His eyes flick briefly to mine before he takes a shuddering breath and steps away.

My heart races as I pull myself onto the wall, and not from exertion. I force myself to focus. I slowly traverse the wall, making sure every motion is intentional. I feel

Eli's gaze on my back like an itch I can't quite scratch. It makes me nervous, especially after our *whatever-that-was* on the ground.

When I get to the top, my muscles are shaky and fatigued. I wipe sweat from my forehead and rest my fingers in the crevice between the wall and the ceiling, my chest heaving. After another minute, I give Eli the signal—a thumbs-up—that I'm going to belay down the wall.

I start a graceful descent, kicking off the wall with both feet and running the rope between my fingers, feeling as close to being an astronaut as I'll ever get.

That's when everything goes wrong.

The upper tie-in loop on my harness snaps, sending me careening at an awkward angle, my entire body weight now supported by the rope that's running through my leg loop. I scramble for one of the grips but can't catch hold with my sweaty fingers, tired and clumsy from all the climbing.

I imagine the scene from afar—me frantically pin-wheeling my arms, flailing about fourteen feet in the air. I'm in for a world of hurt and there's nothing I can do to stop it.

Adrenaline courses through my veins, the pounding of my heart a cacophony in my ears. I let out a desperate wail as I fall backward away from the wall.

It happens so fast Eli isn't expecting it. He's thrown off-balance as I plummet toward the ground.

They say your life flashes before your eyes during a near-death experience. For me, it's more of a stream of consciousness. I think of my winery, my dream turned sour. I think of my family, my parents and Liam, and Zin, who will think I *actually* forgot to feed her. And I think of myself, how much I still have left to do.

Please, let me walk away from this.

I squeeze my eyes shut in anticipation of the impact, bracing myself for serious pain.

A moment passes, and then another.

When I don't hit the ground, I hesitantly open one eye to find myself frozen in the air, suspended mere feet above the ground.

Eli must have reacted just in time, tugging on his end of the belaying rope, which is luckily secured at a different point of my harness.

He shakily lowers me to the ground and helps me regain my balance. My fingers dig into his shirt, the material worn and soft.

I collapse onto the mat, pulling my knees to my chest. I can't think about what would've happened if Eli hadn't caught me in time, or if I'd been climbing with someone less experienced.

Eli kneels beside me and rubs my back reassuringly. His scent is like a day spent climbing on a subdued mountain trail—pine trees, sweat, and climbing chalk.

Around us, the steady rhythm of the gym continues as if nothing happened. No one but Eli and I seem to realize what a close call I had.

Eli looks between me and the wall, eyes narrowed. "I know you're too good to let anything like that happen under normal circumstances."

"My tie-in loop ripped," I say, gesturing to the frayed fabric on my climbing harness. "I—I wasn't expecting it. It threw me off-balance and I couldn't catch hold of anything."

Of course there are dangers associated with climbing, but there's a *wrongness* surrounding this accident. If it was an accident.

"How old is this harness?" Eli asks.

"I got it for Christmas, so five months ago, but I've hardly climbed with it." My thoughts gravitate to the same place as his: this harness is too new to have snapped in this way naturally.

Eli assesses the orange straps, his eyes calculating. "This isn't ordinary wear and tear. If it was, it would've been the belaying loop for sure."

The belaying loop holds the brunt of a climber's weight and thus is the most durable piece on the harness, and the most fatal if anything happens to it. "I got lucky. If it'd been the belaying loop, you'd be scraping a puddle of Parker off the ground."

Eli smiles, but it's a grim smile. "I wouldn't call this lucky."

"What would you call it?"

"Sabotage." He holds my gaze, his hand still resting on my back. To outsiders, we look like we're pausing our climbing session to whisper sweet nothings into each other's ears. If only.

I dip my head between my knees and try to slow my breathing. I've gone straight from a racing heart to hyperventilating. I hate that Eli is seeing me at all my low points.

He keeps one arm resting on my back while pulling his phone out of his pocket. "I'm calling this in."

I lift my head up too fast, stars dotting my vision. "No, don't," I say. "We don't even know it was foul play." While it's the practical thing to do, I'd rather not spend the next hour rehashing what happened.

"Yes, we do," he says, squaring his shoulders. "This could be related to the case. It's my job." He presses dial before I can offer up another protest. His tone is professional as he conveys the events of my near catastrophe to whoever is on the other end of the line. The creases around his mouth let me know he's worried. I'm worried, too.

I force myself to stand, away from the safety and warmth at Eli's side. I wobble slightly, my feet unsteady as I survey the climbing wall.

Who had access to my harness between this morning when I left my apartment and this evening when I closed Vino Valentino? That would be Reid—I stashed my bag under our table at the Laughing Rooster—and anyone who came into my winery today since I kept my bag under the tasting counter, which isn't exactly private. I know of Anita and Jason, but someone else could have slipped in while I visited Max.

One thing's for certain: if Gaskel's killer damaged my harness, that means I've struck a nerve.

Eli drives me to the police station. He claims it's because I shouldn't be alone right now, but part of me wonders if he doesn't trust that I'll go on my own. Can't say I blame him.

It's my first visit to the Boulder County Sheriff's Office and I'm impressed by the sleek building—a mesh of western and modern styles with a flagstone exterior and more windows than I can count. In an open office shared by all the detectives, with a backdrop of desks scattered haphazardly throughout, I relate my story to a young officer who seems keen to impress Detective

Fuller. Eli waits, steadfast, at my side, listening intently even though he already knows the details.

After I finish giving my statement and fill out a lengthy form, I'm drained, grumpy, and sick of being referred to as a victim. My stomach rumbles and I realize I haven't eaten anything since lunch. I add hungry to my growing list of complaints.

While I could navigate public transportation or order an Uber, I accept Eli's offer to take me home, especially when he suggests we stop for food on the way.

He parks outside a restaurant on the east end of Pearl Street called Mountain Sky, its vibrant sign of a sun rising over mountain peaks giving it a hippie vibe.

"When I said we should have dinner together, this isn't what I had in mind," Eli says.

"You mean this isn't how all your dates start?" I quip, sashaying into the restaurant.

The interior is homey—wooden tables, welcoming murals in the same style as the sign outside, and a large chalkboard spanning the entire back wall with the day's specials handwritten in colorful chalk. The best part about this place is that it's known for its microbrews, and frankly, I could use a night away from all things related to fermented grapes.

Eli and I slide into a booth, a general chatter rising around us to effectively muffle our conversation. I order a Belgian Tripel and a burrito smothered with green chili. Eli orders the same, only pairing his with an IPA.

We sip our frothy beers. The warming hints of caramel, cherries, and cloves wash over me, soothing my shaking hands. A headache blooms as my mind races from Gaskel's murder to my failing business to my climbing tumble. It's a toxic cycle.

"Is there anything I can do for you?" Eli asks in an even voice. He's clearly experienced in dealing with distraught citizens.

"Distract me." I grip my pint with white knuckles, the exterior dewy. "Tell me how you became a detective."

He stares at the ceiling and rubs his chin, a shadow of scruff barely visible. The longer he stalls, the more curious I become. "I suppose it started when an officer saved my life."

Now that gets my attention. I lean forward. "What?"

"As you know, I was kind of a stoner in high school."

"Oh, I remember." I recount a particularly colorful tale in which he stumbled into my AP calc class mistaking it for the restroom, and the teacher's desk for a urinal. *Area under the curve* took on a whole new meaning.

He clears his throat and drains a good portion of his beer, his angled cheekbones splotchy. "My dad's a piece of work and pot was a way for me to escape. I'd already had two possession tickets when I got caught with both alcohol and weed. I had just turned eighteen, so the third strike would've meant serving time and a record as a felon.

"The officer knew I'd had a tough life and took pity on me. He threw me in jail to detox overnight and then drove me to a federal prison, showed me where I was heading if I didn't get my act together. It scared the shit out of me." He takes a deep breath, his eyes downcast, haunted. "It was the motivation I needed. I graduated high school and took community college classes until I completed the prerequisites for the police academy."

I blink rapidly, readjusting my headband. "I had no idea."

"Sometimes you become your reputation, at least to the outside world. When that happens, it's hard to change the perception."

I think of the barrage of negativity my winery and I are receiving on social media; hopefully I'll get the chance to set the record straight. "Well, you've officially been promoted from resident pothead to detective, at least in my book."

Our waitress sets a plate in front of each of us, the rising steam smelling of roasted chili peppers, cumin, and crisp potatoes. I sigh in contentment, chewing a mouthful of thick green pork chili and gooey cheddar cheese. "Do you ever feel ripped off now that weed is legal?"

He snorts, diving into his own burrito. "No, I sometimes feel like what I went through made me a better detective." He points his fork at me. "Not that I was a hardened criminal, but I definitely have a unique perspective into how the delinquent mind operates."

"What do your spidey senses tell you about the delinquent mind in this investigation?"

"That we're dealing with someone desperate." He looks at me warily and with a touch of fear. "Watch your back, Parker."

Goose bumps break out on my arms and a chill that has nothing to do with the temperature settles over our table. We finish our meal in silence.

Chapter Eight

I show up at my parents' house early the next morning with two Laughing Rooster coffees in tow. My childhood home is a picturesque brick two-story in North Boulder with large pine trees dotting the front yard and sleek solar panels on the roof. It's only as an adult that I've come to appreciate the value of such an abode.

I went casual today, skinny jeans with a blouse and flat leather sandals, perfect for tromping around their yard in order to reach the separate basement entrance in the back where Liam resides. My parents have probably already left for work anyway, not that I particularly feel like chatting with them. My mother would smother me with concern over the investigation and my father would shift into professor mode, and underneath it all would be this unspoken, simmering tension: I'm not sure they believe in me.

My parents have what they jokingly refer to as the Liam Fund. This represents a sum of money set aside for when Liam needs to be bailed out of whatever situation he's gotten himself into, like the massive debt he incurred from the day-trading debacle.

That by itself is fine. I get it; parents love unconditionally. But here's the thing: my parents have never helped *me* out financially.

Sure, my dad's role at the university meant I basically got a free education. Which I don't take for granted. I paid for room and board through work-study programs and, after college, landed a gig that helped me pad my savings account.

But when I voiced my desire to open Vino Valentine, they didn't see fit to give me a single penny. Even as they were paying for Liam's base amp for his dream to become a mega-star musician.

I was scraping together funds, living on ramen and coffee, and talking with investors when my aunt Laura passed away. What she'd given me was more than just money, it was proof that someone in my family believed in me. And I would trade it all in for the chance to talk with her again, even just once.

If my parents truly believed in me, wouldn't they have at least offered to help me out when I needed it? Wouldn't they have found a way to attend my opening? Wouldn't my mom have refrained from making a spritzer out of my carefully crafted wine? These are questions my fragile ego can't handle right now.

I'm darting under a pine tree branch when I hear my mom's voice, like shattering glass in the silence. "Parker, what are you doing here?"

I freeze and turn, chewing my lower lip. "Um, going to see Liam about something."

"Tell him we had a deal about the smell," she says with a sniff, leaving me perplexed. Her purse and lunch tote are slung over one shoulder and the keys to her Nissan LEAF are at the ready.

She peers over the top of her glasses, piercing me with her analytical blue eyes as if I were a chemical formula that could be balanced. "Have there been any developments in the investigation?"

My mom can always tell when I'm lying, so it's best to keep it vague. "Not really."

She utters a swearword that takes me by surprise. I'm tempted to go hug her, because sometimes, no matter how old you are, all you need is the comfort of your mom. Then she speaks again . . .

"I talked to my boss and there's an entry-level analyst position open." She fidgets with her car keys, her beaker key chain glinting in the sunlight. "Let me know if you're interested."

I see red, as if looking at the world through a rosé filter. I hear the clink of ice cubes and fizz as if she's making a spritzer all over again. My own mother doesn't think I can do this.

I square my shoulders and force myself to say, "I'm not giving up on Vino Valentine yet."

"I figured you'd say that," she says, pursing her lips.

I raise both to-go mugs in her direction. "I'd better get moving before the coffee gets cold."

A debate plays out on her face, like there's more she wants to say, but she opens her car door and waves me off. "Remember to tell Liam about the smell."

"Of course," I answer with a forced smile.

I continue around the house at a brisk pace, only relaxing when her car finally backs out of the driveway.

After a few minutes of persistent knocking, Liam answers the door in a wrinkled undershirt and pajama bottoms, his dark hair sticking out in every direction. He rubs his eyes and yawns. "One of those had better be for me."

"With a splash of hazelnut, just how you like." I take a large gulp of my own latte, letting the caffeine give me energy. I didn't get much sleep. Eli graciously gave my apartment a once-over when he dropped me off, but I was still awake most of the night, perched on the couch with Zin in my lap, wide-eyed and twitching at every noise.

Liam grunts and guzzles his coffee, waving for me to follow him inside. The basement is like a lair, only the upper half of a single window allowing light in. The mixture of college-era posters, cast-off furniture, and storage boxes makes the space feel chaotic, and an aroma similar to dill pickles wafts through the air, a scent I know is from the chemicals Liam uses to develop film. Now I know what my mom meant about the smell.

Liam disappears into what used to be a linen closet but now serves as a makeshift darkroom. A paper cutter and trays of chemicals line the built-in shelves, and a thick black curtain hangs over the doorway.

While I wait, I peruse the photographs pinned to a clothesline draped along one wall, a variety of landscapes, stills, and portraits. I pause in front of an especially poignant one, a picture of a street performer playing the violin. The woman's face is lined with wrinkles and her eyes are shut, the barest hint of a smile on her lips. She's completely absorbed in her music, passion pouring from her fingertips into her instrument. In short, it's beautiful. A tear prickles at the corner of my eye.

Liam is good. *Really* good. I just hope he sticks with it.

Liam returns with a handful of prints. "These are amazing," I say, gesturing to the photographs, my gaze lingering on the musician.

He gives me a noncommittal shrug.

"Seriously, you should enter them into a contest or something."

"I'll think about it." He frowns and it's clear he'll do no such thing. He passes me the stack of prints. "Do you want to look at these or not?"

"Coward," I mumble, shaking my head. I can't blame him; criticism is tough. I still haven't fully recovered from Gaskel's negative comments about my wine, even after discovering there were other influencing factors. You know, like poison and bribes.

Liam flops onto the couch and resumes gulping his coffee. He closes his eyes and leans his head back. "Just gonna rest my eyes for a sec."

I sort through the black-and-white prints, shocked by the quality. The lighting and style are unique and edgy, and there's an authenticity to each one.

There are decent shots of wine and decor that will be perfect for the Vino Valentine website, but where Liam really shines is with people. He managed to snap a picture of pretty much everyone at the opening and, moreover, at vulnerable moments when they've let their guard down.

He captured Moira staring down her husband, one

hand clenched into a fist and the other holding the glass of wine that would soon become a projectile, a look of utter desperation on her face. Sage gazing at Jason, the latter distracted by something offscreen, which pretty much sums up their relationship. Another of Sage, this time laughing, her eyes twinkling. Anita smiling sweetly, the light reflected in her glasses, and Max in the background checking her out. Maybe he's not as infatuated with his new girlfriend as I thought.

Then there's one of me with a giant grin on my face and my shoulders thrown back in pride. I look so happy. Naive. I click my tongue and continue.

The next photo features Gaskel pawing at his empty glass mere minutes before his fatal sip. I scan the image for clues. His fancy watch glints on his wrist, and there's no sign of the piece of paper that was sticking out of his front pocket. He has the same haughty demeanor I remember so well, but at this particular instant, Gaskel appears distracted, his eyes cast to the side and his neck craned as if he were searching for someone. Then I recall he said he'd been waiting for someone. I would bet a case of Cristal he attended my opening for another reason besides my craftsmanship. If only I knew what that reason was, and who he was supposed to meet.

No one ever did turn up looking for him, unless the flashing lights of the police cars and ambulance scared them off. But maybe the meeting was a ruse, a way to get him to my winery at that specific time.

In the background, fuzzy and out of focus, a shadow falls over the bottle of chardonnay on the counter of the tasting bar, and in the upper-left-hand corner are what look like fingers and a large ring hovering over his glass.

I home in on the shadow and the pale fingers, faintly

wondering if this could be the hand of the murderer. Was there any hesitation, a slight tremble, at the gravity of taking another life? There's no telling, and nothing distinguishing apart from the ring, and I don't recognize the gaudy accessory.

I flip to the last print—Reid holding a glass of wine to the light, his hair mussed and sleeve tattoo barely visible. I may stare at the picture a moment too long.

"You've got it bad," Liam says, one eye open as he nestles deeper into the couch.

I stammer an excuse. "I was looking at the background."

Liam doesn't buy it. "I don't know why chicks like that guy so much," he says. "It's impossible to go out with him anymore. He's the worst wingman."

I shift from one foot to the other, leaning against the armrest. There's no great way to segue into checking someone's alibi. "Was Reid helping you frame shots at my opening when Gaskel walked in?"

"Yeah, but I'm not gonna let him take all the credit."

I smile as if artistic attribution was why I was curious. "Did you know he wants to open his own restaurant?"

"Sure, he's been planning it for the last year or so."

"He wants to feature my wine." I wait for Liam's reaction. Even though my brother is a mess professionally, I value his opinion.

"Really?" Liam asks, eyebrows raised.

"Is that so hard to believe?"

"Guess not. He's into the whole local scene." He peers at me from the couch. "Seriously, though, don't start something with him. It won't end well for either of you."

"Hypothetically speaking, why not?"

"Because he's not a relationship guy and you're, well, opinionated."

"You say *'opinionated'* like it's a bad thing."

"It is when you're the reason my former best friend ghosted me."

Guilt prickles at the back of my neck. I try to rub it away but, like a pesky itch, it remains. "That was on him." Mostly. "Look, I promised it wouldn't turn into another Guy situation and I meant it."

His face a map of skepticism, Liam stands and stretches, downing the rest of his coffee. "I've gotta get to work."

"Work?" I ask in disbelief. "As in a job?"

"Landscaping. I'm on a crew for the city." Our skin is naturally olive, but now that he mentions it, he's a deeper tan than usual, and fitter—healthier. The dirty work boots he wore when we had lunch make sense now.

"Good for you," I say, meaning it.

He acts like it's no big deal, although I can't remember the last time he earned a steady income. "I don't want to live here forever and I've gotta support my photography somehow."

"You know what would help?" I say, tapping one finger against my depleted to-go mug. I toss it into the trash bin. "Actually sharing your photography."

"Man, you're worse than Mom."

I wince. "Hey, that's harsh."

"Fair enough," he says with a snort. "I'll make it up to you. Reid and I are going out on Pearl later, wanna tag along?"

"Can't. Sage and I are going tasting at Murphy's Bend, but maybe after." I start for the door, applying an extra coat of lip gloss, saying, mostly to myself, "I need to talk some sense into her, but subtly."

"About what?"

I sigh in exasperation, clicking my purse shut. "Jason is going to propose."

A shadow passes over Liam's features as he blinks several times, scratching his head. "Good for her," he says. "Take the prints if you want, I haven't called the detective yet. Lock the door behind you, all right?"

"Wait," I shout, scrambling after his retreating figure. "What just happened?"

He turns to me, a heaviness hanging about his shoulders. He's on the verge of saying something but then swallows once, his throat bobbing. I can almost pinpoint the moment he shuts down.

"It's nothing," he says flatly. "Just go. Please. I don't want to be late."

Without another word, he stalks into the bathroom, closes the door behind him, and turns the shower on, leaving me completely baffled. I add Liam's reaction to my ever-growing list of puzzles to contend with.

I slip out, taking the prints with me, wondering if the key to Gaskel's murder is hidden somewhere among the glossy sheets.

There's something in Liam's photos from the opening, I can feel it. My forehead scrunched in concentration, I study them for the umpteenth time at Vino Valentine. Anita is on her lunch break and with #KillerChardonnay still trending, I have the place to myself.

My eyes dart between the picture of Gaskel before his last sip to the empty barstool where he sat. The silence presses in around me as I struggle to pinpoint what's bothering me. I relax my mind, close my eyes, and take a deep breath, a practice I've learned helps me identify aromas in particularly complex wines. It yields nothing.

I'm grinding my teeth in frustration when Reid surprises me with a visit. I hurriedly stash the prints under the bar and greet him, not having to fake the smile on my face.

His amber hair is brushed to the side and he's wearing a T-shirt for one of my favorite indie bands. "I was testing new recipes and thought you could use some lunch," Reid says, holding up a carryout bag sporting The Pantry's logo. Working with a renowned chef could have its perks. "And maybe I can have that tasting, if you're not too busy."

"As you can see, we're completely slammed," I quip, gesturing to the empty tables, my heart lodging itself in my throat.

There have only been two measly RSVPs to my VIP party. I keep reminding myself it's only been twenty-four hours since I sent out invites, but I still feel a fluttering of panic rise in my chest. What if the event is a complete bust?

"No work today?" I ask.

"The restaurant is closed Tuesdays. It's usually when I experiment or hit the farmers market."

"My gain. Have a seat and I'll get you a glass," I say.

"Come on, Parks." He utters my nickname with familiarity, as if we've known each other for years instead of days. He continues, radiating charm, "Don't make me drink alone."

"I need to keep my wits—and my taste buds—about me. I'm going to Murphy's Bend later."

He commandeers an oak-barrel table for our impromptu picnic, pulling containers and cutlery out of the paper bag. "Hot date?"

"With my best friend, so the hottest. Obviously." I crinkle my nose, delivering ice waters and a clean wineglass to the table. "Did you consider their wine for your restaurant?"

"They were next on my list if I didn't care for yours. Lucky for both of us, that didn't happen."

I nod, my lips twitching into a half smile. "What's on the menu?" Palate cleansers are important with tastings. Based on the heavenly scents wafting from the containers, Reid went above and beyond standard fare.

"Bacon-wrapped dates followed by an arugula-and-roasted-beet salad. Focaccia with garlic-infused olive oil on the side." He offers me a date with his fork. "Bon appétit."

My jaw literally drops. I close it around the bacon-wrapped date, sighing as the heavenly pillow dissolves in my mouth, salty, sweet, and sinful. "You'd better be careful, a girl could get used to this."

He winks at me. "Wait till you try my breakfast."

The innuendo is heavier than a French Burgundy. Color creeps into my cheeks. "Maybe over a *business* meeting."

"We can call it whatever you want." His green eyes meet mine, flashing dangerously as he draws my attention to his mouth by taking a slow bite. Thankfully, he changes the topic before I combust. "So what wine should I start with?"

I pour him a taster of the Mount Sanitas White. "A blend inspired by a sunset hike up my favorite Boulder trail."

Reid studies the splash of wine, swirling, sniffing, and holding it to the light. "Pale yellow color. Aromas of apples, peaches, and something tropical." He pauses, pondering. "Maybe guava."

"Very good," I say, impressed.

"I don't mess around when it comes to flavor." He takes a sip, swishing the wine around in his mouth before swallowing. He taps a few notes into his phone. "This will pair nicely with our salad, although I'd go lighter on the herbs to not overpower the nuances of the blend."

I munch my salad, the fresh and tart flavors dancing on my tongue. Reid's suggestion is spot-on. It tastes like summer with its crisp garden vegetables and tangy citrus. His food is entirely deserving of Gaskel's rave review. I tell him as much.

"It doesn't matter." He takes a large mouthful of greens.

"You really don't care what other people think?"

"I learned a long time ago life's too short to worry about making anyone but yourself happy." He shrugs, wiping his mouth with a napkin, but I can tell there's more to his story. "What am I tasting next?"

"The infamous Chautauqua Chardonnay." I raise one eyebrow, leaning forward. "Scared?"

A weird expression comes over his face, a crack in his otherwise confident demeanor. It's gone a moment later, replaced with the spark of a challenge. "Not of your wine."

I pour him a taster and he praises it immediately.

"Oaky and buttery, but not overly so. The acidity gives it a nice balance. You should be proud."

"Thanks," I say, a warm and fuzzy feeling rising in my chest. I squash it down and remind myself of the reasons Reid is off-limits.

First off, Liam wouldn't be happy if he found out I was dating another one of his friends, one he's explicitly warned me away from. Secondly, since Reid and I are conducting business together, we need to keep our relationship professional. And third, with a murder investigation afoot, it's hardly an appropriate time for a new romance.

Reid furrows his eyebrows. "Speaking of your killer chardonnay, I talked to the owner of The Pantry about Gaskel."

I freeze mid-chew, crispy focaccia turning to sawdust in my mouth. "Did you find anything out?"

"Apparently Gaskel was part of the reason Brennan decided to make the leap from tech and open a restaurant."

"Wait, are you talking about Brennan Fourie?"

"The one and only."

"Interesting . . ." The guy was a legend in my house growing up, my dad idolizing the advances he made in mobile technology and renewable energy before randomly turning his golden thumb to the restaurant industry. "Were they on good terms?"

"It sure seems that way. Brennan was pretty shaken up by Gaskel's death." Reid downs the rest of his chardonnay, smacking his lips in approval. "I guess they were old friends, met years ago when Brennan was in town for a conference. He likes to have the best of everything—gadgets, cars, meals. He immediately sought out Gaskel, wanting to know which restaurants to try in Denver. That was ten years ago."

Even the best friendships can sour over time, and just because Brennan wasn't at my opening doesn't mean he didn't somehow orchestrate the whole thing. I drum my fingers on the table, my brain churning through possibilities.

"Did you learn anything about Gaskel's morally questionable side business?"

"It didn't come up naturally, and this sort of accusation . . ." He trails off, running a hand through his hair. "Once I say it, there's no backpedaling."

"Fair enough," I say, trying not to sound too disappointed. I pour Reid a taster of the next wine on the list, the Pearl Street Pinot. "Did he know of anyone particularly upset with Gaskel?"

"Brennan said that Gaskel wouldn't have been doing his job if he didn't upset people."

"I suppose that's true."

I gaze at my winery, sadness and frustration roiling in my stomach. If Gaskel had ruined my business with a negative review, would I be upset enough to kill?

Of course not.

I have a support system, friends and family to keep me from falling to pieces. But what if I wasn't so lucky?

Reid drapes his arm lazily over the back of his chair, the light catching on his oven-burn scars. "Brennan also mentioned there's a memorial service tomorrow morning at North Star Lutheran."

"Good to know." There are dozens of reasons I shouldn't attend, namely, no one will want to see the woman social media has deemed responsible for Gaskel's demise. Still, I tuck the information away, just in case. "Have you told Brennan about your restaurant?"

He shakes his head, jaw clenched. "Not yet." He hesitates. "I just haven't found the right time."

"Uh-huh," I say, entirely unconvinced.

Reid swishes wine in his mouth and swallows. "There's always something—the dinner rush, menu planning, prep work—but I will. Eventually."

"Right," I say knowingly. "Look, I know you're upset with him for paying off Gaskel, but you owe him a heads-up."

My phone buzzes with an unknown number. I answer and give my customary greeting, "Parker Valentine."

There's heavy breathing on the other end of the line.

"Hello," I say sharply, certain it's some sort of political survey or phishing scam. "Is anyone there?"

I'm ready to hang up when a shaky voice says, "It's Max—Max Jackard. I need to talk to you."

I excuse myself from the table, holding one finger up to Reid.

I dart into the back, my voice echoing off the cool stainless-steel equipment. "It's about Gaskel, isn't it?"

He breathes into the phone. Loud music turns on in the background and I wonder if he's trying to camouflage his voice.

My fingers tingle in anticipation. "Are you ready to tell me how you heard about my opening?"

It takes an eternity for him to answer. "Yes. To both." Another long pause. "I have to tell someone, but I can't go to the cops."

Fear snakes it way up my spine. I add honey to my voice, all soothing and supportive. "It's okay, Max. You can tell me."

Our connection blips out and I'm afraid I've lost him. Then he makes a sound, a cross between a sob and a groan. "I didn't know what I was doing."

Oh God, this call is taking an ugly turn. Is it possible he's going to confess to the crime? I wish I'd had the forethought to record it. "Max, this is important. What did you do?"

There's a disturbance on the line and all I catch is one word: "Pocket."

"Hang on." I walk farther into the back until my cell signal clears. "What did you just say about a pocket?"

There are shouts in the background, mixing with the loud music, his roommates calling for him to *hurry his ass up.* Max grows even more agitated. "Look, I can't talk now. Meet me outside the theater building on campus." He's talking so fast I have to cover my other ear to make sure I catch every word. "Tonight, ten o'clock."

Then he hangs up.

I grip my phone with white knuckles, staring at the blank screen, completely dazed.

Classes are out and it's that odd week before summer session starts, meaning campus will be deserted, especially at that time of night. No doubt what Max is going for.

I think of my climbing harness, the accident that wasn't an accident, and shiver. This could be a trap, in which case it would be stupid to go alone. But dare I tell Eli? He's so straitlaced now, he would probably insist on my staying out of it and then we might never learn what Max has to say.

Anita walks in the alley-side entrance, bright sunlight following her through the open door like an aura. She's in wide-leg cropped pants and an off-the-shoulder blouse, her long blond hair loose.

"I tried that new kebab place. It's amazing. You know, in case you haven't had lunch yet." She smiles at me, clutching her purse to her side, her cheeks rosy. "No offense, but it looks like you could use some fresh air."

It's like I'm coming out of a coma. I shake my head, my hair brushing against my shoulders. "I already ate."

"Were there any customers?" she asks, optimism seeping into her voice.

"Technically, no," I say, remembering the hunk of deliciousness currently waiting for me out front. And I'm not talking about the focaccia.

I book it back into the tasting room, only Reid isn't there. He's cleaned up our lunch and on the table is a clear plastic container with a single chocolate truffle—dark chocolate, by the looks of it—sprinkled with cocoa powder. Next to it, there's a note scribbled on a napkin: *Thanks for the tasting. No meal is complete without dessert. Talk soon.—R*

My mouth waters as I stare at the truffle, its sugary scent somehow permeating the plastic. Under normal circumstances I would already be one with the chocolate. But Max's call left me rattled and full of uncertainty.

I consider the decadent morsel and the man who made it for me.

My brother vouched for Reid and confirmed he was nowhere near Gaskel when the critic was poisoned. I've had multiple meals with him and remain unscathed, *and* he even offered to help with the investigation. Now, unprompted, he brings me dessert.

Unable to resist anymore, I pop the truffle in my mouth, letting out a contented sigh. My eyes shut in ecstasy as flavors of dark chocolate and espresso dance on my tongue, a perfect combination of bitter and sweet.

When my eyes flutter open, I officially cross Reid off my list of suspects.

And I know what to do about Max.

I have to meet him, of course. There's no way I'm going to let this killer run my life any more than he or she already is.

Chapter Nine

"Wait, tell me what to do again?" Sage asks, practically bouncing on her stool.

We're seated at the tasting counter at Murphy's Bend. The decor is traditional—a curved chestnut countertop lined with high-backed stools and pictures of the Murphy clan covering the walls. They're not just selling wine; they're selling their family story. And clearly it's working for them. The place is packed, even though it's a weeknight. In fact, Sage and I are lucky we managed to secure two spots.

Gaskel's review didn't upset their business nearly as much as I thought. Maybe Moira was right that his opinions weren't the be-all end-all. Then again, the renowned critic didn't die after trying their wine.

"Stick your nose in the glass—all the way—and breathe in." Sage does as I say, getting a drop of wine on her nose. "List the first scents that come to mind. The more specific the better."

"Cream soda and apples." She looks at me questioningly, her fiery red hair like an exclamation point to her black slacks and stark white blouse. As always, there's some nerd canon present, today a *Deathly Hallows* pendant around her neck.

I hold a hand over my chest in pride. "You'll be a master sommelier in no time."

"Really?"

"Well, no," I say. "It takes years of hard work to achieve that level, but you're well on your way."

Sage raises her glass to her lips, but then pauses. "Do we drink now?"

I nod enthusiastically and we clink our glasses together, glasses I surreptitiously rinsed with water from a community pitcher before our tasting began. I don't trust anyone.

Their chardonnay is good, but not great. There's an artificial flavor, like movie theater popcorn, that gives it an unpleasant muskiness. Gaskel's review was actually pretty spot-on. I dump the remainder and munch on a cracker to cleanse my palate.

"So how are things?" I ask.

Sage finishes the subpar wine with a shrug. "The Manual is pushing me to decide my next step career-wise. We've been having lots of *'what do you want to be when you grow up'* talks," she says with air quotes. "Not sure I'm ready to move on, though. Things are good as is."

Sage has no idea she'll be making multiple major life decisions very soon. "You'll rock whatever it is you decide to do. Just take your time. There's no reason to rush into anything." Hopefully she'll remember those words when Jason proposes.

"If I took a job in corporate, my workload would be more manageable." She frowns. "Jason's always on me for working too much."

"Pfft," I say with a wave. "Jason could stand to work a little bit harder. What's he doing tonight, anyway?"

"Frisbro practice."

"Hopefully the rest of his teammates show up," I say, thinking of my meeting with Max later. If he's exhausted, he might be less guarded.

"Yeah . . ." She trails off and sighs. "He's acting weird. Standoffish. Last time this happened, he planned a trip to Vegas with his buddies and neglected to tell me about it."

I click my tongue and gently remind her, "That's because he had just borrowed money from you."

"Sometimes I worry I'm wasting my time with him."

My throat bobs, all my opinions threatening to burst forth. Really, there's only one thing that matters. "Does he make you happy? Like, legit, happy?"

She opens and closes her mouth, hesitating. She stares at the photos of Murphy family members smiling down at us from behind the bar as if they hold the answer. "Of course he does," she finally says, a little too quickly. "He's always been there for me. He's a nice guy."

"You deserve pure, undiluted happiness. If Jason doesn't do it for you, there are plenty of *nice* guys out there."

"You know it's not that easy. Remember Guy?"

"No one will let me forget," I mumble, my earlier conversation with Liam fresh in my mind.

Guy and I let our relationship drag on six months

longer than it should have, both of us clinging to what was easy because we were too scared to face the unknown. He was the shoulder I desperately needed to lean on until, all of a sudden, he let me fall. I was just the idea of what he wanted in a girlfriend instead of the real thing.

I continue, "In retrospect, I wish I'd ended things sooner. Love and comfort are two different things."

"Everything is always clearer in retrospect." She waves her empty wineglass. "Hey, how do we get more?"

As if on cue, Moira glides over, the epitome of chic in a fitted jumpsuit and suede pumps. Her long blond hair is loose around her shoulders, the maroon highlights adding dimension to her style. "What did you think of the chardonnay?"

"Delicious," Sage answers, saving me from having to fumble around my rather harsh opinion. "What's next?"

"The Bend It Red, light-bodied and fruity." She pours a splash into each of our glasses. "Carrick, get over here." She waves her husband over while Sage and I go about sniffing and sipping.

Even though Carrick was at my opening, I didn't get a good look at him. Granted, he'd been covered in cherry wine at the time and, frankly, I'd had other things to worry about. But now I give his looks the full appreciation they deserve. Carrick is ruggedly handsome, dimpled chin and dark hair with streaks of silver running through it. I may drool a little bit on the counter.

He rests a hand on Moira's lower back and addresses me. "This one will not stop gushing about you and your wine," he says in a thick French accent. "It's a pleasure to meet you." He flashes his pearly whites at me.

I steal a glance at Sage. Her rosy cheeks say she's as

smitten as I am. "You have an impressive setup here." I gesture to the crowded area.

"It keeps us busy. Too busy sometimes." He slides a hand in the pocket of his fitted khakis, eyebrows furrowed.

Questions flood my mind. How did this worldly pair meet and come to own this winery together? How is it their chardonnay is so lacking when their Bend It Red is so superb? I snap back to the present. These are mysteries for another time.

"We got the invitation to your party," Moira says, beaming at me. "Consider this our formal RSVP."

"What party?" Sage asks.

"A last-ditch effort to save my winery." I cross one leg over the other, bobbing my foot up and down.

"We went through a rough patch a few years ago," Carrick says, a weariness entering his eyes. "It takes a toll, but your wine is good. You will be fine."

This seems as good an opportunity as any to slip in a reference to Gaskel. "Opinions vary. Gaskel certainly wasn't impressed with my chardonnay, although that could have been the poison. Unfortunately, we'll never know." I cock my head to the side, studying their reactions.

Moira looks at me imploringly. "Darling, I told you to move on from that. Focus on the next harvest. That's what we're doing, right, dear?" She squeezes her husband's shoulder, but there's an unspoken tension between them.

Carrick gives a tight-lipped smile. "Excuse me, please. I must see to our customers."

He wanders to the other end of the tasting bar and dutifully pours tasters for a group sitting there.

"I should help," Moira says. "If I recall correctly, this was your favorite." She winks at me and then pours Sage and me each a full glass of the Bend It Red before traipsing off.

"That was weird," I say when Moira is out of ear-shot, drumming my fingers on the countertop. I stop when I realize my mom does the same thing when she's nervous.

"No kidding," Sage grumbles. "Talk about relation-ship problems."

"Maybe. They seemed fine until I mentioned Gaskel." I stare after Moira, absently touching my leather purse, which is hanging from the back of my stool. Li-am's prints are tucked inside. I have a sudden urge to reexamine them, to see if there's one that places Carrick anywhere near Gaskel's glass.

"I suppose my invite to your fancy party got lost in the ether," Sage says, half of her wine suddenly gone. I can't blame her; the wine is really quite delicious.

I swivel toward Sage while shamelessly rubberneck-ing Moira and Carrick. "I didn't want you to feel pres-sured, especially with everything else you have going on."

"Count me in," she says. "We can continue my wine education."

At the end of the bar, Moira whispers something into Carrick's ear and then disappears down a hallway in the back corner. Carrick laughs with a patron, but his good humor is obviously forced. He excuses himself, all charm, and follows after his wife.

I only have a split second to make a decision. It turns out the threat of professional failure is a wonderful mo-tivator.

I slide off my barstool. "I'll be right back."

"Where are you going?" Sage asks, but I shush her.

"Just have to check something," I answer vaguely, darting down the hallway after the troubled couple.

Their hushed voices beckon to me. I tiptoe down the hallway, my leather sandals padding softly against the hardwood floor. The air smells dank, of spilled wine and cardboard. I stop in front of a doorway that leads to what I'm guessing is one of many storage rooms. A stack of wine crates blocks my view.

"I cannot keep pretending everything is okay," Carrick whispers, his accent imbuing his words with even more passion.

"We just have to get through the summer," Moira says.

"And then what?"

There's a long sigh. "We've been through this. I can't take a season off, not when my family's legacy is at stake."

One of them paces back and forth—Carrick, I guess, by the weight of the footsteps. "You forget, this is my legacy now, too. Not just yours."

"Of course, dear. I only meant—"

"I know what you meant," he says, exasperated. "One season will not matter. Our wine will be better because of it, not this weak *tord-boyaux* we are making now."

I wince. I don't speak French, but I can tell *tord-boyaux* isn't a good thing. Carrick might be a dreamboat, but insulting his wife's craftsmanship doesn't seem very sensible. At least neither of them has a glass of wine in hand. I'd hate to see more wine—even mediocre wine—wasted on another one of their fights.

That is, if their argument at my opening wasn't a well-orchestrated diversion.

"Those people out there expect something new."

"Then let's give them something really special." Carrick paces again, his steps growing faster and more agitated. "We need to keep the promise we made to each other. You must follow through."

I chew on my bottom lip, puzzling over Carrick's words. What promise? What is it that Moira has to follow through on?

When Moira speaks next, it's in such a hushed tone I almost miss it. "I wish you could forget Gaskel's review."

"And live in denial like you?" He snorts and utters something in French. "What is she doing here, anyway?"

Wait, are they talking about me? My breath hitches as I press myself closer to the doorframe. If I could, I'd melt into the wall.

"Parker is welcome here, just like every other customer."

Oh God, they *are* talking about me. I feel a sharp stab of embarrassment.

"The last thing we need is to be associated with her," Carrick says.

I'm tempted to defend myself, but I stay frozen, continuing to eavesdrop on this bizarre conversation.

"Come now, she had nothing to do with Gaskel's death." The certainty in her voice takes me aback. I'm honored to have her on my side, unless her confidence stems from knowing who is actually responsible.

"Do you remember how hard it was to start something on your own?" she asks. "I don't know the story with her parents, but I didn't get a strong sense of familial support at her opening." I feel another stab, this time of vulnerability at a near stranger picking up on my family drama. Moira continues, "It seems like she could use some guidance."

"You have always had a soft spot for strays."

"It's served me well in the past."

"Me also," he says softly, making me feel like I'm intruding on a private joke.

Having heard more than my fair share, I slink away from the door and attempt a stealthy retreat.

I fail miserably, tripping over an exposed floorboard.

I curse under my breath. Damn these sandals and their overextended toe. Over my shoulder, the door creaks open. Carrick freezes in place, his dark eyes widening.

Heat rushes to my face. "I was just . . ." I trail off, searching for a feasible excuse. "Looking for the bathroom."

He frowns, chiseled lines etching deeper into his face. "It's by the entrance. You cannot miss it."

Carrick watches me for a moment too long. He knows I was eavesdropping. That I heard their conversation. Sweat beads on my upper lip.

I hate playing the ditz, but it's my only option. "Right," I say, giving what I hope comes across as a flirtatious giggle. "I'd better slow down my tasting." I feign a slight wobble, even though I've never felt more sober.

When he responds with a full-bodied laugh, I relax, but only slightly. "It happens to all of us. A hazard of the trade."

"Who are you talking to, love?" Moira's hand rests

on Carrick's shoulder as she gently steps around him and into the hallway. "Oh, Parker, were you looking for us? You're probably anxious to continue your tasting."

I mentally kick myself for not thinking of that excuse. "Something like that," I mumble.

Moira links arms with me and we stroll back to the main room, Carrick following close behind. I feel his gaze on my back, silent and calculating. My skin crawls. I want nothing more than to hightail it out of here, pronto.

But if I flee, I may as well confess to spying on them. My best bet is to act normal and finish the tasting.

We return to the tasting bar, where Sage has bonded with a couple of dames over their shared lack of wine-tasting knowledge and, more recently, their lack of wine. Moira and Carrick get busy pouring tasters, much to Sage's and the dames' satisfaction, and I get busy pretending my stomach isn't twisting itself into knots.

The next hour is excruciating. We sniff, swirl, and sip our way through mediocre wines, none of which come close to the flavor achieved in the Bend It Red.

I squirm in my seat, my eyes flitting about. I'm hyperaware of everything, the back of the stool digging into my shoulder blades, the laughter bubbling up around me, and the way Carrick's eyes bore into me when he thinks I'm not paying attention.

How is their business doing so well? Are all of these people loyal to the legacy of Murphy's Bend? Or are they newbie tasters like Sage, who don't know decent wine from *tord-boyaux*?

I rub at the nape of my neck where my hair stands on end. Sage side-eyes me, mouthing, *What's wrong?*

Guess I'm not as subtle as I thought.

I shake my head and mouth back, *Nothing*, and we proceed to taste an overly tannic cab.

We finally finish with a dessert wine, a syrupy port that clings to my throat as I swallow. I dump the rest of my glass, exhale a sigh of relief, and stand up quickly, ready to be rid of this place. Sage shoulders her purse and follows my lead, bidding a cheery farewell to the dames.

I flag down Moira and try to hand her my credit card to pay, but she waves me off. "It's our treat, darling."

"Thank you," I say.

"Of course," she gushes. She pulls Carrick to her side and away from the crystal glass he was drying with a towel. Her knuckles are white as she clings to his shirtsleeve. "We're glad you came in."

She's so good-natured, her eyes kind and understanding, I almost feel bad for eavesdropping. That is, until I catch Carrick studying me. He smiles when I meet his gaze, but it's less Prince Charming and more Big Bad Wolf.

"Yes," Carrick says. "We will see you at your party." The way he says it sounds like a threat.

Chapter Ten

Owning a cat is supposed to lower stress levels. I have yet to see proof of that this week.

After Sage and I part ways, I wear down the carpet in my apartment, pacing back and forth. Zin watches from her perch on my couch, her ash-colored tail swishing in time with my strides, until she eventually falls asleep, leaving me alone with my nerves.

My mind cycles through the same questions over and over. What does Max know? Who is he afraid of? What if my meeting with him is an elaborate ruse?

I can hardly stand it.

When it's finally time to go, I grab a black hoodie from my closet and say goodbye to Zin. I scratch my furry companion's ears and give her an extra scoop of food. If this is a trap, I don't want her starving before someone can see to her.

Jeez, Parker, as if you weren't twitchy enough.

I shake off the morbid thought and lock the door behind me.

My Uber driver's name is Tom. He drives a Cadillac, listens to smooth jazz, and has a five-star rating, although I quickly learn this is only because it's his first night on the job.

"I'm still not sure I like the idea of having strangers in my car, but I could use the extra money," he explains, eyeing me warily in his rearview mirror. "Why are you going to campus at this time of night, anyway?"

"Just feeling nostalgic," I fib, my knees jiggling.

I direct him to a parking spot on Euclid Avenue, a short jaunt from where Max told me to meet him. Streetlights illuminate the brick architecture and green ivy vines. Leafy trees fan in the breeze, their shifting shadows sending a shiver up my spine.

"Actually," I say. "There's twenty bucks in it if you wait here for me."

"You got it." Tom flips a book open and turns up his jazz. "Don't take too long."

I shut the car door behind me and pull my hood over my head, tying the drawstrings into a neat bow.

Even though I graduated years ago, I can easily recall the campus layout. The theater building borders Norlin Quad, a large grassy field that, while ideal for studying in the sunshine, offers little in the way of camouflage. Instead, I decide to take the narrow path behind Hellems, a multipurpose building where a variety of classes are held. That way I can sneak around the side and approach from the back.

Still, thinking and doing are two very different things.

I take a steadying breath and then force myself forward, turning my head in every direction to monitor for movement.

At one point, I think I hear footsteps. I pick up my pace and so do the footsteps. It's not until I turn the final corner that I realize I've been racing my own echo.

I crouch behind a bush and peek through crisscrossing branches. I have a clear view of the steps leading up to the entrance of the theater building. There's a solitary bike without a seat locked to the railing. No one is around.

Careful to keep the backlit screen hidden, I check the clock on my phone. It's ten o'clock on the dot. Any moment now, Max should appear and provide the answers I so desperately crave.

Time is a slippery entity. As crickets chirp lazily and clouds drift over the waning moon, I'm not sure if seconds or minutes pass.

My legs cramp and I shift on my feet, giving in and checking my phone again. Max is fifteen minutes late.

I have two simultaneous thoughts. The first is worry since Max seemed determined to clear his conscience. The second is fear, confirmation that this is some sort of setup, in which case, I need to vamoose.

My phone vibrates, the ringer silenced for my rendezvous. Reid's name lights up the screen. My pulse speeds up. I try not to let it go to my head that he's calling me on his night off.

I press ignore and continue my vigil, figuring he'll leave a voice mail, one I'm very much looking forward to listening to. He calls again a second later. I furrow my eyebrows, thoroughly confused, as I swipe to answer.

"Hey," I whisper.

"Parker?" Reid shouts over a loud bass in the background.

"Yeah. What's up?" I ask, still whispering, my eyes glued to the front of the theater building.

"It's your brother . . ."

My heart plummets as he trails off. I stand up so abruptly that stars dance in my vision, and not the ones overhead.

I grip my phone with white knuckles, already jogging toward where I hope Tom and his Cadillac are still waiting for me. "Is Liam okay?" I ask, breathless.

"He's fine." Reid's voice takes on a hint of desperation. "But he's in rough shape. You'd better come down here."

"Where are you?"

"The Sundowner," he says, referencing Liam's favorite bar on Pearl Street.

I spot headlights on Euclid and sigh in relief. "On my way."

I hang up and slide into the Cadillac's backseat. "How do you feel about making one more stop tonight?"

"Where to?" Tom asks, setting his book on the passenger seat and shifting gears.

"Pearl, just off of Broadway," I say absently, gnawing on my lower lip.

I send a text to the number Max called me from earlier, letting him know I couldn't wait any longer. Then I throw myself back in the leather seat and watch as downtown Boulder flies by in a blur, silently willing Tom to go faster.

*   *   *

Pearl Street is hopping, the night young and full of promise. At least for those in their early twenties cruising from bar to bar in search of a good time. Guess I'm getting too old for this scene.

With the promise of another twenty bucks, Tom agrees to wait for me in an alley that doubles as a parking lot.

The Sundowner is the type of place where I would only use the bathroom in an absolute emergency. Located below street level, at the bottom of a dubious staircase, the place is a quintessential dive. Worn bar, mismatched tables and chairs, hole-riddled dart boards, and hard alcohol and squandered dreams on the nose. I'm oddly fond of it.

I push the door open and scan the crowd, quickly spotting Liam and Reid in a corner booth.

Reid waves me over. His hair is darker in the dim lighting, like a polished penny, and he's wearing a slate-green sweater that matches his eyes. His cocky demeanor is gone, replaced with concern.

As for Liam, well, he's a mess. He rests his head on the table, his gaze unfocused, and prods clumsily at a stack of empty shot glasses. His lanky legs jut out into the walkway, his sneakers looking worse for the wear. I haven't seen him this drunk in a long time. It scares me.

"What happened?" I ask, sliding into the booth, the vinyl scratchy beneath my palms.

"I have no idea," Reid answers, shaking his head. "We were just gonna grab a beer, but he kept going. That was hours ago."

I snap my fingers in front of my brother's face. "Earth to Liam."

He rouses himself and flashes me a lopsided grin. "Hey, sis. You decided to come out." He continues, his speech slurred, "I can give you and Reid some privacy since you're obviously not going to listen to me."

I try to laugh it off, looking anywhere but at Reid. "He doesn't know what he's saying."

"Sure I do," Liam says, pushing himself into a sitting position. "Parker was asking about you earlier. Even though I told her you"—he jabs a finger toward Reid—"go through girls faster than I go through careers, and *that's* saying something."

Reid clenches his jaw, eyebrows furrowed.

"And you," Liam continues, turning his accusatory finger on me, "don't think about anyone but yourself."

My mouth drops open and I scoff in indignation.

Oh, we're gonna have words.

Before I can figure out where to start, Liam descends into a fit of coughs that start to sound suspiciously like sobs.

I take pity on him. I exhale my frustration with a deep breath, setting it aside until he's more coherent. Besides, I have a hunch that, deep down, his outburst is about something else entirely. Reid and I are just the easiest targets.

"You were fine this morning. What changed?" I ask, remembering how put together he'd seemed with his photography, stable job, and aspirations to actually move out of our parents' basement.

"Nothing," Liam says. He unstacks the shot glasses and lines them up, one after the other. I count seven.

"You didn't derail over nothing," I say. "Did I put too

much pressure on you with your photography? You don't have to—"

"It's nothing," Liam barks, clipping the shot glass with his hand and sending it sailing to the ground. The glass shatters on the floor, earning a death glare from the bartender.

"Time to go." I finally bring myself to look at Reid. He's watching me with a puzzled expression on his face.

I grab Liam's arm and slowly shift out of the booth.

"Come on, buddy," Reid says. He grabs Liam's other arm, and between us, we're able to get him to his feet.

Liam staggers forward. "She's going to say yes, isn't she?"

"Who?" I ask, confused and frustrated. This isn't how my night was supposed to go.

"Sage," Liam whispers, his head lolling forward. "She's going to marry that bastard."

Then something finally clicks, something I should have seen ages ago.

We were freshmen in college the first time I invited Sage to a family dinner. As we munched our way through my mom's trademark enchiladas, I didn't think anything of it when Liam snagged the seat next to her. Nor did I think anything of it when he chatted her up at subsequent family events. After all, Guy was often there, too, and we had just started dating; I thought Liam was being polite.

There's a deeper meaning behind his actions now. The way Liam always asks about Sage, tries to make her laugh when they're together, and the close-up pictures of her from my opening. I can't believe I didn't see it sooner. I feel a pang of pity toward my wayward brother.

"I dunno," I answer truthfully. "I hope not." As if I needed another reason to root against Jason.

Liam slumps forward, the sadness in his eyes making my heart clench. A choking sound escapes his throat.

The bartender is making his way toward us now. Reid and I each drape one of Liam's arms over our shoulders and usher him through the bar and up the stairs.

The cool night air is a refreshing dose of reality. Liam is able to stand on his own, but the cobblestones prove to be too much for his clumsy feet. He hasn't said a word since asking about Sage, clearly lost in his own torturous thoughts.

The sign of a true friend, Reid readjusts his grip, shouldering Liam's full weight. He turns to me. "Where's your car?"

"I don't own one." I fiddle with my beaded necklace while I orient myself. "My Uber is over there."

"You Ubered here?" Reid shakes his head in disbelief. His good humor is slowly returning now that we're out of the Sundowner.

"Yes." I start walking, throwing a glance behind me to make sure Reid and Liam can keep up.

"Did you get too many parking tickets or something?"

"Hardly," I scoff. "There's no reason to own a car with public transportation and ride sharing. Besides, Boulder traffic is bad enough without me adding one more vehicle to the mix."

"The trick is to live walking distance from everything," Reid says, a light sheen of sweat beading on his forehead. "I'll make sure you and Liam get home okay."

All I can manage is a nod as I maneuver my brother

into the backseat of Tom's Cadillac, hurry around to the other side, and scoot into the middle seat.

Reid squeezes in next to me. Our bodies are pressed together, warmth permeating my jeans and hoodie. He touches my hair lightly. I stare at his fingers, images flashing through my mind—of his fingers tangled in my hair and running down my back. My breath hitches.

He pulls a twig off my hoodie and twirls it between two fingers. "What were you up to when I called?"

"Wouldn't you like to know."

"Oh, you have no idea."

Liam lets out a loud moan and Tom turns around in his seat, gesturing at him with his thumb. "He'd better not get sick in my car."

"I'd step on it, then." I give Tom my address and he wastes no time accelerating. Needless to say, I don't think I'm convincing him to continue moonlighting as an Uber driver.

Usually I don't mind the three flights of stairs that lead to my apartment, but tonight they're the bane of my existence. Even though Liam thoroughly upset me, I wasn't about to drop him off at Mom and Dad's. They set conditions prior to his moving back in with them, and coming home trashed was—and is—a major deal breaker.

Which is why Reid and I haul Liam's drunk ass up the endless steps. By the time we reach my landing, I'm shaking from exertion and fumble with my keys.

We plop Liam on the couch, where I force him to drink a full glass of water. He falls asleep immediately, clutching the edge of Zin's afghan blanket. Zin hops onto the couch and nuzzles next to him, purring, somehow sensing he could use company.

I set another glass of water, a bottle of Tylenol, and an empty trash bin within reach before going in search of Reid. I find him in my kitchen, peeking in the refrigerator.

"Can I get you something?" I ask, crossing my arms over my chest.

"Habit," he explains. "The best way to get to know someone is to look in their fridge."

"Did you learn anything interesting?"

"Decent amount of fresh ingredients, decent amount of wine." He follows me onto the balcony, slipping his hands into his pockets. "Which tells me you're health-conscious, but also like to kick back."

"Very astute," I say, resting my forearms on the railing and gazing at the stars over the Flatirons. Truth be told, there hasn't been much kicking back lately. "Thanks for your help tonight."

He mirrors me, our elbows barely touching as he takes in the view. "No problem."

"I bet this messed with your plans to pick up some lucky girl," I say, not so subtly fishing for information.

"This is better." He faces me full-on, a sly grin sliding into place. "So, you asked your brother about me?" Apparently, he's doing some fishing of his own.

"I'm going to kill Liam," I grumble, dipping my chin. "Don't read too much into that. We're conducting business together. I could've been asking for a reference, to make sure our styles mesh." And now I'm babbling. I clamp my mouth shut before I embarrass myself further.

He cocks his head to the side. "Doesn't change the fact that you were asking about me."

"Oh, get over yourself."

I nudge his shoulder playfully. He goes with it, dramatically falling back a couple of steps before returning to his perch, only closer this time. So close I catch his scent—citrus, fresh herbs, and a hint of peppermint.

"What did you want to know?" he asks.

I'm momentarily distracted by his eyes. They're a rich green, like the leaves of a grapevine, and spark with emotion.

"Oh, um, how he knew you, your band, that sort of thing."

He rests one arm casually on the railing, positioning his foot so it might as well be touching mine. "Did you get the answers you wanted?"

"Eh," I say with a shrug and a coy smile, purely to mess with him.

He laughs and then brushes a strand of hair off my cheek, tucking it behind my ear, his fingers leaving a trail of heat on my skin. "Hopefully I'm more satisfying in real life."

My pulse quickens at our proximity, my heart pounding in rhythm with the sound of the crickets serenading us. I glance at his lips and, though I can't be certain, I'm pretty sure he does the same to me.

Our breaths blend as we lean toward each other. Our foreheads touch and his hand cradles my cheek.

I trace a line down his bicep, the soft fabric of his sweater a contrast to the hard muscle underneath, and lick my lips, mere centimeters from his.

It would be so easy to kiss him. To give in to the unfiltered hotness that is Reid. But I hesitate.

I think of all the reasons we shouldn't—the rules I've put in place to protect myself and my business, and Liam's harsh words. *You don't think of anyone but yourself.*

Maybe Reid is thinking about what Liam said, too, because he pauses.

Then my phone vibrates, a persistent buzzing that finally gets my attention. I shake my head to clear the Reid-induced haze.

I glance at the screen; it's a number I don't recognize. I try to focus, which is nearly impossible with Reid still standing so close, his gaze full of such heat it makes me blush.

"Hello," I say, slightly out of breath.

"Parker, this is Detective Fuller." His tone is professional, as if he's trying to impress someone. Gone is the friend I had dinner with last night.

"Eli—"

Reid raises one eyebrow at me and mouths, *Boyfriend?*

I shake my head and correct myself. "I mean, Detective Fuller. What can I do for you?"

"I need you to come down to the station."

My spine goes ramrod straight and I pace to the edge of the balcony, suddenly chilled. "Why? What happened?"

"There's been a development in the Brown case."

"What sort of development?"

"A man was found dead this evening."

I hold a hand over my mouth. A tingling sensation starts in my fingertips and snakes up my arms to my neck as I force myself to ask, "Who?"

"Max Jackard," Eli says.

The world goes fuzzy around me and it feels like I'm

spinning. I grip the wooden railing, the splintering paint grounding me. As if from afar, I notice Reid has moved to my side and is rubbing my back.

Eli continues, a hint of anger entering his voice, "We discovered a text message sent from your phone. I need to know why you were meeting him."

Oh God, that's why Max didn't show earlier. When I feared for his safety, I never imagined *this*.

"How?" It seems I can only ask one-word questions.

"Suicide."

Chapter Eleven

I get a strange sense of déjà vu as I peer at the Boulder County Sheriff's Office. Its flagstone exterior, white-paned windows, and printed placards are meant to instill confidence in the justice system. Instead, all I feel is a building dread.

Reid escorts me to the entrance and squeezes my hand chastely. Neither of us has mentioned what almost happened on my balcony. "Holler if you need anything." He rubs the back of his neck. "Seriously, I'm at your beck and call."

"I'll be fine," I say, as much for my benefit as for his. Then I take a deep breath, square my shoulders, and walk through the gleaming glass doors.

When I gave my statement after the climbing incident, I did so with an amiable officer prompting me with questions and Eli steadfast at my side. Tonight, however, I'm escorted into a cold room enclosed by mirrored walls. There's a lone table in the center surrounded by metallic chairs so uncomfortable my butt immediately protests with a sharp twinge of pain.

Eli sits across from me, his notepad and a folder on the table before him. His tie is loose around his neck and there's a wariness in his eyes that tells me to proceed with caution. I bite back the myriad questions I'm dying to ask.

Eli doesn't greet me before flipping open his notepad and stating, "Describe in detail your whereabouts this evening, Ms. Valentine."

Not Parker; Ms. Valentine. It seems we've regressed from old friends who rock-climb to casual acquaintances.

I shift in my seat. "At six o'clock I left Anita to close up and went to Murphy's Bend with my best friend. After that, I went home for a bit and—" I pause, fiddling with my necklace, not wanting to spill the next part. "At nine thirty, I took an Uber to campus. I was supposed to meet Max, but he never showed."

My eyes flit to Eli's, trying to gauge his reaction. His face is smooth, unreadable, and completely void of emotion. I may as well be staring at the stainless steel of my winepress.

I continue, "I stayed until a little after ten, when I got a call to go to Pearl Street to pick up my brother. He'd had too much to drink. The rest of my night has been dealing with that." Absently, I touch my lips, deciding not to mention my almost-make-out session with Reid.

Eli leans forward, dark hair escaping his gelled side part. "Let me get this straight. After I warned you to stay out of the investigation, you went to a competitor's winery—"

"To teach my friend, Sage, how to taste wine," I interject, my excuse weaker than a glass of Franzia.

He ignores me, ticking transgressions off on his fingers. "Then you went to campus. At night. Alone. To meet a man you barely know in a murder investigation." He punctuates each statement with an angry jab. "Jesus, Parker, I thought you'd be more careful after your climbing gear was sabotaged."

I feel like I've been slapped. "I can't just sit around and wait for the killer to try again."

Eli rolls his shoulders, struggling to keep his composure. I can't tell what he's more upset about: that I put myself in danger or that I interfered in his case. His voice is detached as he asks, "Were you and Mr. Jackard close?"

I cross my arms over my chest, staring at the initials etched into the tabletop. "I'd only met him twice. At my opening and when I went to his house the other day. Then he called and said he had something important to tell me about Gaskel." Goose bumps break out on my arms as I recall his raw fear, discernible over our spotty connection.

"Did you tell anyone you were meeting him?"

I shake my head. "Honestly, I wasn't convinced I'd actually go through with it."

He lets out a long exhale, hurt entering his brown eyes. "You should've reported this. Why didn't you call me?"

"Because I knew you wouldn't have let me go and I was afraid Max would refuse to talk to anyone else."

"You bet your ass I wouldn't have let you go. This isn't some game."

"You think I don't know that?" I snap, my voice bordering on shrill. I push my bangs back from my forehead, blinking back tears. "I could lose my business, everything I've worked for. I had to do *something*."

"Try a promotional gimmick," he says, completely deadpan.

I grind my teeth, wishing an ad campaign could solve my problems. "I'm throwing a party later this week for VIPs. Does that count?"

"When is this party?" He holds his pen poised over his open notebook. "I'll assign officers to patrol."

"This Thursday." My shoulders tense as his offer slowly sinks in. "You think the killer might try something?"

"Better safe than sorry." He sets his pen down, appraising me. Whatever he sees must concern him, because he tries for humor. "This isn't my way of fishing for an invite."

I snort but an iciness seizes my heart. Images of Gaskel's body flash through my mind—the vomit, how his limbs jutted at awkward angles, the waxiness of his skin. I can't go through that again. My chest tightens and I close my eyes to hold the panic at bay.

"Look, Parker, I'm sorry for being such a hard-ass, but you can't keep putting yourself in danger," Eli says. "I'm actually a decent detective, if you let me do my job."

"What's your solve rate?" Frazzled nerves have apparently disabled my verbal filter.

"Better than most, not as good as some," he answers vaguely. I wonder if that information is public record. "Now, is there anything else you want to tell me?"

This is my opportunity to come clean, to share all the information I've gathered. Before I've sufficiently considered the pros and cons, words burst forth like bubbles from a shaken bottle of prosecco. I tell Eli everything—the weird conversation I had with Max at his frat-boy house, the fight I overhead between Moira and Carrick, and Jason's untimely proposal.

Eli ferociously takes notes, waiting until the end to say anything. "I'm gonna pretend you didn't keep all this from me." He meaningfully clears his throat. "If, and this is important, *if* you promise to stay out of the investigation. I mean it, Parker. This can't happen again."

"Scout's honor," I say, holding up three fingers. Eli doesn't know I was only a Girl Scout for a month. The cookies I could get into, but the "Kumbaya" sing-alongs, not so much.

Eli nods, apparently satisfied. He extracts a piece of paper contained in a plastic bag from the folder and slides it toward me. "We found this letter at the scene."

I scan the note, written in a hasty scrawl that's oddly familiar and signed by Max. In it, he confesses to killing Gaskel. He claims he did it to get revenge on the critic for an unfair review that ruined his family's restaurant—a place called Jolly's Diner. His final words to the world are full of anger, sorrow, and guilt, the latter apparently becoming too much for him to bear. I swallow the lump forming in my throat.

"Does the name 'Jolly's Diner' mean anything to you?"

There's a niggling in the back of my brain, but there are so many loose threads that I can't trace it. "No, sorry." I make a mental note to Google it later.

From the wrinkles in Eli's brow, I can tell he's as puzzled as I am. He replaces the letter and folds his hands on the table. "Now, your brother said he'd have pictures for me. I'm guessing you know where I might find those."

I give him a wry smile. "Hey, you *are* a pretty good detective."

My apartment has gotten more action in the last twenty-four hours than it has in the past six months combined.

Eli leans against the wall of my entryway looking like a suave detective from the 1920s. All he's missing is the cigarette. He cocks an eyebrow toward Liam, who's still fast asleep on my couch with Zin tucked in next to him. They're snoring together in unison.

"Ignore him," I say. "He's out cold."

"I remember your brother from high school," Eli says. "Not as well as you. But he was always kind, even to a stoner like me."

I smile, padding into the kitchen. "For all my brother's faults, he's a good guy."

Eli follows at a respectful distance, my narrow apartment forcing us to go single file.

I dig the prints out of the junk drawer, relocated there from my purse. There was no way I was leaving them out in the open overnight.

I pass the stack to Eli, who straightens to his full six feet and moves closer to the floor lamp. I watch as he flips through them, the black-and-white images blurring together.

Too soon Eli is at the first print again. I furrow my eyebrows, a pit forming in the bottom of my stomach.

Something is wrong.

"Flip through again," I say.

Eli complies, going slower this time.

Nothing jumps out at me at first. There are the same shots of wine, decor, and people. The close-ups of Sage have more meaning now, but otherwise everything is status quo. Then it hits me; it's not the content of the images, it's the quantity.

"There's a print missing," I whisper.

"Are you sure?"

I nod, hair rising on the back of my neck.

Eli checks the corners of each photograph to make sure two aren't stuck together while I lurch toward the junk drawer, my hands shaking as I sift through takeout menus, bags of dried catnip, and loose batteries. It's nowhere to be found.

I pace back and forth, growing agitated. "The print must have been stolen, which means there was something incriminating in it, right?"

"Let's not jump to conclusions yet." Eli plucks his trusty notebook from his suit pocket. "Can you describe the photo?"

"Gaskel was in the foreground with his empty glass— it was taken right before I poured his taster of chardonnay." My memory is hazy and unreliable, a minefield of nerves and exhaustion. "There was a shadow off to one side, and what looked like fingers, barely visible in the upper corner."

Eli's entire demeanor changes as his jaw tenses, accentuating his strong chin. His eyes bore holes into mine. "Who had access to these?"

"I had them at my winery this afternoon, but was with them every sec—" I stop, tugging on my hair in realization.

"What is it?"

"During my phone call with Max, Reid was alone at the front of my store, maybe he saw something— someone."

I decide not to mention Reid's abrupt departure. True, I never found out why he ran off so quickly, but I'm sure he has a good explanation. And I'd hate to put the investigative spotlight on him when he has no reason to steal Liam's print.

"I'll check with Mr. Wallace in the morning." Eli makes a note. "Anyone else?"

"I didn't have the chance to drop them off at my apartment before going to Murphy's Bend. They were in my purse through the whole tasting. I suppose someone could have gotten to them there."

Eli pockets his notebook and neatens the stack of prints. "Tell your brother I'll be wanting the negatives."

"Of course," I say, smacking my palm against my forehead. "Liam can make another print." I start for where Liam is snoring on the couch, tripping over the geometric-print area rug.

Eli grasps my forearm to steady me. He breathes in sharply and takes a step back. "Morning will be fine. Liam's no use to me inebriated. Besides, I have a couple other leads to track down tonight."

I walk him to the front door, a sadness settling over me like a buzz gone bad. If I'm going to learn anything about Max, now is my chance. "What else can you tell me about Max?"

"Nothing, since you promised to stay out of the investigation," he says in a matter-of-fact tone.

"Even if it's for my own sanity?"

I imagine what he must see: disheveled hair, smudged makeup, dirt-scuffed jeans, a slightly crazed look in my eye. Maybe that's why he answers.

"Max was found alone at Chautauqua Park with an open bottle of wine and the suicide note I showed you," he says in one long exhale of words. "It would seem he killed himself out of remorse for murdering Gaskel, using the exact same poison."

My stomach roils and I force myself to focus on the facts. If Max killed Gaskel, then who was he so afraid of? What could possibly have been his motive? And why would he poison himself the night he planned to meet me? Something doesn't smell right.

"I don't buy it," I finally say, wriggling my nose. "Obviously, you don't either or you wouldn't be continuing with the investigation."

"Whoever is behind all this is getting sloppy." His smile looks more like a grimace in the darkness.

"What kind of wine was Max drinking?"

"Chardonnay from Murphy's Bend."

An artificial buttery flavor coats my mouth at the mention of the wine and I fear I'm going to be sick. I ground myself by staring at the welcome rug in my entryway that reads *If You Forgot the Wine, Go Home.* Finally, I peel my tongue from the roof of my mouth. "This is giving chardonnays a bad rep."

He snorts and scratches his forehead. "Have they ever had a good reputation?"

"Hey, chardonnay is the most popular varietal in the U.S.," I say in defense, crossing my arms over my chest. "I guess it's a good sign my wine was spared this time."

"Maybe," Eli says, eyes narrowed. "There are still parts of this that feel personal. Can you think of anyone who would want to hurt you? Maybe an ex?"

"I haven't talked to my last boyfriend since we broke up." Eli never met Guy, wouldn't know this isn't his style. If Guy wanted to take me down, he'd do so with words, a carefully constructed slander campaign, something that wouldn't jeopardize his image. Besides, he's moved on. After Insta-stalking him one afternoon, I learned he's already snuggly with someone else. I doubt he's looked back.

At that memory, I think of another rocky relationship. "Jason, my best friend's boyfriend, knew Max. He's never been my biggest fan. Not sure he had a motive for killing Gaskel, though."

Eli nods, waving in Liam's direction. "I'm glad you're not alone tonight."

I snort. "Fat lot of good he'll do me."

"Sometimes it's about appearances. The killer doesn't know he's in a drunken stupor."

I watch after Eli as he jogs down the steps, an undercurrent of fear coursing through my body. Correction: *hopefully* the killer doesn't know.

I spend the rest of the night alternating between tossing and turning in bed, searching for information on Jolly's Diner, and anxiously checking social media.

I finally remember where I've seen the name "Jolly's Diner": the archive section of Gaskel's blog.

Jolly's used to be located in Evergreen, a mountain town en route to the ski resorts. It was a beloved community favorite until Gaskel reviewed it nine years ago, right as he was gaining traction in the blogosphere. He claimed their stuffed French toast was undercooked, breakfast burritos were lackluster, and their bacon wasn't crispy enough. Coincidentally, the diner closed one year later.

When dawn breaks, so does news of Max's death. #KillerChardonnay is trending on Twitter again. It would seem the people on social media are more interested in vocalizing their opinions than in gathering facts. Because even though my wine wasn't involved in the murder, the angry mob is calling for my head on a platter. Or a corkscrew, as it were.

Desperation kicks in.

I dress all in black—tailored trousers, a V-neck blouse, and pointy-toed flats. I keep my makeup subdued and let my hair air-dry so it's wavy instead of straight. It's not much in the way of camouflage, but hopefully nobody will recognize me.

I have a memorial service to attend today.

"Morning, sunshine," I say, plunking a mug of coffee and plate of dry toast on the table in front of Liam.

He squints and groans, his eyes bloodshot as they take in his surroundings. "Whadhappened?"

I'm in no mood to tiptoe around his hangover. "You mean when you confessed your love for Sage, or when you lashed out at me and Reid and then we had to carry you up three flights of stairs to my apartment, or when someone else turned up dead?"

He sits up, cradling his head with a wince. "That's not funny."

"Good, because I'm not joking."

His skin takes on a green pallor. "Who died?"

"Max Jackard." My throat clenches as I say his name. "He was at my opening."

"Is this related to the fancy critic?"

"So it would seem." Zin rubs up against my leg and head-butts my ankle for attention. I kneel down and scratch behind her ears; the little traitor cuddled with Liam all night.

"Why didn't you wake me up?" His voice is raspy and there's a mystery stain on the front of his Millennium Falcon T-shirt.

"You weren't really in a state to be woken up." I shrug. "Besides, I handled it. Sort of."

Liam bows his head, his eyes locked on the couch cushions as if he were contemplating burrowing into them. "I'm so sorry, Parker." He frowns through an exhale, running a hand through his dark hair. "I've been a crap brother."

"No argument here," I say, clicking my tongue. "I'm only going to apologize one more time for what happened with Guy. Take it or leave it: I'm sorry."

Liam bows his head. "I know."

"No, I don't think you get it. I can't keep defending myself because he turned out to be a Class-A jerk."

Liam mumbles something unintelligible.

"What was that?"

He clears his throat and, looking me straight in the eye, says, "I forgive you."

"Great, now that's settled . . ." I place my hands on my knees, ready to get up.

Liam picks at the weave on Zin's afghan. She hops onto the couch and starts kneading it, emitting a rumbling purr. "It's okay with me, you know."

"What is?"

"You and Reid." He waves his hand in the air before resting it on Zin's head. She leans into his palm, seemingly starved for attention. "You have my blessing, or whatever."

"Thanks," I say quietly, unsure what to do with that. "There's actually something else I need from you."

"Name it." Liam grabs a piece of toast and shudders as he takes a bite, following it with a large gulp of coffee.

"One of your prints was stolen. I need you to make me another one, preferably before you turn the negatives over to Eli, which he requested, by the way."

"Consider it done." He downs the rest of the toast and coffee, the combo seeming to reanimate him.

The silence lengthens, punctuated by Zin's soft purring. I fiddle with my necklace and change the topic. "So Sage, huh?"

Liam checks the time on his phone and hops to his feet, dodging my question. "We should get going."

His reluctance to talk about Sage speaks volumes. It means he's serious. As in completely head over heels. Which, to my knowledge, is a first.

Normally, I would pester him until he caves, but a murder investigation takes precedence over my brother's love life. "I'll grab my purse."

After a quick bus ride across town, we traipse along the sidewalk of my parents' street. My black attire absorbs the sun's rays, insulating me against the cool morning air. The neighborhood lawns are lush and green and dotted with spots of bright color from petunias and marigolds. Every once in a while, Colorado will serve up a freak summer snowstorm, but fortunately for these blooms, this season is proving to be mild.

When we first approach my parents' house, I think I must be seeing things, that sleep deprivation has led to full-fledged hallucinations.

I squeeze my eyes shut and take a deep breath. When I open them, the same scene greets me.

Toilet paper sways from pine tree branches like flags

surrendering to the wind. Entire rolls have been draped over shrubs, unspooled between raised flower beds, and even launched onto the roof. Crushed PBR beer cans litter the sidewalk.

"Teepeed," Liam grumbles. "I'll be glad when all the graduation celebrations are over."

Hair raises on the back of my neck and a chill slithers down my spine.

I peek over my shoulder, scanning the street. We're alone apart from a runner making his way toward the Mount Sanitas trailhead with weights around his ankles. Because running at altitude isn't hard enough.

"Did you celebrate graduation by teepeeing houses?" I ask.

He chews the inside of his cheek, eyebrows furrowed. "Maybe middle-school graduation."

My unease grows as I realize my parents' was the only house that was vandalized. It was targeted. "Let's go."

We traverse the front yard, navigating around rolls of toilet paper, and follow the path to the back of the house.

My heart plummets when I see the basement door swinging open on broken hinges.

"Wait here." Liam jogs the last few steps to the door and tentatively pushes it open.

"Like hell," I grate, following on his heels. I wrap my fingers around the pepper spray I keep tucked in my purse. While Boulder is a relatively safe city, you can never be too careful.

A harsh stench assaults my nostrils as I cross the threshold.

The basement is a shambles. My brother's photographs litter the floor and it looks like someone took a baseball bat to the glass frames and porcelain lamp. The boxes holding our childhood memorabilia are torn to shreds, our prized toys and artwork strewn about.

The real travesty is the makeshift darkroom. Trays are upside down, chemicals seeping into the carpet, and light shines through the unprotected doorway and onto rolls of undeveloped film.

Whoever did this is long gone.

My pulse pounds behind my eyes as I take everything in. Hands shaking, I tiptoe around the shattered remnants of my family's past.

The posters that used to line the walls have been ripped down, only the pushpins remaining, and the base amp my brother uses as an end table is covered in dust, tiny shards of glass, and mystery liquid dripping from an upended cup.

Glass crunches beneath Liam's feet. Gingerly, he crouches to pick up the broken pieces of his vintage Nikon camera. He cradles them in his hands, dipping his forehead toward his fingers as if he could breathe his equipment back together. His chest heaves as he lets the pieces fall back to the floor.

Something sparkles behind the base amp. I bend down for a closer look, carefully moving torn pieces of paper out of the way like I'm playing the ultimate game of pickup sticks.

My heart lodges itself in my throat at what's underneath.

A chunky old-fashioned ring, its silver band twisted in an overlapping design that features a hefty turquoise stone in the center. There's a clasp on one side of the setting that almost looks like a hinge. It's just like the one from Liam's missing print. And around the ring is a circle of faint green dust.

Liam is suddenly at my side. He reaches for the ring, his eyebrows furrowed in a mixture of hurt and confusion.

"Don't," I say, grabbing his hand.

He looks at me, startled by my panic. His blue-gray eyes search mine questioningly.

I can practically feel the blood drain from my face as I ask, "Have you ever seen this ring before?"

"No, it's not mine."

I dip my head beneath my knees and try to think. The ring is in my parents' basement, where my brother is currently living. How could it have gotten here?

"Have you—uh—had a girl over recently?"

Liam turns beet red and shakes his head, offering up no other explanation.

No doubt his pining for Sage has kept him occupied.

I get my senses back and lurch to my feet.

"Mom, Dad!" I shout, darting up the staircase that leads to their kitchen, worry gnawing at my stomach.

I burst through the door to find them sitting at their usual spots at the kitchen table. They stare at me quizzically, my dad with a sliver of grapefruit halfway to his mouth and my mom mid-sip in her peppermint tea, the *Washington Post* sprawled between them.

"Thank God you're okay," I say, holding a hand over my racing heart.

"Why wouldn't we be?" my mom asks.

I wave toward the window, where toilet paper visibly wafts in the breeze.

"Don't let that trouble you," my dad says, pushing

his grapefruit bowl aside. "Sometimes students get upset if they don't receive the grade they think they deserve. This has happened before."

"Have you seen the basement?" I ask. "It's completely trashed."

"I heard a commotion last night. I thought your brother had guests over," my mom explains, the lines in her forehead deepening. She rises to her feet, growing frantic. "Where is Liam? Is he all right?"

My brother materializes behind me. "I'm fine, Mom." Liam turns to me, the severity in his gaze filling me with dread.

My voice is quiet, fearful. "What is it?"

"The negatives from your opening . . ." Liam trails off. "Parker, they're gone."

The Valentine family's behavior is a foregone conclusion. We succumb to our coping behaviors like sugar to yeast.

My dad, cool and calm, focuses on what needs to be done, in this case phoning the police. My mom channels her frantic energy into brewing cups of tea that no one will drink and cleaning every surface in sight. Liam provides comic relief, cracking joke after stupid joke, even though he's clearly heartbroken.

As for me, I'm ashamed to admit, I leave.

I tell myself it's because I have Gaskel's memorial to attend, answers to discover, and a winery to save. But the truth is I'm scared.

First, there's the ring's ominous presence. Then there's the fact that nothing besides the negatives is missing from the basement. Which means the break-in—

and likely the teepeeing—are related to the murder investigation. Whoever is behind all this is smart, desperate, and knows where my family lives. Unfortunately, thanks to the wonder that is the internet, this intel is easily accessible. It could be anyone. I feel nauseated and slightly light-headed, as if I've swallowed wine that has long since turned to vinegar.

I slip out the front door when everyone is occupied. Well, almost everyone.

Liam catches me on the front walkway. He's still in his stained T-shirt and there are dark bags under his eyes. "Not so fast, Houdini."

I wince, tucking my wavy hair behind my ears. "I have to go."

"Can't your winery wait?" There's a bite to his words, anger blended with sadness.

"It's not about my winery," I say quietly, my gaze locked on a strand of toilet paper tucked into a crushed PBR can. "Gaskel's service is this morning."

He rubs his chin, his face grim. "Parker, I'm worried."

"That makes two of us." I cross my arms over my chest, toeing the sidewalk. "What do you remember about the print that was stolen?"

Liam recalls more than I do. Gaskel's sideways glance and tense posture, the phantom fingers and flashy ring in the upper left-hand corner, and the shadow cast over the chardonnay bottle. The shadow allegedly belonged to Reid; Liam wanted it included because it gave the shot more texture.

But without context, these details are as meaningless as categorizing varietals based purely on color.

"Do you really think the print is important?" he asks.

"The killer is working awfully hard to make sure no one sees it again."

What did Liam inadvertently capture on film to make the killer panicked enough to steal every trace of it? Was it their fingers, the focus of Gaskel's attention, or something else entirely? I stand up straighter, my eyes opening wide in realization. There is one other missing piece of evidence. Maybe the key is with that.

"Do you remember Gaskel having a piece of paper? It could've been on the tasting bar, sticking out of his pocket . . ." I trail off, my shoulders creeping up toward my ears.

"No," Liam answers. "Why?"

"Just curious." I let out the breath I'd been holding, checking the time on my phone. "I really have to go."

"Get outta here." He stuffs his hands in his pockets. "This gives me the chance to finally secure the status of favorite child."

"Yeah, right." I force out a chuckle. "I'm sorry about your camera, your photographs—" I swallow, not sure what else to say.

He casts his gaze skyward, blinking into the sunlight. His lips twitch into a lopsided grin, but it doesn't reach his eyes. "The robber probably did the art world a solid."

"Don't say that. Maybe there's a picture you can salvage, send into a magazine or something." No words will be able to repair his precious camera.

"I have enough to deal with right now." He clenches his jaw, waving at the mess in the yard.

"What about work?" I ask. A part of me worries he's

going to completely self-destruct after learning about Sage's imminent engagement coupled with the basement disaster.

"They won't miss me."

I narrow my eyes at him. "You're just not going to show?"

Here I thought Liam was finally getting his act together, but it's the same bottle, different glass.

"Let it go, Parker." He turns his back on me and picks up a long strip of toilet paper, crumpling it into a ball.

I massage my temples and then try a different strategy. "Look, at least call and let them know what happened. Now isn't the time to make any rash decisions."

He heaves a dramatic sigh. "Fine."

I nod, secretly relieved. "We'll get to the bottom of this." If I say it with enough conviction, perhaps I'll actually start to believe it. "Call me if you need me."

"I will." He bows his head and continues, his voice so quiet I almost miss it, "Don't say anything to Sage. Please."

"About what?" I ask with a wink. Then I hightail it to North Star Lutheran.

Chapter Twelve

Devil's Thumb rises out of the mountainside like a stone hitchhiker against the blue-sky panorama. Sunlight peeks through the leaves of a giant maple tree that borders the church, dancing over the brick siding and stained glass windows.

I slip through the sturdy oak doors and loiter in the foyer. I'm late, although considering the events of my morning, I'm lucky to have made it at all.

Through the arched corridor, the pews are full of well-wishers there to commemorate Gaskel. I look at the sea of bowed heads, every sniffle and rustle of the program amplifying my discomfort.

I don't belong here.

I may have witnessed the final moments of Gaskel's life, but that doesn't give me the right to encroach on his family and friends in this manner. Still, if I want justice—for Gaskel, for Max, and for my family—then I need answers. Answers that inevitably lie in learning more about his character.

The service is formal; a pastor drones through Scripture with occasional chants from the congregation. I shift from foot to foot and scan the crowd, wondering if the killer is here, murmuring prayers, all the while congratulating themselves on the inside. My stomach churns at the thought.

A shadow catches my eye as a lone man appears at my side. He has dark curly hair and an earring in his left ear. He gives off an aura of money, a cavalier disinterest that reminds me of Gaskel. He shakes his head with obvious disgust when the pastor invites everyone to a luncheon reception in the adjoining room. Curious . . .

Caught in a wave of mourners, I lose track of the mystery man. I'm swept into a ballroom with linoleum floors that smells of flowery Febreze and stale coffee. I don't pretend to have known Gaskel on a personal level, but the paper tablecloths, folding chairs, and plastic cutlery don't really seem like him.

I claim a seat at one of the circular tables and do my best to blend in.

Although I crane my neck searching for him, the man from the foyer is nowhere to be found. I do, however, spot two faces I recognize: Moira and Carrick. They're dressed in head-to-toe black and hover near a banquet table lined with carafes of coffee and trays of store-bought pastries. Their hands are clasped, but there's a distance between them, an invisible barrier lodged between their torsos.

I furrow my eyebrows. From the fight I overheard,

they weren't fans of Gaskel. In fact, his review clearly led to friction in their marriage.

"I hoped I'd run into you today, Parks," Reid says, materializing at my side. He looks dapper in black slacks and a matching collared shirt that has the top button undone.

I usher him into the seat next to me, whispering, "Don't let on who I am."

"I like your hair." He twirls a wavy strand around his pointer finger and my pulse races. Stupid, naive heart. We're at a memorial, for chrissake.

I tilt away from him, putting a respectful amount of space between us. "I didn't peg you for the suit type."

"I'm like an onion."

"You make people cry?"

"No, I have layers." He rests his elbow on the back of his chair. "How'd it go with the detective?"

"He got mad at me for interfering in the investigation."

"And your response is to skulk around Gaskel's memorial service incognito?"

"Naturally." I wring my hands in my lap, the paper tablecloth crinkling with each twitch. "Did Detective Fuller talk to you this morning?"

"About what?"

"About something taken from my winery yesterday. One of Liam's prints. Did you notice anyone come in or out when I left you alone?"

"No, and I didn't take it, either, if that's what you're implying. Liam's my friend, I would never do that to him." He maintains eye contact for so long that I believe him.

"I never thought it was you," I say truthfully.

"Good."

If it wasn't stolen while Reid was there, it had to have been later yesterday afternoon, either at my winery or Murphy's Bend.

But there's another mystery Reid can solve for me now. "Where did you go?"

"Why, did you miss me?" he asks, but when I don't laugh, he continues, "The Pantry. I had to take care of something."

Despite his vague answer, I'm inclined to believe him.

My attention is drawn back to Moira and Carrick, who are now speaking with a rather stout, sour-faced woman. Next to her is a young girl who looks about five years old holding the leash of Gaskel's dog, Pico. I recognize the small brown dog from the picture on Gaskel's website. He sniffs longingly at the pastries and the girl slips him a croissant.

"Ava, don't," the woman snaps, so loudly the scolding echoes through the rafters. She continues in an unnecessarily loud voice, "Why he left that rat to me, I'll never know."

Moira crosses her arms over her chest and reengages the woman in a conversation. Carrick kneels down to pat Pico on the head, and I catch him wink at the little girl. He seems harmless enough from a distance, but then again, so do mountain lions.

"What do you think Moira and Carrick are doing here?" I ask.

Reid gives a full-bodied shrug. "Probably the same thing everyone else is."

"But they didn't even like Gaskel. He gave them a bad review."

"How many times do I have to tell you, reviews aren't everything," Reid says through an exasperated sigh.

"That may be," I concede. "But it's still weird."

"Come on." Reid pulls me to my feet, the contact sending a jolt of electricity up my arm. "I'll introduce you to Brennan. You can finally ask him about Gaskel's side business and review of The Pantry."

We weave between dozens of tables, crowded with people sharing their favorite Gaskel anecdotes, blog posts, and what the beloved critic meant to them. His name fills the air, harmonizing the overlapping dialogue.

Self-conscious, I keep my chin tucked and my gaze locked on Reid's back. I only let my guard down when we reach the far side of the room, quieter for its proximity to the bathrooms.

"Hey, Brennan," Reid says. "There's someone I want you to meet."

I feel a twinge of nerves to meet this former tech giant turned restaurateur. Then Reid steps aside and I come face-to-face with the man from the foyer.

Brennan Fourie towers over me both in stature and personality. Surprise registers on his face when Reid says my name.

"It's bold of you to come here," Brennan says, crushing my hand in a viselike grip. He speaks with a faint accent—British or maybe Australian. "I respect that."

"Uh, thanks." I force myself not to shrivel under his intensity. "This is quite the turnout."

"Gaskel would have hated it," Brennan says. He glares at the sour-faced woman as if he could sting her with his disapproval. "Even in death, that sister of his won't let him have his way."

Reid and I glance at each other, eyebrows raised. He signals me to take the lead with a nod.

If there's one thing I understand, it's complicated sibling relationships. "He and his sister didn't get along?"

"That's putting it lightly." Brennan crosses his arms over his broad chest, biceps bulging. "Vera resented Gaskel—I think, for his success."

Now, I know Liam and I have our problems, but *if*—and it's a big if—my winery somehow survives this mess, I can't imagine him being anything but supportive. And vice versa with his photography. Or his band. Or his podcast. Or whatever it is he decides to do.

I study Vera Brown as she holds court across the room. The only resemblance to Gaskel is in the slight angle of her eyes and her extra-large forehead. Her cheeks are rosy and her frumpy black dress clings to all the wrong places. She clutches a Kleenex in one hand that she periodically lifts to her nose. Yes, everyone grieves differently. But she seems to be trying awfully hard to appear upset.

I click my tongue. "You knew Gaskel well, I take it?"

"'*Well*' is relative," Brennan challenges. "But to someone like Gaskel, I suppose so. He valued his privacy. I got the impression he didn't have many confidants."

Reid rolls up the sleeves of his collared shirt, the tines of his fork tattoo just visible. "He always ate alone at the restaurant."

"It was one of his rules," Brennan says, smiling fondly at the memory. "He didn't want anyone else's opinion to impact his reviews. Gaskel was careful like that."

Reid snorts and grumbles, "Yeah, careful no one found out he made up his mind before ever taking a bite."

Not the most eloquent delivery, but Reid isn't the subtle type.

Brennan's smile falters. "Don't tell me you believe those rumors?"

"Rumors?" Reid asks, jaw clenched. "I saw you pass him an envelope the last time he ate at The Pantry."

"An envelope with tickets to see *Hamilton* at the Buell. The mayor gave me tickets to watch from his private balcony." He shrugs like this is no big deal, even though most would kill for *Hamilton* tickets. "Since I've already seen the show in New York, I thought Gaskel would appreciate them."

Reid isn't convinced. "You didn't get anything in return for those tickets?"

"You actually believe I would stoop to that level?" Brennan asks, his voice a mixture of disbelief and hurt. "Or that I would need to?"

Reid shakes his head. "I don't know what to think."

I sense it from the slight twitch of his mouth, the way his eyes flick briefly to the ground: there's something Brennan isn't owning up to. Whether it has to do with Gaskel or a completely unrelated matter, I don't know.

"You earned that starred review. Gaskel considered you one of the best chefs in Denver—hell, probably all of Colorado." Brennan bellows the last bit, waving his arms for emphasis. "He counseled me to never let you go. I failed on that account, part of the reason I offered to invest in your restaurant."

I gape at Reid. He must have taken my advice and told Brennan about his plans to go out on his own. I'm touched he listened to me, although I'd rather not be present for the fallout. I shift awkwardly, wishing I could climb into the floral-print wallpaper and disappear.

Reid clears his throat and tugs at his collar sheepishly. "I'm sorry."

Brennan claps him on the shoulder, dude code for "*it's all good*," and turns back to me. "Reid tells me your wine is top-notch. I might have to add it to The Pantry's menu."

Seriously, who does Brennan think he is? The fairy godfather of the food and beverage industry?

Somehow I keep my jaw from hitting the floor. "R-really? Even after what happened to your friend?"

"I don't blame you." Brennan hesitates, an action that seems entirely alien to him. "Gaskel wrote honest reviews. Brutally honest. It was something I admired about him, but others found threatening."

"Have you ever heard of Jolly's Diner?" I ask. "It might be one of those that felt threatened." And, consequently, one that could have bitten back.

"No, but Gaskel was very prolific." His eyes dim like champagne gone flat. I've bothered him with enough questions.

"Please come by my winery sometime for a free tasting." As a rule of thumb, I always carry business cards with me. I pull one out of my purse and pass it to Brennan. "Better yet, we're having a party tomorrow night, VIPs only. You're welcome to stop by."

"I'll consider it." He tucks my card into his wallet. "Now, if you'll excuse me, I'm going to pay my respects to Vera."

Brennan strolls away, the crowd parting for his giant figure. Pico wags his tail at Brennan and yips affectionately, earning a surprisingly tender pat on the head. Pico sits at his side while Brennan addresses Vera. Brennan sure has a way with animals . . .

"I can't believe Gaskel's reviews were legit, that Brennan never . . ." Reid trails off. He holds a hand to his forehead, his skin paler than a New Zealand Sauvignon Blanc. "I feel like an ass."

I throw his words back at him. "Reviews aren't everything."

He just grunts and continues staring off into space.

His uncertainty is unnerving. "Would knowing have changed anything?"

"I might have waited to open my own restaurant. Timed it a little better." He rubs at the oven-burn scars lining his forearm. "I've been pushing myself, working at The Pantry and putting together plans to go out on my own. It's been hard. A lot of late nights and early mornings. Last night was the first time I've been out in ages."

I see now, beneath his cocky grins and bravado, he's terrified—terrified of failing, and probably, to some degree, of succeeding. I felt the same way before opening Vino Valentine.

"There's never a perfect time to pursue your dream." I search his green eyes, willing a spark to enter them again. "You just have to take the plunge and hope for the best."

Reid finally looks at me, the corner of his lips twitching. "How's that working out for you?"

"Ask me next week," I say with a halfhearted chuckle. "Let's talk to Gaskel's sister, Vera. I've been watching and there's something bugging me about her."

"You got it, Parks." Reid drapes his arm over my

shoulder. As we make our way across the room, I'm not sure if I'm holding him up or if he's supporting me. Perhaps it's both.

I prompt Reid to introduce me as his girlfriend.

This has the benefit of gaining Vera's trust. It wouldn't sound the same if I introduced myself as the vintner who inadvertently poured the glass of wine that killed her brother. On the downside, Reid trips over the word *girlfriend* as if it started with four consonants strung together instead of a simple *G*. Not that it matters. We have a professional relationship, nothing more.

Vera Brown is the model of a grieving sister. Her body language is reserved as she graciously thanks well-wishers for coming. I notice that up close her skin has a grayish tint to it, accentuated by a thick layer of foundation. But I recall the way she snapped at her daughter and referred to Pico as "*that rat.*"

Ava and Pico have since retreated into the church courtyard to play fetch. As I watch them through an open window, her laughter and his wagging tail eases a knot in my chest. Maybe it's the sheer innocence of the scene, or maybe it's knowing they have each other.

"I'm so sorry for your loss," I say. "Gaskel was a local treasure." And I mean it. Even if the man didn't like my wine, he was just doing his job. Besides, there are worse things than a failed business. This could be my funeral, for example.

Reid echoes my sentiments, his hand resting casually on my lower back.

Vera dabs at her eyes, which don't have any tears in them as far as I can tell. "How did you know my brother?"

"He made my career," Reid says. "Everyone in the restaurant world will miss him."

She frowns, her expression distinctly toadlike, and grumbles, "Not all of them, apparently."

I can't help but pick at that thread. "What do you mean?"

"Go read his blog," she croaks. "There are loads of people happy he's gone, sullying our family name." A sadness passes over her features, probably the first genuine emotion I've seen her show.

She must be referring to the comments. I recall username *"devils_food99"* even accused him of ruining their family.

"Like Jolly's Diner?" I ask.

Reid shoots me a quizzical look, one eyebrow raised; I'll have to explain my fixation on the bygone diner later.

There's no flicker of recognition. In fact, Vera's only reaction is an aggrieved sigh. "Who are you again?"

Reid's hand tenses, his fingers digging into my spine. I ignore him and answer, "Someone who wants to see justice served."

"There's no such thing as justice, sweetie," Vera says. "Ask my ex-husband."

Ah, she's a cynical divorcée. I almost feel sorry for her. "You really didn't get along with Gaskel, did you?"

"Not after he left me to care for our ailing parents. Alone. Didn't even come visit Dad when he was on his deathbed." She snorts and then remembers to pretend-dab her tearless eyes. "And he thought leaving his estate to Ava would make up for it. Yeah, right."

I change tactics, appealing to her negativity. "Some people take family for granted." I'm one to talk. Color dots my cheeks in shame at how I left my parents and brother to deal with the vandalism of my childhood home. I make a silent promise to check in with them, pronto.

"All families have their problems," Reid starts. "That's what makes family, you know, family."

Vera harrumphs and shouts out the window, her voice shrill, "Ava, get inside right now or no iPad."

I decide to call it before Vera revokes my screen privileges.

"Our condolences," I say as I back away.

Reid falls in stride beside me, his hand still on the small of my back. For how much he struggled with the dreaded *G*-word, he plays a surprisingly devoted boyfriend. *Fake boyfriend*, I remind myself.

We exit the church in time to see Moira and Carrick peel out of the parking lot, sending a cloud of dirt swirling in the air behind them. I swear under my breath at having missed them. At least this proved to be a fruitful expedition. Now I know two key pieces of information: Gaskel's reviews were honest and he left everything to his niece.

"What's with the questions about Jolly's Diner?" Reid asks.

"Max mentioned it in his suicide note, found at the Chautauqua Park crime scene." How surreal to be in a situation where I need to differentiate between crime scenes. I chew on my bottom lip. "He claimed he killed Gaskel out of revenge for his bad review, which basically shut the diner down. Jolly's is at the center of everything. I can feel it. Only, nobody has heard of it."

"Where was it?"

"Evergreen," I say with a sigh. I was planning on Ubering up there but, it being a significant trek into the mountains, the ride would break my quickly diminishing bank. "You doing anything now?" I ask, inwardly wincing at how girlish and hopeful I sound.

Reid's gaze softens. "Driving you to Evergreen."

"You sure?" I ask, relieved. "You don't have to work?"

"I planned the menu yesterday and had a good haul of fresh ingredients from the farmers market. My sous chef can get started on prep." Reid jogs toward a forest-green Jeep. "Come on. We'd better get going."

I catch up to him, my excitement growing. "Maybe a neighbor or someone remembers Jolly's."

Reid opens the trunk of his car, which is littered with spare bike parts and reusable grocery bags. He unbuttons his collared shirt and tosses it in, leaving him in a snug-fitting undershirt.

For the first time, I hesitate, rocking back and forth on my feet. "Wait, why did you leave so suddenly yesterday? Where did you go?"

"I thought that was obvious." Reid says. "I went to tell Brennan about my restaurant. That was one helluva guilt trip you sent me on."

My unease recedes, but only slightly.

"You don't trust me?" Reid grins and I'm struck by just how attractive he is with his bronzed skin and amber-and-gold-streaked hair. "Even after what almost happened on the balcony?"

My mind reels back to late last night. His eyes gleaming from the electricity coursing between us. His fingers caressing my cheek. And his lips, a hairsbreadth from mine.

I cross my arms over my chest. "*Because* of what almost happened on the balcony."

He flinches and rubs the back of his neck. "Look, I'm not very good at this."

"At what?"

"Relationships. Not that we're in a, you know, but—" He swallows, his voice rough. "It's like I told Vera, every family has their problems."

I bite my tongue, waiting for him to continue.

"I wasn't supposed to be a chef. I was supposed to do something more worthwhile—be an engineer or a doctor of some kind."

"What you do is important. Everyone has to eat."

"It's not enough." He shakes his head, gravel crunching beneath his dress shoes. "Truth is, I haven't talked to my family in almost a year."

No wonder he doesn't care what other people think; he can't afford to. His confidence is a shield, a carefully constructed defense mechanism to keep from getting hurt again.

My heart melts and I'm one step away from throwing my arms around him and never letting go.

Truth is, I've trusted him all along. With my auxiliary investigating. With our future business plans. And now, maybe, with something even more personal.

"We all have to decide who we let in, Parks." Reid's green eyes pierce mine and a smile plays at his lips like a dare. "I guess that was my way of saying you're in." He opens the passenger door for me.

Chapter Thirteen

The inside of Reid's car smells like a condensed version of him, a delicious mixture of citrus, herbs, and peppermint. I could breathe it in all day.

His car is clean, but not so clean I'm afraid to touch anything. Recipe cards are neatly stacked in the console and there's a pair of hiking boots on the floor behind the driver's seat.

Reid dons a pair of sunglasses and taps his hands against the steering wheel in time to a French electronic band I've never heard before. I make a mental note to download their album. I'd almost forgotten he and Liam were in a band together, Reid being the drummer.

While he jams out, I make two phone calls. The first one is to Liam to get an update on the home front.

His phone rings and rings and rings until, finally, he answers in a strained voice. "What's up?"

"I was calling to check in," I say. "Did Detective Fuller stop by?"

"Sure did," he says in a clipped tone.

"Did something happen?"

"It's nothing."

"Withholding information won't help anyone right now," I say. I can't help but think of the massive secret he somehow managed to keep from me. Who knows how long he's had feelings for Sage?

"They brought me in for questioning," Liam says. "I've only just got back to Mom and Dad's."

My palm grows sweaty and I switch my phone to my other hand. "What do you mean 'questioning'?"

Reid side-eyes me, his drumming slowing to a stop, lines of concern etched in his forehead. The look on my face does nothing to reassure him. I turn away, watching scenery out the window flash by. We're on the outskirts of Boulder now, the houses becoming farther apart and the shops slightly more conventional.

"As part of the investigation," Liam says, almost sounding out of breath, "Detective Fuller tied the ring you found in the basement to the crime scene. Thanks to you, I didn't touch it, so there were no fingerprints to—I quote—give them sufficient evidence to arrest me."

"Oh my God," I say, holding my hand over my mouth.

"Then, after answering the same question, asked in slightly different ways, about a dozen times, I managed to convince them I had no idea how it got there. They told me not to leave town and released me."

"Sorry you had to deal with that, Liam." I lean back in my seat, my heart going out to my brother. He's having an utterly shit day. And it's not even noon yet.

"It's okay," he says, an ironic cheeriness entering his

voice. "At least I got to ride in a cop car. Never done that before."

I hear the distinct rustle of a trash bag and picture Liam cleaning up my parents' front lawn. Alone. Because no doubt they're already en route to work.

"Leave some for me," I say. I don't like picturing him picking up that mess on his own.

"I've got this. Be careful, sis." I hear the clanging of empty aluminum cans before our connection ends.

Something is bothering me about the PBR cans. Something that feels obvious, like when I can't remember the name of a celebrity. It will only come to me if I don't focus directly on it.

My second call is to Anita asking her to open the shop. She agrees, but there's a catch in her voice before she answers. I try not to worry about her hesitation, or what it might mean. I know for a fact this isn't the work experience she was counting on. Though, if she quits, I suppose that means I won't have to fire her when—if— I can't save my winery.

The drive goes by quickly. Highway 93 passes through the contaminated site of Rocky Flats, a former nuclear-weapon facility turned nature reserve. It makes me think of the poison in my own life. You can't see it in the inconspicuous shrubs or tumbleweeds, but you can sense maleficence lurking beneath the surface.

We merge onto I70 and head west into the mountains. Buffalo graze in grassy vales and, in the background, majestic peaks soar into the crisp blue sky, seeming both close and far away at the same time.

The conversation with Reid flows easily. I learn that he grew up in Connecticut and is the youngest of three brothers, his older siblings in careers his parents deem *important* (one a lawyer and one a doctor, though he doesn't hold their success against them). After high school, Reid defied his parents and, instead of going to some fancy schmancy Ivy League college, attended the Culinary Institute of America in New York. He then worked various stints as a sous chef before eventually landing in Boulder.

In turn, I share about my family—my fear that I'm not living up to my parents' expectations, either, how I worry about Liam with his perpetual hobby-hopping, and the way the death of my aunt Laura first destroyed me and then motivated me to open my own winery. How I wished she were here with me now.

When we reach our exit, I switch into copilot mode, navigating us through the heart of Evergreen, a busy downtown street lined with restored historical buildings, quaint shops, and pine trees. I direct Reid down a side street on the edge of town that runs parallel to a ravine.

"Here," I say, leaning forward in my seat. "Pull over."

Reid parks his Jeep on the shoulder and we hop out. Below us, Bear Creek babbles and a herd of elk freeze, marking our every move.

The building that used to house Jolly's has fallen into disrepair. It's small. There was probably only room for five or six tables plus an economical kitchen. Even though it's been nearly ten years since the diner was open, the space hasn't been used for anything else. A weathered sign is hidden behind overgrown trees, and dirt and pine needles litter the patio where customers used to eat. Boards cover the windows.

Reid and I approach the padlocked door, almost stepping on a bouquet of flowers.

That's right, flowers.

Someone has been here, and recently, given the freshness of the violet tulips.

Reid crouches down to examine the blooms. "That's not creepy or anything."

The cardboard covering one of the windows has slipped, leaving a corner exposed. The floor creaks as I peer inside, holding my hands over my face to block out the sun. The interior is bare, stripped of all tables, chairs, and personality. Faded wallpaper peels from the walls, suspended in a state of perpetual decay. On the opposite side of the room is a counter, where I imagine customers used to sit and have a cup of coffee and exchange gossip. Now the only thing being exchanged is dust.

I rub my arms and whip my head in every direction. Birds chirp in the surrounding woods, competing with a *whooshing* sound from a car wash down the street.

"Let's see if someone at the car wash can help us."

We leave Reid's car and walk farther down the street. It would be a relaxing stroll, romantic even, if it were under different circumstances.

The car wash is the old-fashioned kind where you actually have to get out of your car and hose it down yourself. I didn't know any of those still existed. A truck caked in mud is parked in one of the stalls; the others are empty. There's a small shedlike structure that doubles as a convenience store. Inside, an unenthused teen is distracted by his smartphone. He doesn't even look up as we approach.

"Excuse me," I say.

The epitome of customer service, he asks, not sparing us a glance. "'Sup?"

"Do you know anything about the old diner?"

He blinks slowly as if I'd asked him a calculus question. "What?"

Reid tries. "Is there anyone around who's lived in the area for a while?"

"My family, I guess," he says. "But Grans is the only one home."

I cling to this tiny speck of hope like legs to the side of a wineglass. "Any chance we can chat with her?"

He shrugs, slouching deeper in his chair. "Our house is the one behind the car wash."

"Great. Thanks," I say curtly, but the kid is already glued to his device.

Despite the welcome mat, the house doesn't seem very friendly. Pots of withering plants and snow shovels line the porch. Reid knocks on the door and a lady with a Brillo pad of white hair answers. She's wearing a blouse, baggy slacks, and slippers. She looks a little too excited to have company.

"Sorry to bother you," I start, raising my voice when I notice a hearing aid in her ear. "We were wondering if you remembered anything about the old diner, Jolly's."

"Yes, of course." Her smile falters and she leans into the door for support. "Pity what happened to the family."

My mouth goes tannin-dry. "What happened? Can you tell us?"

She shakes her head. Her voice wobbles as she answers, "It was a long time ago."

Reid interjects, breaking out the dimples. Bless those dimples. "Anything you tell us would be great— I'm sorry, I didn't catch your name."

Apparently, no one is immune to his charm.

"Deloris," she answers, holding a hand over her chest.

"Please, Deloris," I say, tempted to fall to my knees and beg. "It could be important."

"Oh, very well. You'd better come on in." She opens the door wide and shuffles inside, waving for us to follow her. "Would you like some lemonade?"

"Love some," Reid answers, winking at me.

I clutch his forearm, giving it an appreciative squeeze, before stepping over the threshold.

Deloris McGuffin has lived in Evergreen her whole life.

In her dated living room, complete with shag carpet and a landline, she tells us about her family (of which her slacker grandson is her pride and joy), her two cats (Maine coons named Lucy and Ethel), and her recent purchase from the home shopping channel (some sort of creepy doll).

The only thing she *doesn't* talk about is Jolly's. A pit forms in the bottom of my stomach at her reluctance. Something terrible must have happened.

I polish off my glass of lemonade, lips puckering from the tartness, while she recounts how the town has changed over the last few decades.

"No new businesses have moved into the old Jolly's location?" I ask.

Her good humor melts away and she shakes her head. "The property is still owned by the family."

"Did you used to eat there?"

"Everyone did. It was more than food, it was community."

A long-haired cat struts into the room, tail in the air, and makes a beeline for Reid. He scratches behind its ears obligingly.

"Lucy likes you, and she's picky," Deloris says with a chuckle, her eyes twinkling behind thick spectacles.

"She must smell my cat," Reid answers.

A man with a cat, be still my heart.

Reid continues, oblivious to the two smitten broads lapping up his every word, "I'm opening a restaurant soon and want to provide that, create a space where people can come together. How did they do it?"

"The Joneses owned the place, Matthew and, of course, Holly." Her voice takes on a reverent tone when she mentions the name "Holly." "Though everyone called her Jolly on account of her cheery disposition. Always had a smile on her face, Jolly, and never turned anyone away, not even Old Walt."

"Old Walt?" I prod.

"The town drunk," she says distastefully, picking lint and cat hair off her slacks. "He had a bad habit of passing out in the post office vestibule. Jolly would bring him hot coffee and flapjacks."

Deloris gives Reid a pointed look. "You want to create community, you have to be welcoming like that."

Call me a cynic, but I'm overly suspicious of people who are too angelic. "That was awfully generous of her."

"That was Jolly, generous to the core." Deloris stares into space, lost in her memories. "It was her dream to own a restaurant, to share her love through cooking. Her husband was a good man. Matthew moved heaven and earth to make her dream a reality, sold his landscaping company, and helped run the diner."

She falls silent.

A sense of foreboding grows in the quiet, so ominous I can almost taste it. I peel my tongue from the roof of my mouth and ask, "What happened?"

"That food critic came to town. He stopped by Jolly's on his way down from the mountains like most out-of-towners. Jolly was so flustered, she—" Deloris pauses to regain her composure. "After he left, she told me she'd made a mess of everything, that he'd never give her a good review.

"I told her it didn't matter, that we'd always be there for her." She sniffles and takes a shaky breath. "As it turns out, I couldn't speak for the rest of the town. Soon after that, Jolly's closed."

I brace myself, somehow perceiving that the worst is yet to come.

Deloris continues, unbidden, "It broke her. The diner was Jolly's dream, her livelihood. Without it, she just . . . faded."

"Faded?"

"She got sick. Cancer." Her voice wobbles and then breaks. "She passed away a year later, and her husband—he was so devastated he followed not long after."

My heart aches like it's been stomped on, crushed under dozens of bare feet, happiness oozing out like grape juice.

I hold a hand over my mouth. "Ohmygod."

Color drains from Reid's face and his eyes seek mine out. In that moment, I can tell he's feeling everything that I am—an overwhelming sadness, anger at the injustice of the world, and the tiniest ray of hope that maybe, just maybe, we've stumbled on the motive behind Gaskel's murder.

The clock chimes noon and Deloris starts as if waking from a nightmare. "I need to bring Dylan his lunch."

Reid and I follow her into the kitchen, carrying our empty lemonade glasses.

"You said the property still belonged to the family," I say. "What family?"

"The child," Deloris replies absently, assembling sandwich ingredients.

My head snaps to attention.

"Child?" Reid asks. He goes about cleaning our glasses, setting them on a dish rack to dry. "Holly and Matthew had a kid?"

"Oh yes. Ragamuffin of a thing, always helping Jolly in the kitchen." She gazes out the window over the sink and shakes her head. "Such a shame."

The hair at the nape of my neck stands on end and I can't help but think of Max. Even though I question whether his death was really suicide, maybe there was some truth in his letter. "Do you remember anything else? If it was a boy or girl?"

Deloris fumbles with two slices of bread. I realize her hands are shaking. "It was a long time ago."

"A name, what happened to them, anything?" I can't keep the desperation out of my voice. Maybe that's what tips Deloris off, for a steeliness enters her eyes that wasn't there before.

"I'm afraid not."

"Does the name 'Max' ring a bell?"

She shakes her head. She focuses so intently on the package of deli meat it leads me to believe she knows more than she's letting on. Perhaps as a final favor to Jolly, she's protecting the identity of her baby. Wherever they are. Hopefully with some good-natured relative, far away from this place and its constant reminders of loss. But what if they're not? What if this person is nearby, close enough to have exacted revenge on Gaskel?

Reid returns to my side. I open my mouth to plead

our case, but before I get the chance, Deloris herds us to the front door and practically shoves us outside. For a grandma, she's got some pep.

"That's enough sad memories for one day," she says. "I have to see to my grandson. You drive safe, now."

"Thanks for your—" I start, but Deloris has already shut the door in our faces. "Hospitality."

Chapter Fourteen

Fun fact: grapes take on the flavor of plants that grow around them. If they neighbor a peach tree, they'll have a tangy sweetness. If they're near an apple orchard, they'll taste crisp and citrusy. I wonder if people are like that, and what would happen to someone made to ripen alone.

The diner looks different now. Haunted. The cheerful purple paint has gone the same way as Jolly's dream, and there are three handprints pressed into the cement walkway, two adult size and one that clearly belonged to a child. My heart breaks afresh for the family.

Reid's Jeep is a comfort, his scent like a soothing balm I'm all too happy to apply.

We spend the drive back to Boulder speculating on what became of Jolly's progeny. I don't know anyone with the last name of Jones, and it's too common a name for Google to be of assistance. They could be anywhere.

"I wish Deloris had trusted us," I say for probably the dozenth time, fiddling with my beaded necklace.

Reid drums his fingers on the steering wheel along with a melancholy song that fits the mood perfectly. "Can't blame her. Two strangers showing up, asking random questions. I'm shocked she told us as much as she did."

"I suppose I have you to thank for that." I study his profile, scruff just starting to appear on his chin. "So what's your cat's name?"

"William," he says with pride, casting furtive glances my way.

"Cool?" I venture, since he seems to be waiting for a response.

He looks at me again, eyebrows furrowed in concern. "As in William Wallace from *Braveheart*."

"Never seen it."

"What?" He shakes his head, eyes wide in disbelief. He switches into a phony Scottish accent and continues, "That's something we shall have to remedy, isn't it?"

I chuckle at his terrible impersonation. While I have reservations about how much I'll enjoy a biopic about a Scottish war hero, I'm hung up on the way he said *we*.

Excluding our almost-kiss on my balcony, I've refrained from mixing business with pleasure. I've never really been tempted. But with the future of Vino Valentine on the line, I can't help but wonder, who is my rule really protecting?

My phone buzzes and I lunge for it, seizing the distraction. I answer to an excited squeal.

"I'm engaged!" Sage says breathlessly.

My chest constricts as a surge of disappointment

rushes over me. Jason didn't waste any time, a smart move on his part. If he'd given Sage one more day to mull over their relationship, her answer might have been different. I cringe, thinking of how I'm going to break the news to Liam.

"Congratulations." My attempt at enthusiasm is flatter than a flute of day-old champagne. I rally by asking her how it happened.

"Jason surprised me with a picnic lunch at work. We ate along the Boulder Creek Trail. He hid the ring in a piece of cheesecake."

"But you don't like cheesecake," I blurt out. "You've always called it an insult to cheese."

"Because it is," she says with an audible shudder. "But it's the thought that counts."

"Mm-hmm." I study my fingernails. "What does the ring look like?"

She proceeds to describe the amethyst ring Jason showed me the other day, wrong for her on so many levels.

"It sounds . . ." I search for an appropriate word. "Pretty."

"It *is* pretty." There's an edge to her voice, like she's trying to convince herself as much as she is me. She sighs into the phone. "Can't you just be happy for me?"

And now I feel like the worst friend ever. Because honestly, the ring, the proposal, none of that stuff matters in the grand scheme of things.

"If you're happy, I'm happy," I say. "Let me take you guys out later to celebrate. We can toast to your engagement."

"Yeah, okay," she says, a hopeful uptick to her voice. "Hey, I've gotta get back to work."

I can picture The Manual standing beside her desk,

adding one more case on top of her already hefty workload.

"I'll text you the time and place," I say before hanging up.

I lean back against the headrest and stare out the window. We're back in Boulder, the number of pedestrians and bicyclists growing the closer we get to downtown.

Reid interrupts my brooding. "Did I hear you need somewhere to celebrate tonight?" It's only now that I notice his drumming has stopped. He almost seems nervous.

"Yep, my friend is officially engaged." Luckily, I have a few hours to put my big-girl pants on and show Sage I support her. "Why, do you know of somewhere?"

"How about The Pantry?" Reid asks, and then adds, "I can show you what I'm thinking of making for your party."

I twirl a strand of hair around one finger; it may be the same one Reid touched earlier. "That sounds perfect. Thank you."

I catch his eye, just long enough to feel a warmth blossom in my chest. He looks away quickly and I do the same, color dotting my cheeks.

We're driving by the Hill with its eclectic cafés, hip restaurants, and tattoo parlors, when I realize what's been bugging me about the PBR cans. Namely, who willingly drinks cheap beer: college students. And I can think of one house full of PBR-swilling dudes related to Gaskel's case who could have vandalized my parents' house. I just don't know why.

"Can you make one more stop for me? On Grant Street." I bounce on the edge of my seat. "I have a hunch I want to follow up on."

"A murder-related hunch?" Reid asks, creases forming on his brow.

"I don't have any other kind right now."

The Hill operates in a different time zone than the rest of Boulder. Even though it's technically afternoon, the streets are empty and the houses are quiet.

Reid and I stand shoulder to shoulder on the porch of Max's house, camping chairs, cigarette butts, and Frisbees strewn about in place of a welcome mat.

I swallow nervously. Maybe this wasn't such a good idea.

Images of my family from this morning flash through my mind—my dad's somber resolve, my mom's distress-cleaning, and Liam's camouflaged sadness. I'm doing this for them.

I lift my chin, leveraging every bit of my five-foot-four-inch frame, and knock.

The same guy who answered the door the other day greets us with a scowl, thankfully wearing more than boxers and a graduation cap.

"You again," he says, his eyes flicking to Reid before returning to me. "I know you're not Max's girlfriend. She stopped by after hearing about his death."

I lift my hands in defense. "I never said I was."

It sometimes amazes me how death brings people together. After Aunt Laura died, relatives I hadn't seen since I was a kid flew in from all over the country. We hugged one another and, through our tears, found a way to smile again. In this case, it sounds like Max's roommates finally got to meet his mystery dream girl, albeit too late for him to show her off.

The guy barricades the entrance, but he's too scrawny to block everything from my line of sight, like the rolls of toilet paper stacked at the bottom of the staircase.

"So what do you want?"

I decide bluntness is the best strategy. "Where were you and your roommates last night?"

"None of your business." He hocks a loogie and spits, his saliva landing dangerously close to my shoe.

I inch closer to Reid. "Well, you see, it *is* my business. My parents' house was trashed and my brother's—"

"Your brother had it coming," the guy says with clenched fists.

I cock my head, perplexed. I mean, Liam isn't the most reliable, and no doubt he's upset people, but not to this extent.

"What exactly did Liam do?" I ask.

"He's the reason Max"—he chokes out his friend's name—"is gone."

Okay, now I'm really confused. I glance at Reid with one eyebrow raised. He appears to be just as lost as I am.

"Wait, back up," I say. "What?"

"He killed him." The unfiltered anger in his voice makes me break out in a cold sweat. "He picked a fight with Max, and when Max became too much for him, he forced poison down his throat."

"No, he didn't," I say stupidly, unable to think of a better response.

I will my brain to catch up, but none of this jibes with what Eli told me about the crime scene. One thing is clear: his friends don't believe Max's death was suicide.

Reid comes to my rescue, speaking in an even tone, "That's impossible. Liam was with us last night. He was indisposed."

"That's right, so he couldn't have poisoned Max." At least Liam's drunken stupor was good for providing an alibi. Now that's a thought I never expected to have. I shake my head, something dawning on me. "Who told you he was involved?"

Doubt crosses the dudebro's face, his lips twitching into a frown. Then he crosses his arms over his chest and widens his stance. "Wouldn't you like to know?"

"Obviously," Reid says dryly.

Another of Max's roommates comes to the door, this one taller, broader, and sporting a black and gold CU Buffaloes jersey. His nose is crooked, as if it has been bashed in more than once.

"Who are you?" he grunts. "What's this about?"

"We need to know who told you Liam was involved in Max's death," I say. "Please, it's important."

They both open their mouths at the same time, but with very different intentions.

The first one spits out, "None of your business."

While the new arrival looks like he's on the verge of giving us something—a name, a chance—he hesitates. He clamps his square jaw closed, and soon his scowl matches that of his roommate.

Before I can respond, Reid steps in front of me, matching their menacing glares. "I get it. You guys are protecting your own. That's what we're trying to do for Liam."

The behemoth's nostrils flare. "You know that bastard?"

"Say that again," Reid dares, cocking his head to the side and clenching his hands into tight fists. Apparently, he's a bad boy in more than just appearance.

As much as I'd like to defend my brother's honor—or see Reid defend it, as it were—it's not worth the hassle. These guys are clearly hurt over the loss of their friend, and lashing out at anyone who gives them reason to.

I grab Reid's hand and give it a gentle squeeze. "We'd better be going."

"But—" he starts.

I shake my head infinitesimally and tug on his arm. "Come on."

He follows, begrudgingly, and together we jog down the steps.

"You'd better not come back," the dudebro shouts from the porch.

I feel Reid's hand tense in mine and, for a split second, I'm afraid he's going to turn back, but he just lets out a string of expletives. We climb into his Jeep and Reid wastes no time shifting into gear and getting us the hell outta Dodge.

I glance in the passenger-side mirror, my heart pounding. Max's roommates are still glaring after us when we turn on Broadway.

Without meaning to, they gave me exactly what I wanted: confirmation that they were the ones who vandalized my parents' house, conceivably because they thought Liam was responsible for Max's death. The real killer must have used them, and the distraction they caused, to steal Liam's film and plant the ring. I would be impressed by the killer's resourcefulness if I wasn't so terrified.

"I could've taken those guys," Reid says. "Could've gotten more out of them."

"Yeah, at what cost?" I challenge.

"You're probably right, but still . . ." He glowers, pacing back and forth on the sidewalk outside of Vino Valentine, his Jeep idling in the parking lot.

As expected, my shop is empty save for Anita. Next door, the Laughing Rooster is bustling, the sound of the espresso machine and earthy smell of coffee, cinnamon, and toasted bread wafting into the parking lot.

"Are you okay?" I ask, leaning against the hood of his Jeep.

"Yeah, great." Reid clasps his hands over his head and takes deep breaths. "I should be asking you that."

I'm not sure how to sum up my current state, so I go with the simplest answer: "I'm fine."

He stops pacing and gives me a puzzled look, similar to the one he gave me at the Sundowner. His green eyes are disarming, as if they see straight to my core.

"What?" I ask, shifting on my feet.

"Nothing." He rubs his chin and continues wearing a path in the sidewalk.

It's clearly not *nothing*, but I have more pressing matters to deal with at the moment.

I dig Eli's card from my purse and am dialing his number when said detective pulls into the parking lot.

Eli steps out of a nondescript navy car that pairs nicely with his crisp suit. In one fluid motion, he removes his aviator sunglasses and tucks them into his jacket pocket. I glimpse his gun, strapped to his chest by a shoulder harness, and hope he never has to use that thing.

"I came by to check on you," Eli says to me, his caramel eyes warm and full of concern. He nods curtly at Reid. "Mr. Wallace."

"Is there any news?" I ask hopefully.

"Handwriting specialists analyzed Max's letter. While convincing, there are subtle differences. Enough to question its veracity."

"Which means it wasn't suicide." I'd assumed as much, but a feeling of dread washes over me at having confirmation.

"Correct," Eli says.

"Actually, I'm glad you're here," I say, proceeding to rehash Reid's and my adventures. I fill him in on everything, our conversations at Gaskel's memorial, our spontaneous day trip to Evergreen and the sad tale we heard there, and our confrontation at the Grant Street house.

Eli takes dutiful notes, his stance rigid. I can practically feel the stress radiating off of him, especially as I describe the almost-fight we got into at our last destination.

"You shouldn't have gone there alone," he says.

"She wasn't alone," Reid says. Is it me or is he hovering a little closer than usual?

An icy note enters Eli's voice. "It was dangerous." He focuses on me, lips pursed. "You promised you would stay out of the investigation."

"That was before my family got involved." I cross my arms over my chest. "The game changed."

"This isn't Monopoly, Parker. There is no Get Out of Jail Free card."

Instead of making me feel chastised, his comment goads me. "Why exactly did you drag Liam in for questioning? You saw him passed out at my apartment last night. You knew he couldn't have been involved in Max's death."

Eli considers me, his face void of emotion.

Reid watches me intently as he listens to our interchange. I shift under the weight of both men's gazes.

Finally, Eli sighs. "Because we found traces of aconitine at his residence."

"The green powder," I say, remembering the circle of light green dust around the ring.

He nods. "There was a secret compartment in the ring that contained the poison, although given how it was positioned, someone wanted to make sure it was found."

"Who?"

"That's what I'm trying to find out." He turns his focus to Reid. "Mr. Wallace, I need to ask you a few questions." With a pointed glance at me, he adds, "In private."

"Lead the way, Detective," Reid says with a flourishing wave. He winks at me, "See you tonight, Parks."

My cheeks flush; Reid has that effect on me, regardless of the situation. "Thanks for the ride, and for all your help. Really."

Eli clears his throat meaningfully and leads Reid out of earshot.

I have the best assistant.

Vino Valentine is pristine. The scent of oak barrels and the lavender from Anita's perfume greet me when I open the door. Clean glasses have been artfully placed on tables, sparkling beneath the wine-bottle lanterns, and ambient acoustic music plays in the background.

"Hi, Parker," Anita says from her perch behind the tasting bar. She pushes her trademark thick-framed glasses up her nose and shuts a hefty Econometrics textbook.

"Studying already?" I ask with one eyebrow raised. "School isn't even in session."

She shrugs, playing with the end of her ponytail, swiveling back and forth on a stool. "I wanted to get a head start for next semester."

"Have you read anything enlightening—trends, predictions, venture miracles—that might save my business?"

She frowns.

"I'll take that as a no," I say, stashing my purse beneath the counter. "Thanks for opening this morning."

"Sure thing."

"Have there been any customers?"

Anita shakes her head, her eyes glued to her blond hair as if she were searching for split ends.

I shouldn't be surprised. #KillerChardonnay is back with a vengeance. That damned hashtag has been trending all day, and my personal accounts continue to be attacked. Despite my efforts to defend myself with carefully crafted posts, my winery is still barren of customers. As I survey Vino Valentine, I feel like the wind has been knocked out of me. I try not to let my hurt show and refocus on my troubled assistant.

"Is everything okay?" I ask gently.

When Anita doesn't answer, I lean against the counter and cross my legs out in front of me, a casual way of cornering her. I recall her jumpiness with Eli and the way she rocked back and forth on her heels when I broached the topic later.

Panic roils in my stomach. "It's time you tell me what's bothering you."

She sniffles quietly, a single tear plopping onto her textbook.

I wait, arms crossed over my chest, and watch her steadily. After the day I've had, nothing will surprise me.

Anita shrivels like a grape left on the vine for too long. She says in a small voice, "This isn't really the experience I was hoping for."

I try for a joke to lighten the mood. "You mean you weren't interested in working at a crime scene?"

It doesn't work.

My heart plummets. I look down at the hard maple countertop. "Are you quitting?"

"I really appreciate everything you've taught me, but if I want to start my own business someday, I need to actually learn how to conduct one," she says. "With a profit margin and, well, customers."

I wince and push my bangs away from my forehead. "What better experience is there than helping a struggling business survive?"

She shakes her head.

In a final cast of desperation, I throw her own words back at her, the ones she said to me that made me feel hopeful earlier in the week. "What happened to this being a storm my winery can weather?"

"I still believe that. I'm just not sure I can weather it with you."

"Why not?" I press.

Her face twists in anguish. "Because I'm scared."

"Scared?" I ask, the word echoing through my mind.

Tears trickle down her rosy cheeks, leaving trails of black mascara. "I'm terrified during every shift. Afraid"—she hiccups—"afraid something else might happen."

I recall the hitch in her voice when I asked her to

open earlier and feel a surge of guilt. My sole employee doesn't feel safe working here. Can't say I blame her.

"I've put a lot of thought into this," she says, imploring me to understand with her eyes. "You're such an awesome boss, I hate disappointing you."

I pass her a cloth napkin. "You're not disappointing me," I say. "Honestly, if I were in your shoes, I would probably do the same thing."

"R-really?"

"Can you work through the VIP party tomorrow night?" I ask, not ready to face that task alone. "Detective Fuller said he'd have officers stationed here, so it'll be perfectly safe. And if you change your mind, as long as I have the resources, your position will always be here."

"Of course. Thank you for understanding," she says. "I should go freshen up."

Anita disappears into the restroom to touch up her makeup, leaving me staring at the husk of my dream. Everything I care about is slowly being peeled away from me, like my life is going through a giant de-stemmer machine. I have to hope that there will be some remnant of myself left once all is said and done.

Chapter Fifteen

After Anita leaves for a yoga class, I savor a solitary afternoon in my winery. After all, I don't know how many more there will be.

I push the murder investigation to the back of my mind and focus on the VIP party. Of the thirty people I sent invites to, about half accepted, which is honestly more than I expected. Everything is coming together nicely—linens and cutlery will be delivered tomorrow morning, Reid is giving me a preview of his pairing dishes tonight, and my wines are ready for their do-over debut.

I feel the tiniest ray of hope. That is, until Moira Murphy waltzes through the door.

She's wearing the same outfit as she was this morning at Gaskel's memorial, a black sheath dress with pumps so chic they give me closet envy. With her long hair twisted into an elegant knot, her maroon highlights are as subdued as her demeanor. Her skin is ashen and there's a sadness in her eyes that puts me on edge.

Murphy's Bend hasn't escaped the virtual onslaught of #KillerChardonnay, although they haven't gotten hit as hard as I have. Still, I wonder how she and her business are faring. If her sadness is because of that, her crumbling marriage, or whatever promise Carrick is challenging her to keep.

Sneakily, I palm my phone and find Eli's number in my recent call log. Then I give Moira a welcoming smile. "What can I do for you?"

Moira slides onto a stool and folds her hands on the bar. Her fingers are bare. It's not like I expected her to be wearing the nefarious poison ring; that's safe with Eli, tucked away as evidence. But she isn't even wearing a wedding ring.

"I'll have a taste of something," she says, her voice as silky as port. "Your choice."

I reach blindly for a bottle and wind up pouring her a splash of the Mile High Merlot. She holds the wine up to the light and analyzes the burgundy liquid before taking a sip, the motions looking ridiculously glamorous.

I find myself leaning forward, eager to hear what she thinks.

"I love a full-bodied merlot," she says, sighing contentedly. Wine trickles down the side of her glass like a shiver. "I saw you at Gaskel's memorial."

And I'm right back on edge. "You and Carrick left before I could say hello." I remember the lengthy conversation she had with Gaskel's sister and ask, "Had you met Vera before?"

"Never, and can't say I want to again," she says with a huff.

I'm not sure why—a large part of Vera's grief was obviously fabricated—but I rush to her defense. "She just lost her brother."

"I know, darling. That's why we went." She swallows the rest of the merlot and I pour her another taster. "It was important that Carrick and I share with Gaskel's family what he did for us."

I rest my elbows on the counter, fiddling with my beaded necklace. "But didn't Gaskel give you a bad review?"

"Well, yes, but he also forced us to confront a few things."

"Like what?"

Moira stills and pierces me with her gaze. "Parker, don't ever let business consume your life. Never lose sight of what is most important: family." She frowns as she twirls the stem of her glass. "Carrick and I forgot. Gaskel reminded us, in a roundabout way."

I recall the argument I overheard at Murphy's Bend, the tension I sensed between her and her husband. It's ironic that those who are closest to us have the greatest opportunity to cause us pain.

"We could all use that reminder once in a while," I say. "Preferably before it's too late."

"That's the catch, isn't it? It's impossible to know until it's gone." She touches her naked ring finger.

I consider my next words carefully, not wanting to overstep. "You know, with the merlot you're tasting, I thought the whole batch was ruined." I let out a long sigh, pausing for effect. "It was bitter and sour with no depth of flavor. Particular grapes, I guess. But I couldn't afford to give up on it. I extended the maceration time, let it continue aging, and, with a little extra coaxing, it turned into a damn good wine."

"Extended maceration is a fabulous technique," she says. She tilts her wineglass, studying the way the liquid changes color in the light. "Although it's important to know when to let go, too."

"True." I ditch the heavy life metaphors and say with a wink, "But I really like merlot."

An easy smile returns to Moira's face and she takes another sip of wine. "How is the VIP party coming along? Are you ready?"

Fleetingly, I wonder why she cares so much, why she's so eager to help a business that could eventually take market share from hers.

"As ready as I can be," I say. "Actually, while you're here, can I run a couple things by you?"

"Absolutely. Who will be attending?"

I grab my laptop and show her the guest list.

She dons a funky pair of reading glasses that obscure half of her face and peruses the screen. "This is a good group."

"Here's the tasting menu." I click to a separate Word doc, chewing my thumbnail nervously. "I'm adding the syrah for good measure. I was hoping to let it age another year, but desperate times and all."

"Something to make the guests feel special, excellent." She nods in approval. "What else?"

"My friend is a chef." My voice catches on the word *friend*, but I power forward. "He's going to make appetizers to pair with my wine."

"That's awfully generous of him." Moira gives me a

knowing look over her funky circular frames. "Is he talented?"

"Yes. Very." I leave out the part about Reid opening his own restaurant and wanting to feature my wine. Oh, and also the part about him being drop-dead gorgeous.

"Perfect." Moira reaches across the bar and grips my hand. She says with conviction, "Parker, this will work. Your winery will survive this."

I give her a forced smile, wishing I had a fraction of her confidence. "And what about your winery? I heard it was your chardonnay found at the last crime scene."

If possible, her face pales even further. "It seems we both need to see the culprit brought to light."

"Any idea who could be behind it?"

Her throat bobs before she answers, "I would tell you if I knew, dear."

Would she, though, if it meant betraying her husband?

A question takes root in my mind: Why their wine? Was it perhaps a strategic move to cast suspicion on them? Or was it simply because it was the most accessible for the killer?

The bell over the door jingles, signaling the arrival of an actual in-the-flesh customer, a slim girl a couple of years younger than me with a bright pink faux hawk, a colorful rose tattoo coiling up her right arm, and piercings galore. I have to stop myself from doing a happy dance.

Moira raises one eyebrow at the new arrival and finishes her merlot. "I'll let you tend to your customer. See you tomorrow night for your party, dear." She clutches her purse and turns back to me, a gleam in her eye. "Be sure to have a little fun, splurge on a new dress for the occasion."

The mystery lady sets up shop at an oak-barrel table. She unslings a mesh messenger bag from over her shoulder and extracts a laptop covered in stickers. She has a nose ring, an emerald stud where a beauty mark would be, and three holes in each ear. Her eye makeup is dark and shimmery and twin dolphin tattoos flash their tails from the backs of each hand.

Gotta admit, I admire her bold style.

"Welcome to Vino Valentine," I say with a welcoming smile, handing her a tasting menu. "Let me know if you have any questions. I'll start by bringing you some water."

"Actually," she says, her voice surprisingly perky, "I already know what I'd like. The Chautauqua Chardonnay."

"Coming right up." I busy myself fixing her taster, pouring in a little extra because why the hell not?

I place the glass on her table and she proceeds to sniff and swirl like an expert. "Is it true this killed a man?" she asks, her tone reverent.

Well, that's not the least bit creepy. I struggle to keep my smile intact. "Don't believe everything you read on social media."

She eyes me carefully, her eyelashes buried by a thick coat of mascara. "But it's true, isn't it?"

Seriously, who is this chick? "Technically, it was the poison that killed him, but yeah, this is what he was drinking."

She takes a large swallow and swishes the golden liquid in her mouth, staring up at the ceiling. When she finally swallows, she cranes her neck and waits. For what, I have no idea. Her T-shirt slips off her shoulder, revealing yet another tattoo, a cherry blossom branch along her collarbone.

"Delicious," she finally says, her cheeks splotchy as she bolts upright. "Buttery like bluefin with just the right amount of citrus."

"Uh, thanks," I say hesitantly. "That's an unusual comparison, but I guess I can see it."

"Good mouth-feel, too." She smacks her lips and crosses her legs, her knee poking through a hole in her skinny jeans. "Are you the owner?"

"At your service," I say proudly, extending a hand. "Parker Valentine."

"Libby Lincoln." We shake hands, her grip unusually strong. "How long have you owned the place?"

"It just opened last Saturday."

"Bad luck, that murder."

"You could say that." I feel uneasy discussing Gaskel's murder with this stranger and find myself wishing Moira were still here.

"Can I have a full glass of the chard?" Libby asks. She opens her laptop, the stickers covering it bright and artsy and from every corner of the globe. "If you don't mind, I'll park here and get some work done."

I'm tempted to ask what she does for a living, but I know better. People come to wineries for all sorts of reasons—camaraderie, relaxation, peace and quiet— and as the proprietor, it's my job to determine when to pry and when to let someone be.

"Of course." I tuck her unused tasting menu under my arm since she doesn't seem interested in it. "Let me know if you need the Wi-Fi password."

After I pour her wine, I pretend to wipe down the tasting counter and subtly study Libby from across the room.

The click-clack of her typing reaches my ears, mixing with the folksy music Anita left on. Every once in a while, Libby pauses and glances around her as if trying to figure out what to write next. Curious . . .

There's obviously more to this Libby Lincoln than meets the eye. An idea bubbles to my mind and I breathe in sharply.

What if her fascination with Gaskel's murder is more than morbid curiosity? What if she had a personal connection to him, like being the MIA child of a wronged restaurateur? The real question, though, is this: How do I find out without alienating the first legit customer I've had in days?

Trust my brother to arrive at exactly the wrong moment.

Liam pushes the door open as Libby takes her last swallow of wine. I'm still not sure how to politely pepper her with questions, but I'm running out of time. She gazes around my winery—her eyes roving over the lanterns, espresso folding chairs, artwork, and shelves of sparkling stemware—before nodding to herself.

Liam makes a beeline for me. His shoulders are tense and there's a crease between his eyebrows that reminds me of our dad. He looks taller, lighter, and I realize I've grown accustomed to the sight of him with a camera around his neck.

"Hey." I wave at him and then hold up one finger. "Hang on, I'll be right back."

I make to dart around him, but he stops me. "Parker, we need to talk."

"Can it wait a second?" I nod toward Libby, who stows her laptop and hoists her bag crosswise over one shoulder.

Liam shakes his head, lips pursed. "It's important."

I search his face and don't like what I see. "Just give me a—"

The jingle of the bell alerts me to Libby's departure. There's a twenty-dollar bill tucked underneath her water glass, well more than she owed.

I dart outside and whip my head around, shielding my eyes from the sunlight. Folks bustle in and out of the Laughing Rooster with to-go mugs in hand. Subarus, mud-splattered SUVs, and environmentally friendly vehicles fill the parking lot. Across the street, the bus station is crowded with people ignoring each other, earbuds securely in place.

But there's no sign of Libby. She's gone. Now I'll never be able to make sense of her strange fascination with the role my wine played in Gaskel's murder. Or, at the very least, encourage her to come back with friends.

I reenter Vino Valentine in a huff. "Dammit, Liam," I say, exasperated. "She's gone. She could have been Jolly's daughter."

"Who?" he asks, scratching his head. "Never mind. It doesn't matter."

"Of course it does. She could have been the key to finding out the truth about what happened to Gaskel, to saving my business." I grind my teeth, temper flaring. "You wouldn't understand that. You give up on your dreams at the first sign of struggle."

He flinches like I've sucker-punched him, which, given the current state of his camera and photographs, I kinda have.

"Sorry, Liam." I rub my temples and try to calm down. "I'm just stressed."

It's a testament to how serious his errand is that he lets my jab go. "You know how Jason has always been proud of his ultimate team?"

"The Frisbros," I say with an eye roll. "How could I forget?" Especially when they keep cropping up.

"When I was cleaning up the mess at Mom and Dad's, I found something. An official tournament-grade disc."

"This is Boulder." I put my hands on my hips. "It could belong to anyone."

"Maybe," he says. "But I've never gotten a good vibe from that guy."

I level with him, hoping my voice comes across as soothing rather than pitying. "Is it possible you're looking for something to break up Jason and Sage?"

"Very possible." At least he's honest with himself, which is more than I can say for myself. "That doesn't mean I'm wrong."

I open my mouth to respond in the negative, but then hesitate, recalling where Sage said Jason was while we were tasting wine last night: Frisbro practice. With Max.

My mind reels.

Jason admitted he was upset with Max over his lack of devotion to the Frisbros. That hardly seems like motive enough for murder, but there are other factors.

He was at my opening *and* happened to stop by my winery the day my climbing gear was sabotaged. Sure, he could have been in the wrong places at the wrong times, but I'm leery of coincidences.

Jason could have convinced his teammates to trash my parents' basement. Maybe he caught Liam drooling over Sage and wanted him out of the picture. It would be a bonehead move to leave a disc behind, but Jason isn't exactly a rocket scientist. The prospect leaves a bitter taste on my tongue.

It's possible I'm looking for something to break up Jason and Sage, too. But the pieces fit. Too well for my liking.

"Okay," I admit. "There's a chance. A decent one. But we can't say anything to Sage until we know for sure."

He shuffles his feet. "So what do we do?"

I tap my finger on the bar, musing. It's almost like we're conspiring to stay out past curfew rather than tracking down a felon.

"I'm meeting Sage and Jason at The Pantry later to celebrate their engagement." I swallow the bile that rises in my throat. "Why don't you stop by—Reid is working, so say you're there to see him—and we can gauge Jason's reaction, ask a couple questions."

"I'll be there," Liam says.

"So," I start as I clean up Libby's table. "Are you doing okay after everything last night and this morning?"

"I've been better," he says with a shrug. "But I'll survive."

I tuck Libby's money into the cash register, the only green the neglected machine has seen, and steal a glance at my brother. "The police haven't bugged you any more, have they?"

"No," he says. "Detective Fuller has come a long way. I didn't even recognize him until he told me he went to Boulder High with us."

Sadness drips from his words, his actions, like wine from a spigot, no matter how hard he tries to pretend otherwise. At least Eli is cutting him some slack.

"You know I'm here for you, right?" I ask. "If you need anything."

"I know," he says quietly, stuffing his hands in his pockets. "It's time for me to step up, give this whole adult thing a try."

"It's not so bad, under normal circumstances."

"If you say so." He manages a small smile, but it doesn't reach his eyes. "I've gotta clock a couple hours at work. See ya later."

Liam weaves his way through my empty winery, his retreating figure sending a jolt of anxiety through me. He's walking like a man who's had everything taken from him. And when you have nothing to lose, you're apt to take stupid risks.

I make it a point to buy local. I figure, if I expect the community to support my winery, then I have to do my part to support the community. That means shopping at the weekly farmers market, perusing tomes at the Boulder Book Store, and frequenting my favorite boutique on Pearl Street, Brocade.

Brocade's window display features summer dresses in more styles than I have social engagements on my calendar. Each one is unique, embellished with details that boast of a personal attention not found in department stores. They're paired with plush pashminas and funky jackets for those cool Colorado evenings.

In the store, I can't help but touch the soft velvets, slippery silks, and airy chiffons. The scent of cloth and exotic perfume eases a knot between my shoulder blades.

Moira was right. I needed to have a little fun.

Even so, dire thoughts push their way into my brain.

Gaskel dumping his wine in my vase of daisies and desperately reaching for a cracker, poison already coursing through his veins. Max cut down when he had a new girlfriend, a job with the Shakespeare Festival, and his entire life to look forward to. My brother, his camera as shattered as his heart. Anita, quitting because she doesn't feel safe. And my aunt Laura, her belief in me woefully misplaced, her investment going to waste.

My vision blurs from tears, sadness threatening to overwhelm me, and I force myself to focus on the racks of designer duds. My fingers fumble over fabrics until the mist clears.

Two dresses eventually catch my eye. One is a strapless cocktail number the color of golden chardonnay, and the other is a wrap dress adorned with tiny lilies.

They both fit perfectly, cinched at the waist and short enough to show off my legs. I study myself in the communal mirror in the fitting room, brushing the pleated lace of the gold dress.

"That dress suits you," the boutique owner says, joining me in front of the mirror. "The color highlights your olive skin tone."

"I have a big event tomorrow night—do you think this is professional enough?"

"Absolutely." She smiles broadly, smelling a potential sale. "Jazz it up with a blazer and heels. You'll blow them away."

"I'm debating," I say, disappearing into the dressing room and emerging a minute later wearing the navy-blue lily dress.

"Both dresses belong in your closet," she says, circling me like a shark, gently tugging the sleeves of the dress, as if it needs adjusting.

"My wallet says otherwise."

She purses her lips and winks at me. "Tell you what: I'll give you a discount on the second one. Forty percent off."

I hesitate, but then remember Moira's other advice: splurge.

"Deal," I say, and decide to go for broke. "Do you have a blazer that would match the gold dress?"

"I'll be right back."

I stare at my reflection in the mirror, smoothing the folds of the dress, discovering pockets at the hips. In my humble opinion, the best dresses have pockets. I slip my hands inside and revel in the soft lining.

That's when I have an epiphany.

Max uttered one decipherable word during our patchy phone conversation: *pocket*.

Thoughts rush fast, like wine through an aerator.

What if Max was the one who stole the piece of paper sticking out of Gaskel's pocket? But why would he do that, unless . . . could Max actually be Jolly's son? Was he the real reason Gaskel attended my opening, knew about it in the first place? I shake my head, flummoxed.

I leave the store with three garment bags and a severely depleted bank account. Between my shopping spree and the VIP party, my funds are drying up faster than my skin during a Colorado winter.

Hopefully my new ensembles will give me the boost of confidence I need to do what must be done. Because I'm not going down without a fight, and the first round is tonight.

Chapter Sixteen

The Pantry is renowned for its farm-to-table dishes served family style and for its prime location on the west end of Pearl Street, and tonight they're packed. The restaurant balances comfort and class, with chalkboards listing daily specials, rustic wooden tables, and vases full of white hydrangeas. It makes me wonder how much of the ambience is thanks to Reid, and what he envisions for his new restaurant.

I'm the first to arrive. The hostess seems to be expecting me. She eyes me curiously as if to say *her, really?*, which leads me to believe she must be one of Reid's many admirers. Flipping her cascading hair over one shoulder, she informs me in a snooty tone that it will be a few minutes before my table is ready.

I drift away from the icy hostess and make myself

comfortable at the bar. It's all marble, wrought iron, and sparkling glass. Given the posh backdrop, I order an old-fashioned, figuring I could do with a dose of liquid courage for the impending dinner.

"Parker," a familiar silky voice says behind me. "Fancy seeing you here."

I swivel on the barstool to find Moira and Carrick. They're one of those couples who look like they belong together—their perfectly tailored attire, smart footwear, and impeccable hair a study in matched elegance.

Classy broad that I am, I sputter and spit out an ice cube. "Are you two here for dinner?"

"Oh yes," Moira says. She's changed out of her mourning clothes, having figuratively and literally let her hair down. "This is one of our favorite restaurants."

Carrick gives me a forced smile that looks like it causes physical pain. Granted, the last time I saw him he caught me eavesdropping, so I guess it makes sense.

"Do you know the owner?" I ask, bobbing my foot.

"Not well, I'm afraid. We bumped into him recently at that quaint little French bistro in Arvada—" Moira breaks off and turns to Carrick. "What is it called, again?"

"Bistro Paradis," Carrick answers in a heavy French accent. "It's—uh—off the beaten path, as you say."

"That's right," Moira continues, almost as an afterthought. "He was with Gaskel, now that I think of it. I remember we feared Gaskel would ruin the establishment with a poor review."

This tidbit etches itself into my mind. I know Brennan and Gaskel were friends, but Gaskel made it a point to eat alone when he reviewed restaurants.

"We needn't have worried, though," Moira says. "Gaskel never blogged about it."

This only mildly satisfies my curiosity.

Mostly to gauge their reaction, I ask, "Any word on the investigation? Like Moira said earlier, we're in this together now."

Carrick's lip twitches, threatening to unravel his polite façade. His answer is curt: "No."

"You'll be the first to hear when we have news," Moira adds cordially.

Carrick casts about for a distraction and, gesturing toward where Brennan reigns over the hostess stand like the conductor of an orchestra, says, "There is the owner now. I must go beg a table for us. Excuse me."

Moira slides onto the barstool next to me. She fiddles with the strap of her purse and then the frills of her blouse sleeves, more nervous than I've ever seen her.

"So you're not going to let him go, after all?" I ask with one eyebrow raised, referencing our earlier conversation.

"Hopefully things will turn out as well as your merlot."

I click my tongue and decide to see what other information I can needle out of her. "I overheard your fight when I visited your winery."

"Ah, yes," she says. "Carrick told me."

Her candor leaves me feeling vulnerable and embarrassed, an unpalatable combo. I dip my chin, uncertain how to respond.

At my prolonged silence, she continues, "You certainly haven't seen us at our best."

I recall Moira throwing cherry wine in Carrick's face

at my opening, how Sage said they'd continued to bicker, and the vulnerability Liam captured on film. Then I remember Carrick's words from their winery: *We need to keep the promise we made to each other.*

"What does Carrick want you to follow through on?"

She opens and closes her mouth, no doubt considering telling me to mind my own beeswax. After another moment, much to my surprise, she answers, "We promised we would stay true to each other and our joint passion for winemaking. Which has proved to be easier said than done."

Whether that's the truth or a convenient fiction, I don't know.

I flash her what I hope comes across as an understanding smile. "We all go through rough patches."

She relaxes, leaning back on her stool. "Did you know Carrick was the one who came up with the Bend It Red?"

I shake my head. "It's an exceptional wine."

"He's really quite brilliant. He has a keen understanding of how the flavors of grapes evolve during aging." Her gaze softens as it lands on Carrick, who is currently schmoozing with Brennan. "I attribute it to his having grown up in the Loire Valley."

I can picture a younger Carrick—all dimples and dark hair—playing make-believe in a French vineyard. "That's a handy skill in our trade."

"Indeed," she says.

"What did Carrick mean when he said you have a soft spot for strays?"

"You really did hear everything, didn't you?" She tuts and I flush all the way to the tips of my ears. She continues, "It's my fatal flaw. I can't help but . . . well, *help*, I suppose."

I rest my forearm on the bar. "Is Carrick a so-called stray?"

"Suffice it to say, he alienated those close to him due to some . . . decisions he made in his youth." She purses her lips. "But that's his story to tell. Not mine."

Or is there another reason she isn't divulging his past? She's certainly been forthcoming about everything else.

I try to ease the tension, channeling my best girl-talk voice. "How did you two meet?"

Crinkles form around her eyes as the memory takes hold. "I was studying wine at the Institute for American Universities in Aix-en-Provence and Carrick was a server at a small bistro in town. I went there every night for a week; each time we would talk deeper into the night. I told him about my family's winery and the leg-acy I hoped to build, and he shared the depth of his wine knowledge. We haven't been apart since." She pauses, fiddling once again. "We're going back to where we first met and fell in love: Provence."

"When are you going?"

"At the end of the summer. We're going to spend the fall harvest traveling to vineyards in Burgundy, the Loire Valley, and along the Rhône."

"That sounds amazing," I say, cupping my chin with my hand, the utter romance of the trip taking my breath away. "What about Murphy's Bend?"

"It will be here when we get back. There are more important things than the bottom line." Although she camouflages it well, I can tell this decision has taken a toll on her.

Small businesses can't afford to simply close their doors for a month. I wonder how they'll manage it—if they will.

Carrick returns, rests his hands gently on his wife's shoulders, and, with incredible tenderness, brushes her long wavy hair to one side. Her maroon highlights appear a deep burgundy in the dim lighting.

"I hear you two crazy kids are planning a trip," I say.

"Yes, we have much to discuss," he answers, bowing his head. "Our table is ready. Enjoy your meal, Parker."

"We'll see you at your party," Moira says. "We'll be the ones loudly gushing over your wines." She gives me an encouraging smile and, with that, they take their leave.

It hurts how badly I want to trust Moira.

There have been a handful of people who have seen more in me than I have myself. Sage, my constant cheerleader and coconspirator; my college adviser, an intimidating woman who growled at me for three years before revealing that she believed in me; and my aunt, who encouraged me when I doubted myself the most.

Maybe someday I could add Moira to that list. When I'm absolutely sure she and her husband weren't involved in either of the murders, of course. It is a rather conspicuous time to be planning a trip overseas.

Toasted flatbread slathered with hummus and slow-roasted garlic. Grilled jumbo shrimp marinated in mango chutney. Thinly sliced flank steak drizzled with chile verde. An Italian spin on ratatouille with basil, sun-dried tomatoes, and a balsamic glaze.

In short, Reid outdoes himself.

Sage, Jason, and I sit at a four-top in the back of The Pantry with a view of the open kitchen. The sounds of sizzling meats and chopping vegetables serenade us. The best part, though, is the unobstructed view of Reid with his coppery hair and chef's coat rolled up his forearms. His impulsive nature and constant need for movement are assets in the kitchen, honed into a resolute focus that gives him such a commanding presence I'm struck with awe.

And I'm not the only one. I feel the heat of Reid's gaze as he takes in my new lily dress with its plunging neckline and curve-hugging design. My insides go as gooey as the burrata recently delivered to our table. This dress was worth every penny.

Sage faux-fans herself. "Did something happen between you two?" Her nerd is out in full force tonight with her dragon-claw necklace and lightsaber chopsticks pinning her hair into a messy bun. But she's wearing a pale gray suit, which tells me she came straight from work.

"A lady never kisses and tells," I say. "Besides, we're here to celebrate you two."

I raise my glass in a toast. "Congratulations," I say as we clink. "I couldn't be happier." Neither Sage nor Jason seems to notice my clipped tone.

I take a sip of my Mount Sanitas White, one of the wines I carefully packed for this evening. It may seem odd that I brought my own libations, but this way I can make sure the food will pair well with my wine for the VIP party. Not that I doubt Reid; I simply refuse to leave anything to chance.

Once prompted, Sage shares her dream wedding ideas with Jason nodding encouragingly at her side. Even though she's only been engaged for a few hours,

Sage already knows what she wants. Small and tasteful at the Rocky Mountain National Park in Estes, wearing a gauzy dress à la Liv Tyler in *Lord of the Rings* (naturally). She proudly displays her engagement ring as she spouts details. Gone is the uncertainty of yesterday; she's the quintessentially blissful bride-to-be.

However, she's my best friend, and I see the fissures. Subtle things like the way her smile doesn't quite reach her eyes and how she nervously picks at her fingernails.

Jason, on the other hand, seems all too pleased with himself. He dotes on Sage, hanging on her every word and topping off her wineglass when it's only half-empty. He even contributes a few words to the conversation, namely his sole desire for their wedding: that he and his groomsmen wear flip-flops.

I search his face for signs of fatigue, nerves, anything that might suggest he was at my parents' house last night. He gives nothing away.

A long shadow falls over our table and a deep, accented voice asks, "How is everything this evening?"

I spin around to find Brennan Fourie towering over us. He's in jeans, a black T-shirt, and fashionable leather shoes that reek of money.

"Wonderful, thank you," I answer.

He rests his hands nonchalantly on the back of our spare seat, nodding at Sage, Jason, and me in turn. "It's Parker, yeah?"

"That's right." I'm honored he remembers my name. "How long are you in town?"

"Until I wrap up some unfinished business." He has a refined yet somewhat aloof expression on his face. "I'm in need of a new chef."

"Sorry about that," I say.

"Don't apologize for something you didn't do," he says with a sharp look. "Besides, it's business, not personal."

After the last few days, I'm not sure how business can be anything but personal, especially when you've sunk your entire livelihood into it like I have. I don't say this, though.

"I'll keep an ear—er—taste bud out." I switch gears. "I chatted with Vera at Gaskel's memorial. She's an interesting woman."

He blanches and then guffaws. "'Interesting' isn't quite how I would describe her."

"Good point," I say, swirling my glass of wine. "Do you think she had anything to do with Gaskel's death?"

"There are do-ers and there are talkers." He nods at a table of patrons sitting down and says through a smooth smile, "Vera strikes me as a talker, someone who bitches about her problems but does nothing to correct them."

As if offing her brother would have fixed her problems. "Her daughter inherited Gaskel's estate."

He shrugs his broad shoulders. "Small change."

Maybe to someone like him. I take a dainty sip of wine. "Have you thought of anyone else who might have had it in for Gaskel?"

"Unfortunately, no," he says sadly, his curly hair falling over his forehead. "If you'll excuse me, I should make the rounds."

As he turns to another table, he pauses and looks back, his movements fluid and confident. "Oh, and, Parker."

"Hmm?" I peer up at him.

"I'll be at your VIP party tomorrow night. It would be an honor."

After Brennan leaves us, we nibble our way through each dish and I lose myself in the flavors. Savory and bold, but not so much that they'll overpower my wines. They'll complement them, in different ways than I ever expected.

"Ohmygod, this is amazing," Sage says. She shovels another generous portion of ratatouille onto her plate. "You're serving this at your party tomorrow night?"

I nod, sipping the Pearl Street Pinot meant to pair with that dish.

"What's this party everyone keeps talking about?" Jason asks, genuinely curious.

Getting engaged seems to have made him more agreeable. Unless there's another reason for his improved attitude, like getting away with murder.

"The VIP party at Vino Valentine." I cross one leg over the other and steal another glance at Reid. "It's the place to be."

Jason freezes mid-chew, swallowing his food with a gulp of Ralphie's Riesling. "Isn't it too soon to have another party?"

"My business can't really stand to wait any longer. So . . ." I trail off, letting him fill in the blanks. Hopefully he's up to the task.

He shrugs and spears another shrimp with his fork. "I hope it works out how you want."

His statement sends a jolt of nerves through my body. Still, he's making an effort and I can do the same. "Look at that, there's something else we agree on."

"What else did you agree on," Sage asks, looking first to Jason and then to me.

I reach across the table and squeeze her hand. "Your happiness."

Her eyes grow glassy with tears. She dabs her lips with her napkin and excuses herself to use the restroom, leaving Jason and me alone.

I cock my head to the side and consider him without blinking, as if challenging him to a staring contest. "Are you originally from Golden?"

"Why?"

"Because you're marrying my best friend." I lean forward, casting a shadow over the white linen tablecloth. "I want to get to know you." *And to see if you have any connection to Jolly's Diner.*

"Yeah," he answers.

I twitch my lips. Apparently, I'm going to have to drive this conversation, which is fine by me. "Pro tip for the next time you surprise Sage: She hates cheesecake."

He just shrugs. "She said yes, didn't she? She must not hate it as much as you think."

I hope my future fiancé will at least bother to learn my favorite dessert. Luckily for whoever ends up in that esteemed position, my preferences are simple: anything with chocolate.

I continue prodding Jason. "Did you hear about Max?"

"What about him?" he asks with an aggrieved sigh.

"He's dead."

Jason blinks stupidly and runs a hand through his mousy hair. Shock, sadness, and denial flash across his face in turn. He pulls his phone out of his pocket and starts feverishly texting. From his reaction, I gather this is the first he's hearing of Max's demise, which means he wasn't the one who killed him. And he probably wasn't at my parents' house last night.

If I'm being honest, most of my suspicion surrounding Jason has stemmed from my dislike of him. It's time I let it go.

Reid appears at my side. I smell the sugary morsels before I spot the platter of truffles in his outstretched hand.

So. Many. Truffles.

Dark chocolate and milk chocolate, rolled in coconut and crystallized ginger, stuffed with raspberry jam and bitter espresso.

I pick one out at random and take a bite, closing my eyes so I can fully appreciate the sweetness. "My compliments to the chef."

Reid chuckles, a self-satisfied smirk on his face. "Which wine will be paired with dessert?"

Truth be told, I forgot all about my wine. Belatedly, I pour myself a splash and answer, "The Campy Cab." I swish the liquid around in my mouth, noticing how the fruitiness comes to the foreground of my taste buds. "Perfect."

He meets my gaze, green eyes flashing, and in that moment, I forget about the murder investigation, my failing business, and how worried I am about my family and friends.

Then Liam arrives and all hell breaks loose.

On seeing my brother, Jason leaps to his feet, so abruptly he tips his chair over, and takes a swing at him. I might be imagining it, but I even think I hear him growl.

Liam nimbly dodges, skirting out of reach. He's dressed to the nines, in slacks and a collared shirt usually reserved for holidays.

"Square your feet," Liam says, demonstrating the stance for Jason. "It'll help you land more punches."

Leave it to Liam to respond to an attempted assault with a taunt.

"Jason," Sage hisses, recently returned from the ladies' room. Her face turns as crimson as her hair. "What the hell are you doing?"

"That was for Max," Jason says, glowering at Liam.

Guess I know who Jason was texting earlier. My brother is apparently still being blamed for Max's death. Fortunately, not by the authorities. Again.

My muscles tense, at the ready to join the fray. That's when I realize the hubbub of the restaurant has fallen silent. My table has officially become the evening's entertainment. I glance around the sea of faces, faintly recognizing Moira and Carrick at a private booth in the corner, both of whom have their hands braced on their table, at the ready to intervene. Subtly, I shake my head.

Reid side-eyes me as he sets the platter of truffles in the middle of the table, obviously experienced at defusing tension. "Now, now, there's plenty of dessert for everyone."

"Don't mind if I do." Liam waggles his fingers over the tempting truffles and, after popping one into his mouth, claims the empty chair between Jason and me. A bold move that makes me want to smack him upside the head. He doesn't need to be provoking this Frisbro.

Before Jason can react, I gesture for Sage to sit down. She gets the hint and urges Jason back into his seat, too, rubbing his forearm soothingly.

A quiet chatter starts up around us as diners at neighboring tables return to their meals. I exhale in relief. The storm seems to have passed. For now.

Liam licks his fingers one at a time, a carefree grin sliding into place. He focuses entirely on Sage as he says, "I hear congratulations are in order."

Sage beams while Jason broods.

Pots and pans tumble to the floor in the kitchen, causing a loud clamor. "I should get back," Reid says with a wince. He claps Jason on the shoulder as he walks by. "If you try that again, you're outta here."

Jason shrugs him off, sullenly staring at the table, his too-close-together eyes drooping.

I take pity on him. "I'm sorry about Max." I top off his glass of Ralphie's Riesling as a peace offering. "But Liam didn't do it."

Jason snorts. "Like I trust you."

"Jason," Sage snaps, her demeanor distinctly lawyerly.

I've often wondered what would happen if Jason and I were pitted against each other. Who would Sage side with? Now that the opportunity is here, I'd rather not put my friend in that position.

I cut in, explaining how the real killer framed my brother in order to steal his photographs. Jason doesn't seem entirely convinced—the strategic nuances likely beyond his mental capabilities—but at least he isn't shooting metaphorical daggers at Liam anymore.

"That's too bad about your photos," Sage says to Liam, still rubbing Jason's arm. "I would have liked to see them."

Liam waves her off. "No biggie. One print survived,

and I'm gonna enter it into a local contest; the theme is Colors of Colorado."

"Really?" I ask, trying not to sound too hopeful.

"Might as well. It'll be a while before I'll have anything new to showcase." His good humor falters. "Cameras are expensive."

Sage gives Liam a look I recognize, having given Liam similar looks in the past, that of a supportive sister. Even if Jason weren't in the picture, he has a long way to go to woo Sage.

I bring the subject back to the investigation, focusing intently on Jason. "Who told you Liam was involved?"

Jason shifts under my stare. "Guys who know."

"Okay, I'm going to assume you're referring to that houseful of trolls on Grant Street." When he doesn't deny it, I continue, "Text them and find out why they accused my brother. This is important."

Jason gives an elongated sigh as if his phone weighed twenty pounds. He grumbles as he texts, "Knew I should've stayed in and watched the game."

Sage rolls her eyes and I can practically see steam pouring from Liam's ears. As for me, I finish my cab to keep from saying something I'll regret.

A few seconds later, Jason's phone buzzes with a response. "Max's girlfriend."

Wow, that's not what I expected. I furrow my eyebrows and drum my fingers on the table. "Did they mention her name?"

He sighs again as he texts. With all his sighing, he'd better be careful not to hyperventilate. "They don't know."

"What do you mean they don't know?" I ask.

"They never found out, haven't seen her since."

I hold my head in my hands, massaging my temples. This is all so confusing. "Was Max at Frisbros practice last night?"

"Yeah," Jason grunts.

I pepper him with more questions. "Do you know where he was going afterward? If he left with anyone?"

"Probably something to do with the Shakespeare thing. He's been busy with it for weeks."

Liam absently plucks another truffle from the platter. "You weren't at my parents' house last night, were you?"

"No." Jason's voice is full of acid. He scrunches his face and wipes at his nose with a fist. "Screw this, I'm outta here." He storms out of the restaurant without another word.

"Real nice, guys," Sage says, grabbing her purse.

I snap, unable to keep my opinion to myself anymore. "Hey, in case you didn't notice, your fiancé is a complete ass, and he just accused Liam of murder." All my anger at Jason bubbles to the surface. "He remembered you didn't like cheesecake, and that was *still* how he chose to propose. He's a jerk to you and to your friends." My voice cracks as I point at her. "I know you've been with him forever, but you deserve better."

"Is that so?" she asks sarcastically.

"Damn straight. I think you're scared to be alone, to take the time to figure out what will make you happy." I continue, on a roll now, "It's the same with The Manual and your career."

Sage throws a withering glare at Liam, who, to his credit, doesn't shrink away. "Do you have an opinion?"

Liam lifts his chin and looks her straight in the eye. "I came here tonight to make sure Jason wasn't involved in a murder. Because *I wasn't sure*." He tosses his napkin on the table. "That's what a great guy he is."

Sage's jaw drops and she utters something like, "Unbelievable."

"Unbelievable that you have friends who care about you and want to protect you?" I ask.

"Work a little harder on protecting yourself and leave me out of your drama." Sage shoulders her purse and strides after her fiancé.

Waves of emotion course through my body, sadness and a touch of relief. Words, once spoken, can never be taken back. I'm glad for it; I was getting sick of pretending, anyway. But a part of me wonders if our friendship can recover from this.

Chapter Seventeen

After the world's worst engagement celebration, wherein I alienated my best friend and basically accused her fiancé of being complicit in an act of vandalism, I decide to play the dutiful daughter and visit my parents.

I hitch a ride with Liam. We're silent in the car, the same beater he's driven since high school, each of us absorbed in our own thoughts. Liam retreats to the basement as soon as we get to the house. I don't try to stop him; he's had one helluva day.

The house is dark and quiet, the dull hum of appliances and soft rustle of turning pages being the only sounds. I find my dad sipping tea in the living room. He closes the Dick Francis mystery he's reading and gives me a hug.

"Did you get everything sorted with Detective Fuller?" I ask. I collapse onto the couch and prop my feet up on an ottoman, draping a knitted throw over my legs.

He nods and returns to his lounge chair. "Nice kid, said he knew you and Liam growing up."

"He's been pretty helpful throughout the investigation." I pick at a loose thread on the blanket. "That is, when he's not accusing me or Liam of murder."

My dad frowns, probably trying to deduce if I'm serious.

"Guess who I met today?" I ask, only giving my dad a split second to muse. "Brennan Fourie."

"Of Fourie Systems?"

"Correct. He also owns The Pantry," I say. "What do you know about him?"

"Not more than the average person, I'm afraid. Enigmatic personality, notorious bachelor, brilliant software developer, and even more brilliant businessman." He pauses to take a sip of tea. "How is your business?"

Tears prickle my eyes and my throat constricts. "Not great," I finally manage to choke out. "I don't know if the VIP party will be enough to save it."

Vocalizing my fear makes it real. I was always taught that if I worked hard enough, I could accomplish anything I set my mind to, but I'm beginning to wonder if that's a lie. Dismal visions cloud my mind—packing up my winery, working some dead-end job so I can afford cat food, squatting in my parents' basement.

My dad calmly sips his tea. There are chalk smudges on his shirt and his smartwatch glows with a notification. He ignores it. "You're doing something brave, venturing out on your own."

"Brave, or stupid." I nuzzle my head back into the

cushion and stare at the ceiling, wondering, for the umpteenth time, why I thought I could do this.

I guess it's the night for candor, because I blurt out, "Why didn't you and Mom come to my opening?"

"Oh, Parker," my dad says. He takes off his reading glasses and rubs his eyes.

"I get that you guys have your jobs and what you do is important, but you knew the date for ages. And it was on a Saturday! You could have gotten the day off." My voice cracks and the tears that were threatening trickle down my cheeks. I wipe them away.

"We weren't sure you wanted us there," my dad finally admits, passing me a tissue.

I blow my nose in a decidedly unladylike fashion. "You're my parents, of course I wanted—needed—you there."

"You were so excited to have your friends in attendance and guests to impress. Your mom and I figured a couple of old codgers like us would effectively, how do you kids say it"—he searches for a phrase I'm certain will be embarrassing—"kill your buzz."

And I was right.

I smile through my tears. "How could you think that?"

"Liam has always needed us, more than he should, but you're different. You've always been independent. We wanted to respect your space."

Sage's words come back to me: *We can't all be an island like you.* Am I so opposed to asking for help that even my own parents see me that way?

"Is that why you never offered to help when I was saving up to open Vino Valentine?"

"We were prepared to, if you'd asked." He taps his thumbs on his book. "But you never did, and it seemed like you had everything under control."

I scoff.

"It's true. And then when Laura—" He pauses and swallows. Even though she was my mom's sister, they'd been close. "Well, after that, you definitely didn't need us."

My anger melts away as I picture myself in their light.

I click my tongue and sit forward on the couch. "Well, I hope you and Mom will come to the VIP party tomorrow night. I would love to have you there."

"We'll be there."

"Really? Just like that?"

"I said we'll be there, and we will. No matter what." He shifts into what Liam and I affectionately refer to as Lecture Mode, the arm of his glasses in his mouth, a no-nonsense look in his eyes, voice imbued with passion. "We're proud of you, Parker. Going for your dream isn't an easy thing to do."

"Thanks," I say quietly. "But what about the wine spritzer?"

"Your mom is stubborn and knows what she likes." He crosses his long legs in front of him, his feet clad in slippers. "Not dissimilar from you."

I let that sink in.

Loud music drifts up from the basement, old-school rock that I know to be my brother's angry music. "I'm worried about Liam."

"Me too. Perpetually." He steeples his fingers. "What is it in particular?"

"He's suffered . . . heartbreak this week, and then this morning with this photography . . ." I shake my head.

"What do you think we should do?"

"I want to get him a new camera," I say. "In business, it's standard practice to turn over a portion of profits to invest in future endeavors. Namely, for expansion. I'm not in a position to do that, and Liam isn't part of my business per se, but I'd like to invest in him."

My dad blinks several times. I can hardly believe myself, either.

"Let me know how much you need," he says. "Now, tell me about the investigation."

I tug at my beaded necklace. "I don't even know where to start. Things are so tangled."

"That's what debugging is for."

"Too bad I'm not a programmer."

He taps his glasses against the cover of his book. "You know, I often give students two pieces of advice. First, you can never challenge your own assumptions too many times."

His words unsettle me, the rich food from earlier roiling in my stomach. "And the second?"

"Sleep on it. Your subconscious will continue working on a problem while you get some much-needed rest."

My yawn in response proves his point.

Many varietals benefit from aging. When left to its own devices, a chemical reaction occurs between sugars and acids that unlocks the true potential of a wine. It's high time I do a little aging myself.

"Do you mind if I crash here tonight?"

"Not at all. You're always welcome."

I snuggle deeper into the couch and, with the sound of my father steadily turning pages of his book in the background, fall fast asleep.

* * *

The next morning dawns with an auspicious red sunrise, casting a dusty pink glow over the Flatirons. *"Red sky in morning, sailor's warning,"* as my mom always says, even though Colorado is a far cry from the ocean. I try not to view it as an omen.

I get back to my apartment complex early, not wanting Zin to freak out about the lack of kibble in her bowl, already planning to pamper her with extra treats.

Birds chirp in a nearby juniper tree, hopping from branch to branch. I climb the stairwell to my unit, daydreaming about a hot shower, cup of coffee, and cuddle with Zin. A good night's sleep coupled with the conversation with my dad, despite its whole *"trust no one"* vibe at the end, left me feeling comforted.

Then I freeze, some primal part of my brain sensing I'm not alone. A chill creeps up my spine.

Shadows move on the landing outside my front door, the sun casting the figures into elongated shapes, accompanied by two deep voices. They're muffled by distance and noisy birds, and completely unrecognizable. I brace myself for the worst.

I inch toward the inside of the stairwell and dig through my purse for my trusted pepper spray. My hands shake so badly I fumble to unlock the canister. I steady myself with a deep breath, conscious of every creak, and get a solid grip on the canister.

My heart races and I force myself to swallow, my mouth suddenly dry. I tiptoe forward and peek around the corner.

And now I feel ridiculous.

"You guys scared the crap out of me," I say.

Reid and Eli both jump at the sound of my voice. They take in my pepper spray and startled expression and immediately mumble apologies.

I take a second to absorb the scene: two undeniably attractive men waiting on my doorstep like Amazon packages. Reid is wearing a sage-green T-shirt that complements his eyes, and Eli is in his customary navy suit, complete with a perfectly knotted tie.

I nudge past them and unlock my door, waving them inside.

Zin greets me and, seeing we have guests of the male persuasion, twitches her fluffy tail. She sniffs at Reid before rubbing up against his leg in approval. She isn't so sure about Eli, eyeing him suspiciously before trotting to her food dish expectantly.

I switch on my funky lamps as I lead the way deeper into my narrow apartment, my living room even more cramped than usual with Reid and Eli in it.

"Did you guys come here together?" I ask, curiosity piqued.

They simultaneously lean away from each other and shake their heads. I wonder what they found to chat about until I showed up.

"So what can I do for you fellas?" I ask.

"I was on my way to the market but wanted to stop by and confirm the VIP party menu," Reid says. His eyes dart to the French doors that lead to the balcony, and then back to me. "Maybe we can pick up where we left off the other night."

Warmth rushes to my core and I shiver for an entirely different reason.

Eli clears his throat meaningfully. "I wanted to follow up on how your parents are doing after the B and

E," Eli says, and goes on to explain to Reid, "That stands for breaking and entering."

Reid gives him a no-duh expression, but seems to know better than to provoke a detective.

"First things first," I say, scooping a generous amount of kibble into Zin's bowl. I coo at her as she trots over to me. She meows gratefully and, not needing further encouragement, tucks into her food.

There's a knock on the door and we all freeze—Reid, Eli, Zin, and me. Four pairs of eyes seek out the entryway.

Eli rests his hand on the gun holster strapped to his shoulder. "Are you expecting someone?"

"No," I say, flummoxed.

Reid glues himself to my side as Eli checks the peephole. "A fiery redhead?"

"That would be Sage," I say, equal parts eager and nervous. I swat them away and let in my best friend. At least, I hope she's still my best friend.

She's carrying a duffel and her face is blotchy like she's been crying. "Can we talk?"

"Sure," I say. "Just give me a minute."

Sage wedges herself in the living room, setting her bag on the couch, the russet velvet clashing with her hair. She takes in Reid and Eli and raises one eyebrow at me. "I didn't mean to interrupt . . . whatever this is."

"You're not." I turn to Eli, clasping my hands. "Detective Fuller—"

"Eli, please," he says.

"Eli," I acquiesce, guiding him to the front door and the privacy offered there. "I just came from my folks' house and can report they're doing fine."

He nods, lips pursed. "I'll be at your party tonight with two officers in attendance. In plain clothes, as requested."

"Thank you."

He looks like he wants to say something more, but hesitates. "I can see you're busy. Call me if you need anything."

Back in the living room, Sage is complimenting Reid's cooking up one side and down the other.

"And, I mean, those shrimp were to die for," she finishes, holding one hand over her chest, a dreamy look on her face.

"She's right," I say. "Reid, your food was off-the-charts delicious."

Cocksure grin in place, he slips his hands in his pockets. "Glad you liked it."

"Liked is an understatement," I say. "Every dish was exquisite. Do that exact same menu for the tasting later." I usher him toward the door, my hand resting on his shoulder, that one bit of contact sending electricity up my arm.

"But—" he says, clearly not expecting to be sent packing so soon.

"Thank you again for everything," I say, gently squeezing his bicep. "I have to be a good friend now, I hope you understand." Before I lose my nerve, I lean in and whisper in his ear, "We'll revisit the balcony another time."

He smiles, a softer smile than I've grown accustomed to, and nods. "Looking forward to it. Later, Parks."

I wink at him before reluctantly closing the door.

Sage owes me big-time.

* * *

There are two things I know about Sage: Never steal her yogurt and never enter into an argument with her lightly. My girl is a fierce contender, which is why, when I go back into the living room, I tread cautiously.

I lean against the wall, arms crossed over my chest, and wait for her to say something.

She's perched on the sofa, freckles standing out against her pale skin. She's wearing yoga pants, a homemade *Firefly* T-shirt, and a headband. Zin, having scarfed down her breakfast, hops onto the cushion next to her and begins kneading the afghan blanket.

Sage scratches behind her ears and, gaze locked on Zin's silky gray fur, says, "Jason and I are taking a break."

My eyebrows shoot up. "Really?"

"The things you said . . ." She shakes her head. "You were right. About all of it."

A weight lifts from my shoulders and I join her on the couch. "I didn't have to attack you like that, though. We were supposed to be celebrating your engagement."

"It was good you said what you did. And Liam, too," she acknowledges with a touch of irony. "How long have you felt that way?"

I stare at the area rug sheepishly. "Ever since he grunted his way through your birthday party freshmen year of college."

"I guess I always suspected. It's not like you hid it all that well."

"I tried to give him a chance." I rub my neck and continue, "At least, I tried early on."

"I hoped you two would eventually see how awesome each of you were. Turns out Jason wasn't all that awesome, after all." Sage clicks her tongue. "Don't wait so long to tell me next time."

"Hopefully there won't be a next time."

"We both know that when it comes to matters of the heart, my judgment kinda sucks." Zin kneads Sage's knee, coaxing a smile out of her. "Which is why I need my best friend to be honest with me."

"I was afraid . . ." I start, swallowing. "I never want anything to come between us. Especially not some guy."

"We won't let it," she says, her voice edged with certainty. "The truth is, I've known for a while that things weren't working with Jason."

"Why did you stay with him, then?"

She slouches back into the couch. "Because we've always been together. He used to be such a sweet and funny guy; it's just that he hasn't grown up and I have. It happened slowly, so slowly I couldn't pinpoint what was wrong."

Jason's obsession with the Frisbros makes an odd sort of sense; he's playing on an ultimate Frisbee team with guys that enable him to continue acting like an adolescent.

"So you're not engaged anymore?"

She lifts her bare ring finger and sniffs. "It just felt good, you know? The promise of love and support and all that jazz." She pauses, sighing. "Forever."

"You'll find it again."

"Maybe. Maybe not."

We fall silent. There's a lot of uncertainty in this world. It's an injustice to ignore the harsh reality, but it's equally dangerous to dwell on what may or may not happen.

"Well, then we'll be old biddies together, wreaking havoc on the world."

"Hell to the yes," she says, a spark entering her eyes. "We can continue my wine education. Who knows, I could become a somme—thingy."

"Sommelier?"

"Yeah, that." Zin purrs softly as Sage resumes lavishing her with attention. "And I've been thinking more about what I want to do with my career. Criminal law seems pretty intriguing."

I cock my head to the side, trying to envision Sage in that role. "As in working to prove someone's innocent?"

"First off, there is no proving innocence. We can only prove they're guilty beyond a reasonable doubt, or not." She adjusts her headband. "But something like that."

Now, that's a terrifying concept. Of everyone involved in this case, is there anyone I can say for sure is not guilty?

Moira, whose marriage is on the rocks thanks to Gaskel's review. Jolly's MIA child, who had every reason to seek revenge. Vera, who never forgave Gaskel for bailing on their family. Brennan Fourie, who clearly knows more about Gaskel than he's letting on.

I shiver unexpectedly, a chill spreading to my fingertips.

I usually don't buy into hunches, but I have a bad feeling about my VIP party. I chalk it up to nerves and lack of caffeine. My business can't possibly be that cursed, can it? Besides, no one would dare try anything with a detective there.

Sage looks at me with concern and I realize I'm starting to hyperventilate. "Is everything okay?"

"Peachy," I say in an utterly unconvincing voice. I get to my feet and stretch. "I just need to cross some things off my to-do list."

"Do you mind if I stay here for a couple days?"

"Mi casa es Sage's casa," I say with a smile that comes across as more of a grimace.

"Your party's going to be a huge success," she says, immediately pinpointing the source of my discomfort. "If anyone tries anything, they're going to get an ass kicking from yours truly."

I nod numbly.

"Do you need any help getting stuff ready later?"

"That you're coming is more than enough," I say. "Thanks, though."

I seek the sanctuary of my room, trying to ignore the dread flooding my mind.

Before I hop in the shower, I open my laptop to look into two people who keep cropping up. First, I go to the About section of the Murphy's Bend website to find Carrick's last name. That acquired, I type the name "Carrick Dumond" into a Google search bar.

I have to know if the secret past Moira hinted at has anything to do with illegal activity. You know, like homicide.

Most of the hits are decades old, and are in French. I scroll through until I find an article featuring a photo of a younger Carrick. With the help of a nifty translation tool, I learn he was arrested for protesting social injustices as a student in the late eighties.

Political differences can cut deep and ruin relationships—just ask my ex, who flitted off to D.C. to be a political consultant. Could this be what Moira was referring to? And what does it really tell me? Mainly, that Carrick is willing to stand up for what he believes in, an admirable quality.

I let it go and type in one more name: "Brennan Fourie."

The results are a mixture of technobabble relating to Fourie Systems, articles speculating about his personal life, and details about his restaurant venture. I click on Images and quickly scan pictures of him at fancy Hollywood parties, keynote speeches, and daredevil stunts. He's always alone.

Laptops are to cats what lights are to moths. So I shouldn't be surprised when Zin hops onto my desk and basically plants herself on my keyboard. She gazes at me with her wise, orblike eyes. If she could talk, I bet she could shed some light on these mysteries. Unfortunately, all she's shedding is fur.

I pull Zin into my lap and navigate to Gaskel's blog. I haven't checked it since my visit earlier this week. The homepage is flooded with more messages of condolences. I scroll through those with successive swipes on the trackpad, stopping when I reach one particular comment. What was a vague accusation a couple of days ago stands out to me now.

devils_food99: You ruined my family. I was orphaned because of you. You deserve what you got.

I feel a prickling at the nape of my neck and text Eli with the tip to look into the user behind *devils_food99,* adding that whoever it is could be related to Jolly. Or her missing child.

But maybe my gut is wrong and the murderer has no connection to Jolly. The diner could be nothing more than a distraction. Same with the fact that it was a women's ring that contained the poison. After all, Eli said whoever was behind this was smart.

Swiveling back and forth in my office chair, I stare at my computer screen until it fades to black. I'm missing something. I can taste it, an unpleasant funk that doesn't belong. And if I don't figure out what it is soon, everything I've worked for could be destroyed.

Chapter Eighteen

Sage has already left for work when I venture from my room. She was kind enough to prepare a fresh pot of coffee. I press the button on the coffeemaker, letting the bitter, earthy aroma wash over me. The anticipation of caffeine is almost better than the caffeine itself. Almost.

My head feels clearer after a hot shower. Not that I'm any closer to figuring out who killed Gaskel or Max, mind you. Whoever it is is still out there, lurking in the background, watching the drama play out.

But maybe they won't crash my party. Maybe they've carried out their heinous purpose. Yeah, and maybe Vino Valentine will be granted a Michelin star.

I zip my new golden dress, a blazer, and ballet flats into a garment bag, having donned jeans and a tank for the hours of party prep ahead of me.

The rental company is delivering the linens, utensils, and banquet table when I get to my shop.

I go about setting up the banquet table along the back wall, underneath the colorful photographs of vineyards from around the world—Italy, France, Napa, and, of course, Colorado. The cream tablecloth complements the oak and espresso decor, and will provide a classy backdrop for Reid's dishes.

Next, I roll silverware, polish glasses, fill decorative vases with fresh daisies, and, when I can't put it off any longer, tackle the restroom. Like some masochist, my eyes gravitate toward the spot where I discovered Gaskel's body. The image of him lying on his back comes back to me, his legs bent at awkward angles, one hand holding his stomach while the other gripped his wristwatch.

In the last moments of my life, what would I reach for? Something to give me a sense of peace, or perhaps, if I were in Gaskel's position, something to help pinpoint the killer? I wonder which category his watch falls into.

With a shiver, I leave the lavatory and its morbid memories, making my way to the back of my winery. It's time to focus on the star of the event.

My wine cellar is sealed by a stainless-steel door with a double glass-paned window that keeps the temperature and humidity at levels ideal for aging wine. I select the usual suspects from the floor-to-ceiling wine rack—Chautauqua Chardonnay, Mount Sanitas White, Pearl Street Pinot, and other wines from my usual tasting menu—but also a special reserve syrah.

I brush my fingers over the label of the Snowy Day Syrah, the crisscrossing grapevines punctuated by rays of sunshine. This was the first wine I produced that turned out exactly how I wanted it to. I remember handling the delicate purple grapes, carefully tracking the fermentation and maceration, and the excitement when I finally tasted the first sip. Sure, it could do with another year or two of aging, but the flavors are there.

I'm carefully packing bottles into cases for easy transport when Anita flounces through the back door. The wind blows her blond hair around her head like a halo. She's wearing black slacks, a white eyelet blouse, and kitten heels, the perfect combo of professional and flirty.

"Any chance a raise would change your mind about quitting?" I ask. If my hands weren't full, I'd press them together and beg her to stay.

"We'll see." She gives me a good-natured smile, setting down her backpack next to a heap of empty boxes and her to-go coffee cup on the de-stemmer. She grabs a case of wine and lugs it toward the storefront while I go to snag another box.

I'm stooping to grab a cardboard divider when I see it. Inside the main compartment of her backpack, unzipped enough to give me a peek, is a hefty textbook with a bookmark sticking out. Only, it isn't an ordinary bookmark.

Scanning the door to the tasting room for Anita, I carefully tug it out.

It's a postcard. Of Jolly's Diner.

With shaking fingers, I flip it over. On the back, written in Anita's tidy script, is the date and location of my winery's opening and a scrawled message: *time to make amends.*

The extra flourish at the end of the letters, the curviness of the *M*s, are identical to those from Max's letter. It was Anita's handwriting that I recognized. That was the detail in the back of my mind that was bothering me.

And somehow, I know without a doubt, this is what I saw sticking out of Gaskel's pocket.

My blood turns cold as everything snaps into place.

There is one person who had the opportunity to kill Gaskel, sabotage my climbing gear, steal the prints, and plant the ring. Anita.

But that makes no sense. This is Anita we're talking about; she's more cherub than human. Why would she kill Gaskel?

Unless Anita is Jolly's daughter. She's just about the right age. Her last name is Moore, not Jones, but that's easy enough to change.

I sense rather than see Anita pushing the door open. Hastily, I stuff the postcard back into her backpack and make a show of selecting an empty box.

I try to calm my nerves, pretend I didn't just learn my assistant is a murderer. Pretty sure I fail, my eyes darting about no matter how much I tell myself to focus. Breathe.

"What is it?" Anita asks.

"Nothing," I say quickly, dipping my chin. "Mind getting one more? I'll follow in a minute."

"Okay." She shoots a concerned glance over her shoulder, her cheeks flushed from the effort of carrying a full case of wine.

As soon as the door shuts, I grab my cell and dial Eli's number. It rings and rings and I silently plea for him to answer. My palms grow sweaty as I stare at the door Anita disappeared through. She'll be back any second.

And still no answer. Dammit, at least switch to voice mail.

"Drop your phone, Parker," Anita commands in an unrecognizable voice, harsh and unfeeling. She must have gone out the front door, circled around my shop, and snuck up behind me.

Something sharp presses into my back and I drop my phone to the floor, the telltale crack of the glass screen echoing through the empty space.

I turn around and come face-to-face with Anita. Her eyes are cold and she bares her teeth like a feral animal.

Gone is the quintessential adolescent, dependable assistant, and brilliant business student. In her place stands a ruthless killer, holding a corkscrew to my chest.

There have only been a few times in my life when I've been truly afraid.

Once, walking across campus after studying late one night, when a large shadowed figure started following me, his footsteps growing closer and closer. If I hadn't run into a group of freshmen returning from the Hill, I don't know what would have happened. That's the reason I always carry pepper spray with me.

Second, when we got the call that my aunt had been hit by a drunk driver. I couldn't imagine a world without her in it, couldn't bear the sad resignation in my mother's eyes as she learned her baby sister was gone.

Third, earlier this week when I was free-falling off the climbing wall.

And now this moment.

"It was you," is all I can think of to say.

Anita digs the corkscrew into my tank top, the point so sharp it breaks skin. Blood blossoms on the thin cotton fabric. "No shit, Sherlock."

My gut was right; Jolly's was at the center of everything. I give myself half a beat to acknowledge my investigative skills. Then I kickstart my brain, suddenly aware of how isolated I am. No one would hear me scream through the thick walls and closed doors of my winery, and I know, thanks to my obsessive time-checking, that I have at least an hour before anyone else shows up.

Damn my pride for not accepting Sage's help when she offered.

I don't mean to be a friggin' island. I'd rather be a continent, like Australia or Europe. Yes, if I get out of this I vow to be more like the United Nations.

Focus, Parker.

My best bet is to keep Anita talking and hope I can come up with a plan. "You're Jolly's daughter," I say. "That's why you killed Gaskel."

At the name "Jolly," Anita's face floods with emotion. "He killed my mom and dad, left me an orphan to bounce around the foster system. All because he wasn't satisfied with the doneness of French toast."

Now, *killed* is a stretch, but I'm not about to argue with a deranged lunatic. "You could have gone to the media with your story, taken him down professionally. You didn't have to murder him."

"I commented on his blog and no one cared, or even noticed." She shakes her head, blond curls bouncing. "He deserved what he got."

"You're *devils_food99*."

"You did your homework."

"I've always been thorough," I say wryly. "How did you poison him without my noticing?"

"One of my prouder moments," she says with a self-satisfied smirk. "I laced the glass with wolfsbane, the queen of poisons, then gave it to him while everyone was distracted by the arguing couple."

Here I thought Anita was just being helpful, dashing about my winery and cleaning up the mess, when really, she was putting her lethal plan into action. Everything is so clear now, I wonder how I didn't see it sooner. "Then I put his glass through the dishwasher and effectively destroyed the evidence."

"Thanks for that," she says. "Couldn't have only my prints found on the rim."

Anita is obviously intelligent; too bad she's a certifiable psychopath.

As I stare down my nose at the corkscrew, I get an idea. A potentially stupid idea that might get me killed. But it could also be my only shot at getting out of this alive.

I take a small step back, into my wine cellar, gingerly navigating the threshold. Anita steps forward, just like I gambled she would, and repositions the corkscrew so it's at my throat. I can hardly breathe without pricking myself.

I force myself to maintain eye contact, not letting my fear show. "And Max? You were his girlfriend, weren't you?"

"God, he was practically drooling all over me at your opening, despite my pleas to keep it professional since I was '*working*.'" She has the audacity to use air quotes with her free hand.

I recall the way Max was checking Anita out in Liam's picture and give myself a swift mental kick for not piecing it together sooner.

"I can't believe Max fell for a monster like you," I hiss, even though we all fell for her innocent act.

"Max was easily manipulated; lonely people often are. We met volunteering for the Shakespeare Festival— bet you never guessed I'm actually a theater major." She pauses for effect.

Even I have to admit she's a brilliant actress. I mean, seriously, give this chick an Oscar.

"You knew all the business professors, the course material," I argue, inching to the side.

"Easily found online." Anita presses the sharp metal of the corkscrew deeper into my skin, her hand beginning to shake. "Stop moving, Parker."

I swallow, my forehead beading with sweat. "Why my winery? I trusted you." The last word comes out as a croak. All of Anita's support, her kind words and sweet demeanor, were a ploy.

"I had to choose a place Gaskel was likely to review anyway, and wine would be potent enough to disguise the wolfsbane." She falters, a crack in her facade. "For what it's worth, you really are a great boss."

"Gee, thanks," I grumble. "That didn't stop you from sabotaging my climbing harness or harassing my family."

"Your climbing harness was a warning to stop snooping around," she says. Her eyes dart around the small space like a caged animal's, the point of the corkscrew digging deeper into my neck. "And I needed your brother's photographs. He captured my fingers—my ring. They would have given me away."

"What about the postcard?" I ask.

"I sent it to Gaskel to jog his memory about my parents' diner. He couldn't resist trying to absolve himself of guilt."

"Then you had Max steal it while I was dialing 911." Curse my weak stomach; if I'd just stayed put, how much trouble would have been avoided?

"Max didn't know what he was doing. He believed me when I told him Gaskel was blackmailing me— thought he was stealing what Gaskel had on me." She tucks her blond hair behind her ear, such a normal gesture for such a bizarre situation. "It wasn't until later he started suspecting me. I overheard your phone call with him and knew I had to do something."

I remember the spotty conversation Anita is referring to, and how she coincidentally appeared at the end of it. To think that's what led to Max's death.

Perhaps Gaskel wasn't alone in absolving himself of guilt, for Anita continues on her diatribe, "I invited him on a romantic picnic date in the park after his Frisbee practice. Max opened the wine and poured the glass that killed him himself."

"And the suicide note?"

"Penned by me. Would you believe he wrote me a love letter for our one-month anniversary?" She shakes her head, a look of disgust crossing her face. "It made mimicking his handwriting easy."

"Then you tried to pin it on my brother? What, as insurance?"

"Cover all your bases. You taught me that." She nods at me, a malicious gleam in her eye. "Liam was convenient. A constant screw-up."

"Liam isn't a screw-up," I say defensively, and then voice something I can hardly imagine but feel I need to know, "If he'd been in that night, would you have killed him, too?"

She doesn't answer; she doesn't need to. There isn't a hint of remorse in her face. She really is ruthless.

"You were the one who left tulips at Jolly's," I say, another piece falling into place.

"I had to let Mom know I was avenging her."

"I doubt she would see it that way."

I shift on my feet, scooting one more iota to the side. Now I'm in position to make my move, but my timing has to be perfect.

"I told you to hold still," Anita hisses, breaking skin on my neck with the corkscrew. Blood trickles down my chest to my navel.

I wince and lift both hands in mock surrender. "What are you going to do with me?"

With her free hand, she pulls a clear Ziploc bag coated in a light green powder from her pocket. That must be where she's keeping her wolfsbane now that her ring is gone. It's not nearly as glamorous, but deadly all the same. I clamp my mouth shut.

"I think I'll mix you a special cocktail so you can toast to your failed dream." She looks around the cellar and nods. "Yes, I think people will believe you killed yourself in here."

"Too bad I have other plans."

Then I duck, spin out of reach, and dash over the threshold of the wine cellar. Anita lunges after me, swinging the corkscrew, but she's too slow. I slam the door in her face.

Chapter Nineteen

I throw everything I've got into keeping the cellar door shut—my weight, my strength, my dignity. I lean against it, digging my heels into the ground for extra leverage, my heart racing.

Anita thrashes against the door over and over and over. It opens a crack with each push. For such a willowy girl, she's incredibly strong. Must be all those damn yoga classes.

I grit my teeth and press my body into the door like my life depends on it, which, oddly enough, it does. My muscles burn and my chest heaves. I can't keep this up for much longer.

I look from side to side, desperately searching for anything to help me. My eyes land on a folding chair not too far away.

If I were climbing, this would be the ultimate maneuver, maintaining pressure with one foot and hand while simultaneously reaching for the chair. Only, if this were climbing, I would have a spotter in case my move went awry.

Dare I risk it? Dare I not?

Anita pauses her attacks and I make a decision.

I stretch my torso across the door, leaning forward to maintain pressure, and brace myself for impact in case Anita senses my strategy. The chair is still a centimeter away, I shift slightly, reaching a little bit farther. It's enough. Climbing the other night paid off, for I'm able to snag the rim of the chair with my fingertips. I drag it across the floor and wedge it beneath the doorknob.

The whole maneuver took no longer than a second.

My makeshift lock won't hold forever, but I don't need forever. I just need it to last until someone else arrives. Hopefully someone who isn't a guest. Otherwise, imagine the greeting they'd get: *Welcome to my VIP party! Would you mind calling the cops so we can arrest a psycho killer? 'K, thanks.*

I blow my bangs out of my face and scan the vicinity for another way out of this mess. Anita's to-go coffee cup is still perched on the de-stemmer, where she left it, and the garment bag with my party dress hangs on a hook by the grape-sorting table, neither of which is of any use to me now.

Anita pushes against the door, softer now, more probing, as if testing for points of weakness. Then she stops, maybe sensing the extra reinforcement, or maybe finding some new way to torture me. I know she hasn't given up.

For a while, nothing happens.

I'm tempted to sink into a puddle on the floor, my

entire body shaking from effort and shock. Instead, I focus on my breathing—in through my nose, out through my mouth.

That's when I hear a sound that shatters my heart into a thousand pieces: the sound of a wine bottle smashing against the floor.

"I'll destroy every bottle, Parker," Anita shouts, breaking another bottle to prove her intent. "Let me out and I'll go. I'll skip town and leave you and your precious winery in peace."

I'm embarrassed to admit that for the briefest moment, I consider her deal.

But even if I trusted Anita, which I don't, there are more important things than the success of my business. Like justice.

I steel myself as another wine bottle crashes against the floor.

I think of my aunt, how she encouraged me to pursue my dream. I feel her presence now, like a warm blanket draped around my shoulders.

Another wine bottle crashes to the floor, and I wonder which of my darlings it was—the chardonnay, riesling, or perhaps the syrah?

I think of my dad when he said he and my mom were proud of me, his eyes warm and comforting. I never thought their approval would mean so much, but it totally does. I let his words shield me against another crash. Another bottle gone.

How many years of hard work will Anita destroy? Can I really afford to start from scratch after this? A business is nothing without a product to sell.

"Ticktock, Parker," Anita shouts.

Burgundy liquid trickles beneath the cellar door,

seeping into the soles of my sneakers. I sniff a bouquet
of aromas; black cherry, currants, and leather. It's the
Campy Cab.

I think of my brother and Sage, who have both stood
by me through thick and thin, and my new community—
Reid, Moira, and even Eli. The future is ripe and full of
potential. Even if my business isn't a part of it, I sure as
hell am going to be.

No use crying over spilled wine.

I stand up straight and peer through the tiny window.
I catch a flash of motion, white shirt and blond curls,
before Anita's stark blue eyes stare back at me, her rosy
lips twisted into a scowl. It's amazing that someone so
lovely can harbor such evil inside of them.

"You may as well enjoy some of that wine," I say,
speaking with bravado I wish I felt. "It could be your
last drink for a while. You're not getting out of there
unless it's in handcuffs."

Anita fumes and, maintaining eye contact, throws
another bottle to the floor. Pale yellow liquid mixes
with the burgundy on the floor, smelling of honeysuckle
and peaches.

I remain steadfast. I channel Reid's cocksure attitude
and force a grin onto my face.

The door opens behind me, casting sunshine over
the space. I spin around as Eli and two officers charge
to my side.

I'm not a damsel-in-distress sort of gal, but I'm mighty
happy to see Eli. My wine needs rescuing, and pronto.

I usher Eli and the officers to my post outside the
wine cellar, glancing furtively between them and Anita.

I explain the situation in a rush of words so jumbled it's a miracle they comprehend.

Eli unholsters his gun from where it's strapped to his chest. He shed his navy-blue sport coat at some point, and the sleeves of his collared shirt are rolled to his elbows. He's all business, cool and calculating as he assesses his surroundings.

He gestures to the officers and they fall back to either side of him, their badges glinting on their pristine uniforms.

I watch the scene unfold in disbelief, as if it were some crime show on television and not real life: Eli warns Anita to stand back and, in two swift movements, kicks the door open and captures her in a hold, pinning her arms behind her back. The corkscrew clatters to the ground amid broken glass and puddles of wine.

Anita's face is full of rage as Eli reads her Miranda rights. She struggles against her bonds, her curses eventually deteriorating into sobs. I tell myself not to feel sorry for her—she's a murderer, for chrissake—but she strikes a tragic figure. Orphaned as a young girl, she had no one to guide her through this crazy world.

Eli places Anita in the care of the attending police officers. She stares me down as she's led away; I meet her gaze.

"Push the Chardonnay at your party," she says, her long blond hair limp around her shoulders. "It's really delicious."

I'm not sure what to make of that, so I just nod and make a mental note to chuck any open bottles that Anita could have gotten her paws on.

An EMT approaches and badgers me with questions as she checks me over from head to toe. Finally, she deems me healthy. I sustained minor cuts on my stomach and neck, courtesy of the corkscrew, but those are easily patched with Band-Aids. Yeah, the neon Band-Aid is really going to take my gold party dress to the next level.

Eli finishes whatever official detective stuff he had to do before seeking me out. He leans against a wine vat nonchalantly, as if apprehending a murderer is routine.

"Guess I have to find a new assistant, after all," I say by way of a greeting.

He raises one eyebrow. "Let me know when you have an applicant and I'll personally vet them for you."

"I could get used to having an in with the Boulder PD," I say, crossing my arms over my chest. "How did you know to come?"

"Thanks to your tip, IT was able to trace the username you sent me to Anita Moore, formerly Anita Jones, who I knew to be your assistant. We had just made the connection when you called. I kept calling back and when you didn't answer your phone, I assumed the worst." He frowns, rubbing his chin with one hand. "You handled her pretty well on your own."

I wince. "To the detriment of my wine cellar."

All told, Anita destroyed a case—twelve bottles—each of the Campy Cab, Snowy Day Syrah, and Mount Sanitas White. It could have been worse, but I hate seeing good wine go to waste.

"If you're as good a winemaker as you are a sleuth, you'll recover just fine."

I give him a small smile in thanks.

There's a commotion at the front of the store and we hurry through the connecting door.

I'm so elated to see Reid I can't help the goofy grin

that spreads across my face. He's arguing with the officer barricading the crime scene. His face is pale, a stark contrast to his copper hair, and he waves his arms in the air with growing desperation. For someone usually so in control, he seems entirely out of his element.

His eyes land on me and I can practically feel his relief. He nudges past the officer, jogs to my side, and pulls me into an embrace.

"I saw the police cars and ambulance out front. Then they said it was a crime scene and I was afraid . . ." He swallows and continues, his breath warm in my ear. "Are you okay?"

"I'm fine." I give him a tight squeeze, letting his scent ground me: rosemary, citrus, and something peppery.

He pulls away and gives me a once-over, just to make sure. He gently tucks a strand behind my ear and lifts my chin so our gazes lock. What I would give to have more time and less of an audience. But we have other things to worry about now.

"Guests will arrive any second," I say, panic turning my voice into a high-pitched squeak. "They'll see flashing lights and hightail it home. Do not pass go. Do not save Vino Valentine."

"That's my cue," Eli says evenly from behind us. "We're about done here. We should be out of your hair in time for your party."

I nod numbly, lists of to-dos spinning through my head.

Eli salutes farewell and makes to leave when I remember my manners. "Wait, I hope you'll consider staying."

Eli glances between Reid and me, considering my offer, an unreadable expression on his face. "Another time, when I'm not on duty."

Then he returns to the back of my winery and shouts muffled orders to the crime-scene crew.

Reid redirects my attention. "What can I do?"

I glance around my winery—apart from lingering law enforcement agents, it's not in bad shape. Thank goodness I did so much prep earlier. Wineglasses sparkle on the tasting bar, at the ready, and candles flicker in the fading evening light.

"Finish setting up the food and distract any guests who show up early," I say, snagging the garment bag I packed earlier. "I'll be back in a flash."

I dash into the restroom and lock the door behind me, trying to ignore the frantic pattering of my heart. I strip down, shimmy into my dress, and slip on my blazer and flats. Next is my hair. I play up the knotted mess and twist my raven locks into a low bun, loose tendrils falling over my forehead. I add fresh powder to my face, clean the smudged mascara around my eyes, and dab jasmine perfume on my inner wrist.

I emerge mere minutes later feeling like a posh business professional. Or at least as close as I can get.

True to his word, Eli and his band of law enforcement agents waste no time vacating the premises.

Reid is putting the final touches on the banquet table, cleaning the edges of simple white platters loaded with the mouthwatering delicacies I sampled last night. In front of each one is a notecard with a short description and which wine to pair it with.

Maybe we will actually pull this off. Maybe I'll manage to salvage my reputation and save my business. Maybe Reid will sneak me a truffle.

Then the first guest arrives and all thoughts of food vanish.

*   *   *

You would think after confronting a murderer, nothing would make me nervous. Apparently, that isn't the case. Butterflies flitter through my stomach and my palms are clammy. I smooth the front of my dress, unnecessarily, and greet my first guest.

She's an elderly lady with chunky amethyst jewelry, a velvet pantsuit, and a judgy disposition that tells me she isn't easily impressed. I don't have time to fret, though, for a steady stream of people traipse in after her.

It's a tough crowd. Half of the guests came as a personal favor to Moira and Carrick, and the other half to satisfy some morbid curiosity. My only goal is to prove my wine is worth the buzz (pun intended).

I play hostess from behind the tasting bar, talking through my winemaking philosophy so many times I could recite it in my sleep.

Swirling, sniffing, and gurgling abound, and I'm pleased to see the discard vases largely remain empty. That's a good sign.

Descriptive words like *full-bodied* and *mouth-feel* waft through the air, and there are enough fruit comparisons to rival the produce section at Whole Foods. Soft acoustic music provides a backdrop, and flickering candles and dimmed wine-bottle lanterns ooze ambience.

Reid handles the food like the pro he is. He's dressed to the nines, khakis and a snug emerald sweater. He describes how the flavors in each dish complement various wines, even giving general pairing tips, which many of the VIP guests seem excited about.

As the evening wears on, I find Brennan standing

alone in a corner, observing the hubbub with an amused grin on his face.

"Cheers, Parker." He lifts his glass to me. "You throw a helluva party. Gaskel would have approved."

"That means a lot coming from you." I hesitate, debating whether to ask my next question. "You and Gaskel were more than just friends, weren't you?"

Brennan's smile remains intact, but his eyes pool with tears. "How did you know?"

"First, no one just gives away *Hamilton* tickets. Then last night, Moira and Carrick said they saw you together at a restaurant, one he never reviewed. After that, I did a little research, and you've never been photographed with anyone—man or woman." I pause for a breath. "But really, it was Pico."

"Gaskel's dog?"

"He was awfully familiar with you."

Brennan rubs the back of his neck. "Gaskel was the one who wanted to keep our relationship secret, didn't want anyone to think I—a restaurateur—held any sway over his reviews. He was a stickler for keeping his personal life separate from his professional life." He shrugs his broad shoulders. "I gave him his watch as a way to think of me whenever we couldn't be together."

I had begun to suspect as much about his watch. "I'm sorry for your loss," I say. "I can't imagine how hard it's been, not being able to tell anyone."

He sniffs and taps his wineglass. "This is delicious. I'd like to put in an order for a few bottles for the restaurant."

I get the contact information for The Pantry's sommelier, promise to be in touch, and then leave him in peace.

Sage and Liam are at the tasting bar, in the middle of what appears to be an intimate discussion, heads bowed together, faces beaming. There's no sign of Jason. I decide it's probably best not to interrupt.

Moira and Carrick are chatting with guests, describing their upcoming trip to France. I wait for a pause in the conversation before pulling them aside.

"Thank you for all your help," I gush. "This wouldn't have been possible without you."

"Of course, dear," Moira answers. She and Carrick look happier than I've seen them, hands clasped and leaning into each other.

"And I'm sorry for sneaking around your winery, and for eavesdropping," I say, eyeing the ground sheepishly. "I was afraid you were involved and, well"—I clear my throat, not wanting to admit how heavily I suspected them—"turns out it was my assistant all along."

"Water over the bridge," Carrick answers in a thick accent. His silvering hair is slicked into a wave, and his dimpled smile makes him look like a real-life Prince Charming.

Needless to say, Moira and I don't correct him.

"Let's have a joint party when we're back in town," Moira says, and adds coyly, "We can have your chef *friend* cater."

My cheeks flush and I start stammering excuses, glancing at Reid. Moira just pats my arm as she and Carrick waltz away.

Next, I track down the two people whose opinions matter the most: my parents.

They're inconspicuous, perched at an oak-barrel table, sipping glasses of wine. My dad is in an elbow-patch jacket, sans chalk, and my mom is all frizzy hair and barely contained energy.

"No spritzer?" I ask my mom.

She gives me a warm smile, folding her napkin carefully in her lap. "Your wine is perfect, as is."

I can't help the tears that spring to my eyes. I give her a tight hug. "Thanks, Mom."

My dad winks at me over her shoulder. "I hear they arrested the culprit."

I tell them an abridged version of the story; no need for them to know how close their daughter came to being shish-kebabbed by a corkscrew. "It means the world to me that you came tonight."

Inevitably, we'll have our ups and downs in the future, but at this moment, I appreciate my family being at my side, supporting my passion.

"Don't let us keep you from your guests," my mom says, shooing me away.

The next hour passes in a blur. My feet ache so badly I can hardly stand anymore when the last guest finally filters through the door.

I flip the OPEN sign to CLOSED, a giddy feeling bubbling in my chest. I sold a lot of wine tonight, and almost every guest promised they would be back, even the grouchy velvet-clad woman. One night can't make up for my dismal opening week, and I'll need to crunch some numbers, but I'm optimistic.

Now, if only I could figure out how the heavily pierced Libby Lincoln fits into everything. Her presence was too coincidental *not* to be connected with Gaskel's murder. But that's a puzzle for later.

I turn back to Reid, who's stacking empty platters to

bring to the dishwasher. They hardly need it since they were practically licked clean.

"We did it," I say.

I approach him slowly, wringing my hands behind my back. We haven't really been alone since our trip to Evergreen and the tension has mounted to an almost unbearable level.

"Correction, *you* did it. I just helped a little." Reid turns serious, wiping his hands on a towel. "Which means we have business to discuss. I hope you won't forget our deal."

"Of course not." I shake my head, a strand of hair falling over my forehead. "I will personally make sure you have all the Vino Valentine labels you want at your new restaurant."

"Good." He flashes me a devilish grin and takes a step closer. The heat in his gaze sends electricity coursing through my entire body. "You probably have some rule about vendors and merchants not getting involved."

How did he guess? Truth is, I used to have rules about a lot of things, but due to recent events, I'm reevaluating. Life is too short for constraints.

I close the distance between us so our toes nearly touch. "You know what I have to say about that?"

"What?"

"Absolutely nothing."

And then, just like that, I grab a handful of his shirt and pull him toward me into a kiss. He wraps his arms around my waist and smiles into my lips. Our mouths open and our kiss deepens.

His lips are soft against mine, giving and taking in equal measure. For the record, there's nothing else soft about Reid. I trace a line from his bicep to his chest, all lean muscle beneath his shirt, while my other hand cradles his jaw, cut like glass.

Heat courses between us as my hands come to rest over his chest, our hearts pounding in sync. Our kiss slows into something unbelievably tender that leaves me warm and tingly.

Damn, he's a good kisser.

"Thank God," he says, trailing kisses across my cheek and down my neck. "You've been driving me crazy since we first met."

"Likewise," I say breathlessly.

"I've never been so captivated by a woman." He tips my chin up and searches my eyes. "To be honest, it's kinda terrifying."

The cracks in his confident demeanor, the vulnerability he's showed, and all the puzzled looks he gave me make sense now.

I break away to pour us a couple glasses of Ralphie's Riesling. "Here's to a future of successful pairings—food and wine, and otherwise."

"I'll toast to that."

We clink glasses and take small sips, our gazes locked as we swish and swallow. In Reid's arms, the motions have never felt so alluring, and it's not long before we get back to kissing.

Chapter Twenty

It's been two weeks since the VIP party and my winery is chock-full of a clientele as varied as the city of Boulder itself. There are posh professionals, liberals bordering on hippies, college students, and the newest addition: thrill seekers.

Because, as it turns out, Libby Lincoln was more than a pink-haired, heavily tattooed customer with a weird fascination with Gaskel's murder. She's a food and wine blogger with a very specific niche, adrenaline junkies. Her forte includes things like puffer fish, scorpion tequila, and, ironically enough, killer chardonnay.

Between that and news breaking about how I helped track down the murderer, #KillerChardonnay has taken on a whole new meaning. Social media is quick to anger, but also quick to forgive.

I'm pouring tasters for two dudes with giant-gauge

piercings in their ears and sleeve tattoos up their arms when the door jingles.

"Be with you in a minute," I say without glancing up.

I deliver the tasters to the far end of the counter with a smile, taking a second to scan my other tables, which all seem content. I really need to hire an assistant, or three. I'm at my wits' end, but for now, I'm appreciating a bustling winery.

The new arrival slides onto a stool at the end of the bar. I hurriedly wipe down the counter and when I finally look up, I'm surprised to see Eli. He's dressed casually, shorts and a T-shirt, sunglasses resting on top of his head.

"I'll take you up on that drink," he says. "Whatever wine you'd recommend."

I select one for him immediately. "Mile High Merlot, for old time's sake."

He chuckles and feigns a wince. "You're never going to forget who I was in high school, are you?"

"Sorry, comes with the territory."

"I came here for another reason, too," he says, swirling the glass of maroon wine. It seems like a completely foreign action for him. "A couple, actually."

I rest my arms on the tasting bar. "Shoot."

"Anita Moore-Jones will have a court date set soon. There's a good chance you'll have to testify. Just wanted to give you a heads-up."

"Okay." I dip my chin to my chest and exhale, ready to put this whole ordeal behind me.

"Second, I put your friend in contact with the district attorney. Her questions were over my head, and my pay grade."

I gave Sage Eli's contact info, figuring he'd be a good

resource for her future career in criminal law. "That's my girl," I answer proudly.

"Lastly, I want to ask you out to dinner." He takes a sip of wine, holding my gaze with his warm brown eyes. "I don't know what's going on with you and that Reid guy, but I wanted to officially throw my name in the hat."

That surprises me more than everything else he said. I blink several times. "I don't know what to say."

Honestly, while I had fun climbing with Eli, things are going great with Reid. Like, too-good-to-be-true great. For a guy not usually into commitment, he's surprisingly keen on the whole relationship thing. Between dating and planning another food- and wine-tasting party, we've been seeing a lot of each other.

"You don't have to answer right now," Eli says, probably guessing what I'm going to say. He is a detective, after all.

I give him a pained smile. "I'm flattered, really. Maybe we can hit up the climbing gym again some time. As friends."

"I'd like that."

The bell jingles, saving us from further awkwardness. Liam saunters in and takes a seat next to Eli.

He gives us both a head nod. "What's up? You said it was urgent." He drums his fingers on the countertop. "I can't stay long, I'm on my way to meet Sage."

"Really?" I say, drawing out the word for emphasis.

"Yes," he says. "She needs a friend right now."

"Right, a *friend*," I say, narrowing my eyes at him. "If she really needed a friend, she could've called me."

He shrugs and gives me a coy smile, which tells me everything I need to know. Then he opens his mouth again, "And this better not be about you and Reid, cuz I told you both, no details."

Eli stares determinedly at the counter. My cheeks flush as I duck beneath the tasting bar for a package wrapped in brown paper. I hand it to Liam. "I got you something. Well, really, it's from me and Mom and Dad."

Liam eyes the package suspiciously. "What is this?"

"Just open it, doofus."

He tears at the paper haphazardly and freezes. He stares at me in stunned silence, his mouth hanging open. "But—wha—why?"

"I know it's not vintage or anything, but the guy at Mike's Camera Store said it was one of the best."

My brother opens the box and inspects the camera, holding it up to the light. It's a Canon Rebel T7i with plenty of features and doodads for the aspiring photographer.

Whatever he expected, it wasn't this. He runs a hand through his raven hair, speechless for maybe the first time ever.

Finally, he finds his voice. "I can't accept this."

"Yes, you can." I rest my hands on my hips. "And I'd like to commission some photos for my website. I need new ones now that summer is officially here."

He snaps a few pictures, testing the light, his way of accepting.

"It's not going to be easy. You'll encounter plenty of bumps on the road," I say, and add quickly, "Hopefully yours won't involve dead bodies."

Eli snorts into his wineglass. "No offense, but I don't want to get another call from the Valentine family."

"None taken," I say, relieved Eli seems to have recovered from my rejection. I focus on Liam again, willing him to believe me when I say, "You can do this."

Liam walks behind the bar and gives me a hug. "Thanks, sis."

I nod and turn back to my crowded winery, full of mingling patrons. It's an odd bunch, but laughter and happy chatter fill every inch of the space. This. This right here is what I've dreamed about for more years than I care to admit.

When you press grapes, the skin and stems are included with the juice. It's the imperfections that give wine tannins, and ultimately add to the flavor and texture. Maybe that's how life is. It's the extra bits, the so-called imperfections, that make it truly special.

Recipes and
Wine Pairings

Mango Chutney Grilled Shrimp

(Serves 4 to 6)

2 tbsp olive oil
1 cup finely chopped yellow onion
¼ tsp crushed red pepper
3 garlic cloves, minced
1 tbsp ginger root, grated
2 cups finely chopped mango
½ cup orange juice
¼ cup white wine vinegar
1½ pounds jumbo shrimp (24 count), deveined, shell on, raw
Salt and pepper (to taste)

Mango Chutney

Sauté the onion and crushed red pepper in the olive oil for 2 to 3 minutes, or until the onion is translucent. Stir in the garlic and ginger and cook for 1 minute. Add the mango, orange juice, and white wine vinegar. Reduce the heat and let simmer for 30 minutes, stirring occasionally. Let cool to room temperature.

Shrimp

Butterfly the shrimp by cutting along the back, from head to tail, almost slicing through lengthwise but leaving the shell on. This will keep the shrimp tender on the grill, and increases surface area for the marinade to work its magic.

Preheat a grill to medium heat.

Place the shrimp in a bowl and add half of the mango chutney, making sure to get some of the marinade in every nook and cranny. Let sit for 20 minutes.

Grill the shrimp 2 minutes per side. To serve, top the grilled shrimp with the remaining mango chutney. Add salt and pepper to taste.

Suggested wine pairing: a citrusy sauvignon blanc with herbal notes on the nose and tropical fruit on the palate.

Italian Ratatouille with Balsamic Glaze

(Serves 4 to 6)

1 tbsp olive oil
2 yellow onions, thinly sliced
Salt and pepper, to taste
6 roma tomatoes, sliced into ⅛-inch rounds
2 small eggplants, sliced into ⅛-inch rounds
2 medium zucchinis, sliced into ⅛-inch rounds
4 garlic cloves, minced
1 tbsp chopped fresh basil
1 tbsp chopped fresh parsley
1 tbsp chopped fresh thyme
2 tbsp chopped sun-dried tomatoes
1 cup balsamic vinegar
¼ cup brown sugar
½ cup grated parmesan cheese
Rustic bread, for serving

Preheat the oven to 350 degrees F.

Lightly oil an 8x10-inch baking dish. Line the bottom with the thinly sliced onions and season with salt. Arrange an overlapping row of sliced tomatoes, wedged at an angle and packed tightly so they're almost standing upright. Do the same with alternating rows of eggplant and zucchini, repeating until all the veggies have been incorporated.

In a separate bowl, mix the garlic, basil, parsley, thyme, and sun-dried tomatoes. Sprinkle on top of the veggies, uniformly. Drizzle with the olive oil, cover with aluminum foil, and bake for 30 minutes. After 30 minutes, uncover and increase the oven temperature to 425 degrees F. Bake for another 30 minutes, or until veggies are tender and the edges are golden brown.

Bring the balsamic vinegar and brown sugar to a boil in a saucepan, stirring occasionally. Reduce heat to low and let simmer for 20 minutes, or until the mixture has reduced by half.

Drizzle desired amount of balsamic glaze (a little bit goes a long way!) over the ratatouille and add the grated parmesan. Serve with a piece of good rustic bread.

Suggested wine pairing: a light-bodied pinot noir with aromas of cherry and vanilla, and bursting flavors of summer berries.

Dark Chocolate Espresso Truffles

(Yields 12)

8 oz (or 2 bars) of your favorite dark chocolate (such as
   Ghiradelli's Intense Dark, which is 72% cacao)

½ cup heavy cream

1 tbsp brewed coffee

½ tsp vanilla extract

½ cup chocolate-covered espresso beans, crushed

Finely chop the chocolate and place in a heatproof mixing bowl. Heat the cream in a small saucepan until it's just coming to a simmer, being careful not to let it curdle. Pour the cream over the chocolate and stir until the chocolate is completely melted. Mix in the coffee and vanilla.

Refrigerate for 30 minutes.

Line a baking sheet with parchment paper. Using two spoons, scoop the chocolate mixture into small balls and place onto the prepared baking sheet. Lightly roll each of the balls in the crushed espresso beans. Refrigerate for an additional 20 minutes, or until the truffles are firm. Serve at room temperature. Store leftovers in the refrigerator.

Suggested wine pairing: a full-bodied cabernet sauvignon that smells like a campfire and tastes like dried cherries.